Born Of War

Born Of War

Based On A True Story of
American-Chinese Friendship

David E. Feldman

Writers Club Press
San Jose New York Lincoln Shanghai

To my wife, Ellen, who is so nearly perfect.

To my sons.

To Aunt Norma.

In Memory of Uncle Howie, Grandma Nettie, and Grandpa Morris.

Preface

At Thanksgiving dinner in 1974, my uncle, Howard Hyman, produced a photograph of himself alongside Mao Zedong taken on September 16, 1945. He then told our astonished family the story of his 30-year friendship with a handful of remarkable Chinese citizens, many of them students, whom he had met during his stint in the 14th Army Air Corps, aka the Flying Tigers, in World War II.

He explained that the photo had been hidden away during the McCarthy years, and had been brought out now for two reasons. First, since Nixon's visit in 1972, the doors to China had been thrown open, making possible the second reason: he was hoping to arrange a trip within a year or two back to Kunming, Chongqing and other cities he had visited so long ago.

Initially, the Chinese Government refused his request for a visa and itinerary. Along with his second application, Howard sent along the photo. Instantly, permission was granted and an itinerary arranged to cities not seen by westerners in decades. At that time, American citizens rarely visited China.

I was seventeen in 1974, and immediately began begging to go along. By the time the trip finally took place in the summer of '76, I had been granted permission.

We visited Kunming, Chongqing, Xian, Beijing, Guilin, and Shanghai. Along with us came former GIs who had also been with the Flying Tigers. Amidst the raised glasses and shouts of *"Gambei!"* were tearful reunions and bittersweet memories of friends long gone. American guests and Chinese hosts alike were moved by the endurance of their friendships despite the world's changes.

Since then, Howard asked me to write his story, but after writing the first draft as reportage, I was asked by one of his Chinese friends to change certain names and details as "a matter of personal safety." I agreed.

Despite these changes, the essential ingredient, the now more than 50-year American–Chinese friendship, a friendship "born of war," remains intact.

Acknowledgements

The following individuals were of great help in the preparation of *Born Of War*. Please accept my thanks.

Ellen Feldman, Enid and Lawrence Feldman, Grace and Saul Gluck, Ed Bell, Ruth Zachary, Paula Hyman, Renee Kasper, C.F. Kwok, Zhang Yan, Ruth Marconi, Carol Butler.

Author's Note

*B*orn Of War is based on a true story. Originally, the story was written exactly as it happened. Upon reading the original, one of the people upon whom a Chinese character is based, objected, fearing for his and his family's well-being were his role in these events revealed. Therefore, certain names and circumstances were changed. At that point, to show the effect of war on various individuals, additional characters and story lines were "imagined."

I attempted through research and interviews to portray these fictionalized events as they might have occurred, given historical circumstances.

The paragraphs below attempt to distinguish between what is and what is not true.

*　　　*　　　*　　　*

What Is True

Henry's family and the love story with Frances, though the barrette is a literary device; the character Jake Singer; their positions in the 14th Army Air Corps and their friendship with the Chinese characters; the Information and Education forums at the Air Corps base (with and without Chinese participation); Lianda University in general and the circumstances in China at that time;

the character Neil Ku Nuli; the characters Mr. and Mrs. Ai (though they were not dumpling makers); some aspects of the character Chong Lingxiu; the students' plan to spirit the soldiers out of danger if Japanese forces were to overrun the American base; the move of the base to Chongqing and the introduction of the GIs to "new" Chinese friends there; the circumstances surrounding the supper with Mao Zedong and Zhou Enlai on Sept. 16, 1945, with the exception of Louis Stabler's presence.

*   *   *   *

What was Fictionalized (though placed in real settings)
American and Chinese characters not mentioned above; all events at Mr. Gong's farm.

*   *   *   *

A Note on Pronunciation
In *Born Of War* I have done my best to use Pinyin (e.g., *Xiang*) as opposed to Wade-Giles (e.g., *Hsiang*) spellings.

Cast of Characters

American Characters

Henry Neiberg: a young man living in Flatbush, Brooklyn, the apolitical son of a clothing factory owner. Hopes to marry Frances. Joins the Army and is stationed in the Statistical Control Unit (SCU) at the 14th Army Air Corps (aka the Flying Tigers) in Kunming, China. Based on a real person.

Frances: from a poor, unionist family in the Bronx. She does not wish to wait for Henry, since he is not sympathetic to those "less fortunate" than himself. Based on a real person.

Jake Singer: Henry's best friend in the Army. From New York. Attended City College where he attended rallies against Spanish fascism, among other things, and where he met his wife, Blanche. Based on a real person.

Stan Freilich: an American soldier in the SCU. A typesetter from Cleveland, plays clarinet, misses his girlfriend, Irma. Fictional.

Major Drum: an officer in the SCU. Fictional.

Paul Danko: a member of the SCU. Fictional.

Ken McPhee: a member of the SCU. Fictional.

Louis Stabler: a member of the SCU. Fictional.

Larry Curley: one of the soldiers at the 14th Army Air Corps. Very involved in general operations, including the PX and giving out mail. Fictional.

Maurice: a member of the SCU. Thought to be a Communist. Fictional.

Colonel Root: one of the ranking officers in the 14th Army Air Corps. Fictional.

General Claire Chennault: C.O. of the 14th Army Air Corps. Considered one of American history's great air men. An historical figure.

Chinese Characters

"Neil" Ku Nuli: grew up in Chengdu, China, where his father, a maker of artist "chops" (signature stamps) was made to kowtow to oppressive warlords. Attended missionary school where he learned to speak several languages and acquired his western nickname. Attends Lianda University. Aspires to become a journalist. Based on a real person.

Ai Wenti: a Communist-leaning dumpling maker in Kunming. Based on a real person. Circumstances fictionalized.

Ai Huida: Ai Wenti's wife. Based on a real person. Circumstances fictionalized.

"Anton" Chong Lingxiu: a Lianda student who is also a political (Communist) activist. He had been married but his wife was killed in prison. He has not seen his son in many years. Based in part on a real person.

Xiang: a KMT-leaning student. Tolerated by the Communist-leaning students because he persists in spending time with them. Fictional.

Tia Ganjing: Mao Zedong's press attaché. Based on a real person.

Bai: a KMT-leaning student. Fictional.

Bing Po: "the-girl-who-talked-too-much." A Communist-leaning student. Later will be Neil Ku Nuli's wife. Fictional.

"Mary" Cha Wulin: the daughter of a Kunming farmer. Runs away from an arranged marriage to Pei Han, the fish-seller, and stays at Lianda University. Fictional.

Cha Siansheng: Cha Wulin's father. A farmer on the outskirts of Kunming (*"Siansheng"* is an honoring title, like "sir" in English). Fictional.

"Jane" Ju Shiyan: Cha Wulin's best friend. A city girl to whose Kunming family's shop Cha Siansheng makes regular deliveries. Fictional.

Pei Han: a fish-seller in Kunming whose family has arranged his marriage to Cha Wulin. Fictional.

Chen Liduo: a young man from Nanking who has witnessed the slaughter of his family. Fictional.

Professor Shin: a Communist-leaning professor at Lianda. Fictional.

Dr. Wu: a KMT-leaning Lianda professor. Fictional.

Colonel Yin: a KMT officer. Fictional.

Gong Fu Ma: a farmer in the countryside. Has twin daughters, Guelo and Ting Siao. Fictional.

Historical Note

The goals of American involvement in China during the Second World War included battling the Japanese war machine that had so devastated cities such as Shanghai and, of course, Nanking, as it raged west from China's eastern coast. Central to that goal was teaching the Nationalist forces, led by Chiang Kaishek, to fight and supplying them with firepower and training for the job.

The senior officer in the China-Burma-India Theatre of War was General Joseph W. Stilwell (aka Vinegar Joe, aka Walking Joe), who had been stationed in China for ten years between World Wars I and II. Stilwell had served as a construction engineer, army language student and official observer of the Chinese Armies. As Military Attaché to the American Embassy to Beijing he was acquainted with all levels of Chinese officials. Stilwell's war journals, arranged by Theodore H. White, are known as *The Stilwell Papers* and are, along with 10–12 hours of taped interviews, one of several sources for this book.

According to General Stilwell, the Kuomintang (or KMT, or Nationalists), who were America's official Chinese allies, were a corrupt and chaotic regime, hoarding equipment acquired from America via the Lend Lease program for their own use against the Communists. The Nationalist Generalissimo, Chiang Kaishek, was ungrateful, Stilwell wrote, and complained incessantly about the meagerness of the supplies and training his armies received. The Communists, Stilwell noted, reduced taxes and rents, and raised production.

The Chinese soldiers and Chinese people in general were, in Stilwell's opinion, fundamentally honest, frugal, industrious, cheerful, independent, tolerant, friendly and courteous.

The Statistical Control Unit (SCU) at the 14th Army Air Corps was in a unique position to track equipment, since the unit was in part made up of accountants whose job it was to catalog equipment, personnel, and activity, in reports to Washington. Members of the SCU, including the individuals described in this book, confirmed what Stilwell learned and what eventually became common knowledge: that our allies were storing American equipment for their own uses, and were less than enthusiastic allies.

The Chinese Communists, led by Mao Zedong and Zhou Enlai, were a thorn in Chiang Kaishek's side. In that early period of Chinese Communism, especially among students and the youth, there was great enthusiasm and optimism for the Communist grass roots political, military and social programs. Added to this was the successful, especially early in the war, defense of large areas of Northern China referred to by the Communists as the Liberated Areas.

That a poorly armed, untrained (in the western sense) band of rebels could hold off the Japanese Imperial Army was astonishing, to say the least, to American military ears. To achieve this feat, the Communists harnessed the bitterness of a massive peasantry that had been oppressed for centuries. Whatever would come later, the Chinese Communists of the 1930s and 40s were a modern miracle of organization, military ingenuity and social mobility for huge numbers of very poor people who had never experienced anything but oppression.

The KMT discouraged and eventually blockaded western contact with Yenan, where the Communists were headquartered. American journalists, including Theodore H. White and Brooks Atkinson, broke the blockade and established friendships with the Communists for a variety of reasons, including the hope of perhaps containing or influencing the approaching civil war. Reports unanimously demonstrated that the Communist region was popularly governed and engaged in successful peasant guerrilla campaigns against the Japanese. These reports were quickly banned by KMT censors.

American Vice President Henry Wallace, the well-known foreign service officer John Service (who grew up in China), and President Roosevelt sought further official insight into the viability of the Communists as a military and possible political ally. They convinced Chiang Kaishek to authorize the dispatch of a small foreign service delegation to Yenan. The United States Army Observation Group was informally referred to as the Dixie Mission because of its location in "Rebel" (Chinese) Territory.

The Communists were, from the American entry into the war, exceedingly pro-American. The American view, as evidenced by reports submitted by John Service in 1944 on behalf of the Dixie Mission, was equally enthusiastic.

Lianda University was the wartime union of some of China's best universities, which had been forced to flee the west-rushing Japanese forces. Its campus in Kunming was not far from the 14th Army Air Corps base (the Flying Tigers) where the events in this book take place. Some Lianda students leaned politically towards the KMT, others towards the Communists, and many were unaffiliated but hopeful and looking only for representative, fair leadership.

It should be noted that General Claire Chennault, the 14th Air Corps' commanding officer and widely thought of as one of the great airmen of American history, was at odds with General

Stilwell politically. It should also be noted that late in the war General Stilwell was recalled to the United States, and his and the Dixie Mission's recommendations were rejected.

The meeting between the soldiers and Mao Zedong actually did take place on September 16th, 1945 and is as accurately portrayed as possible, with the exception of the attendance of Louis Stabler, who is a fictional character. Mao Zedong and Zhou Enlai were in Chongqing at the American Government's request for a (failed) last ditch attempt at reconciliation with Chiang Kaishek and the Nationalist Government.

Prologue

Henry Neiberg held open the heavy glass door and followed Frances from the cold, salt-white Queens sidewalk onto the red pile carpeting of the darkened Chinese restaurant. His knees shook slightly, in part from age and the cold, wet February, in part from nervousness. A white-haired Chinese man, tall and straight-backed, wearing a brown corduroy overcoat, waited at the largest of the room's circular banquet tables. Before the maitre d', who had begun to lift a finger in his direction, could utter a word, Henry brushed past him, leaving Frances shaking her head and smiling in her new dress, pearls and red nails. A plain wooden barrette, long and tan and unstained, pinned back her hair on the left side.

"Chong Lingxiu, my old friend!" Henry approached the man at the table, who looked startled for a moment, and then grinned through uneven teeth.

"Henry!" His voice was deep and resonant. The two men embraced for more than a minute. "After thirty years, Corporal Henry Neiberg! And this must be the famous Frances."

Only then did Henry inch around on creaky knees and hold open his arm to his wife. "She certainly is. Sweetheart, this is Mr. Chong Lingxiu, student leader and, more or less, my long lost brother." On the last word, his voice broke and he rubbed the corner of his eye with a sun-roughened knuckle.

Chong stepped toward her, and Frances saw that he walked with a quick, awkward step on one side, as though his knee did not work properly. He bent forward and kissed her. "I have heard so much about you. Let me take your coat. And Henry, we are in America now. Call me Lingxiu Chong, in the American order. Family name last."

Henry bowed slightly. "Thank you for correcting me. Ah, who's this coming?"

Two couples approached the table. Rapid-fire Mandarin flew back and forth between them and Chong.

"Honey," Henry said, his smile spreading, becoming a glow, "this is Mr. and Mrs. Ai Wenti and Neil Ku Nuli and, I don't remember your wife's name. I'm sorry."

"Bing Po," said Neil Ku Nuli, the thinner of the most recently-arrived men. His hair was gray but full. His wife was all smiles. She waved.

"Hello! Hello everyone!"

Ai Wenti, his hair jet black, eyes bright and teeth perfect, took everyone's coats and hung them on a nearby rack. Everyone sat down around the table.

Henry clasped Frances's hand to his chest, head shaking, his smile small now, and turned inward so that it barely coaxed the edges of his mouth upwards. "This is really something," he kept repeating to himself.

Ai Wenti, or Wenti Ai as Chong insisted he be referred to in the American way, signalled to the waiter, who brought a bottle of *Mao Tai* and tiny glasses.

"How is your son?" Henry asked Chong.

"He is well and working in Shanghai. And I have two grandsons. You have daughters?"

"Two, yes. They are doing very well, thank you. Ah, look who it is."

A short man in his mid-fifties with thick graying hair and a wide, toothy grin was coming towards them, a heavy palm already outstretched. "Well, well!" His booming voice caused heads to turn around the room. "All my old friends are starting without me! I don't understand it. Not like you at all!"

Neil Ku got up from his chair, went around to the other side of the table and embraced Jake Singer. "And where is Blanche?"

Jake's voice dropped and he glanced at the floor. "I'm afraid Blanche passed away last year." His smile returned. "Neil, I can't tell you how wonderful it is to see you. Did you come by bicycle? I didn't notice your black bike parked outside."

Neil laughed and waved him away. He sat down. "This is Bing Po, my wife."

Bing Po waved.

Jake kissed her lightly on the cheek, slapped Henry on the shoulder, and kissed Frances. "Hiya, folks. And Chong Lingxiu..."

Henry interrupted. "He wants us to reverse the names. We're in America now, he says. So call him Lingxiu Chong."

"How about I call him Anton. That was what we called you, right? Your anglicized name?" Jake looked at Frances. "They used their anglicized names to stay out of trouble with the American brass, who put a lot of effort into finding out just who these young Chinese with all the information were."

"I know," Frances nodded. "I've been hearing these stories for thirty years."

Mr. Ai poured a bit of the clear liquor into a glass, indicating to everyone else to follow suit. He then rose and cleared his throat. His English was barely altered by any accent.

"Permit me," he bowed slightly, "to dominate." A neat waiter in white shirt, red vest and black pants brought a tray of appetizers. With a barely noticeable gesture, Mr. Ai signalled for him to wait.

"To old friends and a Chinese and American friendship unbroken by time or distance. *Gambei!*" He took a quick drink, held his glass upside down and took his seat.

Jake Singer stood up, raising his glass. "From Kunming 1944, to Chongqing 1945, to Flushing 1977! *Gambei!*"

"Do you remember," Neil Ku said in his typically soft voice, and everyone quieted at once, "our picnics at Grandview Park? And the forums at the Army base?"

Jake picked up a smooth, red napkin and spread it on his lap. "What I remember is how you pedalled onto the base, Neil, and told us the Japanese Army was advancing towards the base. I remember how you fellows arranged to provide us with an escape into the countryside."

"Not just an escape," said Neil Ku. "A life, as English teachers somewhere in the countryside."

"They would have been AWOL," Frances exclaimed, her palm to her cheek.

Henry grinned and shook his head. "They sure had it all worked out. We'd be taken away in the middle of the night. The Army wouldn't have liked it very much, and we certainly would never have gone AWOL, but these fellas were something. They really cared about us." He stood up.

"I'd like to make a toast."

Jake pointed to his glass. "You should have something to make it with."

"It doesn't matter. First of all, I'd like to introduce our Chinese friends to my bride of thirty one years, Mrs. Frances Neiberg." He waited while everyone applauded. "As you can see, she is wearing the famous barrette. I'm sure you'll all agree that it looks much better on her lovely head than it did in the dusty pocket of my service uniform or in my locker."

There were murmurs of agreement all around.

He took a deep breath. "And I want to thank you all for coming. A serious note: I know there have been some difficult times since we were last together. I for one haven't agreed with everything our respective governments have done since 1945—not by a long shot. But our friendship is not based on governments or politics. It is based on our growing to love each other, despite being in the middle of a war and our being as different from one another as different can be. So thank you for remembering the nights Jacob and I slept on the floor of Mr. Ai's dumpling shop, and our wonderful discussions about American and Chinese life. When I arrived in China, I didn't know where to turn. I was scared and lonely and, to be honest, I missed my own wonderful mother terribly. But you gentlemen..." His voice trailed off and he paused. The rest of the sentence rushed too quickly from his mouth.

"You gave me a new family, on the other side of the world. Thank you!"

Chong patted Henry on the back.

"You're welcome," said Mr. Ai.

Mrs. Ai, tiny and birdlike, shook a finger. "You remember our advice? We did a very nice job."

Henry nodded. "I'm glad I listened. Frances and I wouldn't be here otherwise."

"I'd like to say something." Frances remained seated but lifted her glass. "I must thank you all. Though until today, I never met any of you and our homes are many thousands of miles apart, we truly are family, as sure as my parents and sister and I are family. I thank you because, without you, I would never have agreed to marry my husband." She clasped Henry's hand, smiled into his eyes, and kissed him.

I

AUTUMN, 1941

Henry Neiberg had been humming since they left his mother's house on East Ninth Street, between Avenues I and J. He took Frances's fingertips in his, held her hand high in the air and twirled her around, as though they were dancing. Her new, polished wood barrette added a sunny highlight to her dark, whirling hair.

"Henry, what's gotten into you?"

"You have."

"And what's that you're humming?"

"I don't know. Something old." He skipped from the sidewalk into the street. "Or maybe something new." He skipped back onto the sidewalk, then reached for her hand, but Frances was too quick. She stepped back.

"Henry, this isn't the Audubon Ballroom. And will you tell me where we're going?"

He stopped and seemed to consider her request. "Mmm. I don't think so. Besides, we're almost there. What's the matter? You're embarrassed to be seen with me?"

"No. Well, sometimes." She brushed her hair out of her face, and Henry's eyes were drawn by the gesture. Her perfect skin, delicate nose and small mouth were overshadowed by her eyes, which at times flashed a fierceness that frightened him, while at other times they sparkled and took his breath away.

Before she could move away, he had grabbed her hand again and twirled her into his arms until they were face to face and all but kissing. "What about...now?"

"Yes! Henry, I wish you'd be more serious. You know, that's what I'm talking about. You don't notice the people who are getting polio, who can't eat, or find decent work. Look at that..." She nodded towards two men, one in an old, torn coat from the Great War, the other in a filthy rag of a shirt. The men appeared to be holding one another up under the lamp post on the street corner. They did not ask for money or food, but their eyes followed the dark, curly-haired Henry and pretty, vivacious Frances with a longing that spoke of hunger and poverty.

"How can I notice anyone?" Henry's voice grew melodramatic. "How can I see, when I'm dazzled by you?"

"Henry, you're being silly..."

Henry stopped, taking Frances by the arm. "Franny, I could learn to care about the things that are important to you. You could point them out as we go along. Mama's taught me to care about people."

Frances took his hand and pointed him back in the direction they had been going. "Your mother is a sweet, wonderful lady, but she can't help what your family does. Not that there's anything wrong with owning a dress factory. She can't help the rows of sewing machines."

Henry pulled his hand away. "The way my father makes his living doesn't make my mother one thing or another."

"No one said she was one thing or another. Your mother is wonderful. She does care about people. We're talking about you. It's important that the people in my life, especially the men…"

"Men, what men?"

"…are aware of certain realities. Maybe your mother is aware of those realities. You, I'm not so sure about." Frances smiled and her eyes sparkled. "Maybe you're too dazzled. Stop worrying about me and look around more."

Henry's voice dropped, its animation gone. "I'm aware. I look." He peered from beneath childlike, lidded eyes. In a rush, he pulled her to him again. "I'm also aware of other realities and don't deny it, you are too."

"Henry, this is a public street!" She tried to push him away.

"I'm not letting go until you admit that you feel about me the way I feel about you."

"Shh! Okay Henry. I do. Stop it. I do!"

Henry turned to a middle-aged couple in matching brown sweaters. "See? She said I do. You heard didn't you?" The man shielded his wife, who pulled her sweater close around her shoulders. The couple hurried on.

They rounded the corner and found themselves on the outer edge of a crowd of thousands of people, all pressing towards the avenue. "Ah," said Henry, "here we are."

Frances hung back. "What are they all here for?"

Henry stood as high as he could on his toes, craning his neck as the parade curved around Flatbush Avenue. Confetti and bits of string rushed over the convertible limousines carrying the pennant winning Brooklyn Dodgers. The two made their way to the bend in the road, across the street from Goodman's, where the crowd had thinned a bit, and Henry hoped to get a glimpse of Cookie Lavagetto or the MVP, Dolph Camilli, or any of his beloved "Bums."

"I wanted to see the Dodgers before I left."

"Oh," said Frances, then frowned and looked at Henry, tapping his shoulder. "For where?"

"I'm going to join the Army!" he called, out of the side of his mouth.

The noise of the crowd made it nearly impossible to hear, so Frances leaned close to him, the warm wind billowing her dark hair across his face. He cleared his throat. "I said, if we get into the war in Europe, I'm going to join the Army." He turned and held her by the shoulders. "Will you be here for me when I get back?"

She turned away, and he followed her a few feet back from the thickest part of the crowd. "I'm not going to take my father's offer to get me a desk job either. I'm going where the war takes me, whether that's France, England or Germany."

She covered her mouth, hiding a giggle. "Oh? And who are you, the Lone Ranger?" She took his hand. "It's wonderful to have a hero for a, for a—"

"For a what?" His eyes searched her face.

She shrugged. "I don't know."

He led her down the block, away from the parade, where it was quiet. Two boys on the sidewalk played boxball, slicing and slamming a pink ball with reddened palms into adjacent sidewalk squares. From an apartment somewhere above wafted the smell of homemade soup; from another came the spicy, thick aroma of pastrami; from a third, fresh garlic and tomato puree. The combination of these aromas, mixed with that of the Flatbush streets, was Brooklyn.

They stopped at a sidewalk cart pulled along by an unshaven man wearing a jacket and cap. Henry pointed to one of the four stacks of pretzels on tall rods. "One please." He looked at Frances but she shook her head. "One," he confirmed.

They walked a few steps further down the block. "Frances, please be here when I get back. We'll...we'll make a life together."

She looked up at him. He was handsome, if a little thin. His curly black hair and prominent cheekbones gave him a Mediterranean look. Her eyes softened. "Are you asking me to marry you?"

"Well, maybe. We'll have to see—"

Something on her face changed. "Henry. I—"

"What's wrong?" He took her hand. They stepped around a man sitting on an old box giving nickel shoe shines. "All I'm asking for is...is an understanding while I'm gone."

She didn't answer and wouldn't look him in the eye.

He looked around for help. "Don't spoil such a perfect day. The Dodgers won the pennant, and this parade—well, I don't think the parade is only for them. It's for us too in a way. If you'll wait for me, it'll be like I won a pennant myself, for us. We don't have to call it more than an understanding. No ring. No fancy stuff. I know you don't want anything fancy or expensive, and we don't have to have that."

She paused. "Henry. I don't think I can. It isn't just what you said about fancy stuff."

"What then? My family loves you and I think I've been accepted by your—"

"You have been. It isn't the families. It's you, Henry. And me, too. We're too different. Our views, what's important to us. Last week when we went into that store downtown—"

"For the pants?" He laughed. "Did you see how that puller tried to get me inside? The way he waited on the sidewalk for any *schlump* who walked by to get pulled in by his spiel." He made his voice squeak. "Coomb-een. Vee haf beeen vaiting ver you! Vee haf—" But Frances didn't laugh.

She looked at the ground. "You don't even know what I'm talking about. That's what I mean. There were women fighting across the street. You don't remember that, do you? A half dozen of them beating two others with handbags and umbrellas."

Henry stepped back from her and looked down the street. The aroma of soup and pastrami was stronger now. "This again."

Frances stepped towards him, looking him in the eye. "That's right, this again. Those were union girls fighting scabs. Girls from poor families who work night and day to feed and clothe themselves."

"You sound like that socialist on the soapbox. Who's the one your mother...?"

"Emma Goldman. Is it such a terrible thing I care about poor people? I'm not a rich girl, in case you haven't noticed."

He nodded. "And I know your family are unionists, and that's fine. Say, my father works hard too, you know."

Her eyes flashed and her hair jumped on the soft curve of her neck. "This has nothing to do with your family. They aren't the ones who want me to wait for them while you go off and probably get yourself killed."

He looked at the ground, then squared himself and took her by the shoulders. For a moment he said nothing, aware only of how beautiful she was. Then the words came back. "You're afraid, aren't you? That something will happen to me if you wait."

Despite her best efforts, a tear squeezed from the corner of her eye. Instantly she wiped it away. "Henry Neiberg, don't give yourself so much credit. It's simply that you don't think about the poor or spend much of your free time thinking about anyone less fortunate than yourself."

"And that's so important to you?"

She had turned away, her arms folded in front of her. Her head bobbed.

"So important that you won't wait for me?"

She nodded again.

"Then I guess you're right." He was glad now that she had turned away and couldn't see his face. "I *don't* spend a lot of time worrying about the poor. I do care, though. I'm not inhuman."

"Henry, there's no point in going on about it. Please. Take me home."

*   *   *   *

After taking Frances home, Henry rode the trains. Around him families chatted and laughed; below the windows of the rickety El was the non-stop motion of busy crowds: men in dark suits, women under big hats, children in blue shorts and t-shirts holding their mothers' hands.

He got off at Coney Island and walked around, losing himself in the smell of hot dogs and buttered popcorn and the crescendo of daring crowds on high flying rides. The war and its danger faded amidst memories of strolling on the windy boardwalk, and hot, sunny beaches—all with Frances.

He bought himself a cup of soup and a pastrami sandwich and stood at the railing looking out to sea, but the war intruded on his thoughts and he turned toward an old Chinese man holding an open palm towards passersby. He looked the man up and down, then turned away from the stringy black hair and leathered face. He had to learn to sympathize with such a man? Couldn't this man work? Hadn't he brought his difficulties on himself? Henry turned back to the ocean; he had his own troubles.

He walked a little further down the boardwalk, until he stood in front of the huge metal-spoked Wonder Wheel that turned slowly above the tiny, colorful train and the huge open mouthed clown heads that welcomed one to the ride.

Two middle aged women were walking behind him, kerchiefs on their hair, pocketbooks swinging on their forearms.

"My Jimmy says we should go on over there and fight. The French caved in, the British aren't having much more success. If we don't get involved, the Germans will overrun the whole shebang."

The second woman's voice was no nonsense. "The problem isn't the Germans, Mary. It's the Jews. None of this would've happened if it weren't for them. Think about it. And now we'll likely see our boys: your Jimmy Junior and my Georgie, sent over and God knows what'll happen to them. And all to save the Jews. It's a Jewish war, don't you see? And really now, didn't they bring it on themselves?"

*   *   *   *

Two months later, four boys ignored the December wind and played a game of stickball between the sewers on a tree-lined street in Flatbush. In a two-story brick house nearby, Henry sat at a window, watching them. Across the room, Enid, his twelve-year-old sister, watched. She had never seen her brother as quiet as he'd been since the news had come about Pearl Harbor. He was quieter even than he'd been since he and Frances had stopped seeing one another. No singing, no practical jokes, not even much of his beloved music. Only wide, sad eyes in a kind face turned fearful.

"Why don't you go out and see if you can play with those guys, Hen?"

"They've already got four. Five'll do them no good." He spoke into the sleeve of his shirt as he looked out over the blue slate porch.

"Well you can't just sit there and look like the world's going to end!"

"Sure he can." Their jowly father, Morris, was reading the Yiddish *Forward* in the swivelling armchair under a goose-necked lamp, his glasses down on his nose.

Henry lifted his head. "No Pop, I can't. If the world's going to end, how can I just sit here?" He started to go back to watching the game, but his father folded his paper and slapped it down on his lap, looking at his son.

"You were a real bigshot a month ago. Not going to take the desk job I got you, right?" He rolled his eyes, his shoulders hunching. "Look at me! I'm going in the Army! I'm a fighting man! Well now you're going, and not to any desk job! The Japanese saw to that! So how do you like it now?"

Henry looked at his father, expressionless. "I see you like it well enough."

Morris shook his finger at his son. *"Ven dos mazl kumt, shtel im a shtul!"*[1]

Henry sighed and looked at the ceiling. "Dad, I didn't want the desk job then, and I don't want it now."

"Ach!" Morris opened his newspaper and muttered to himself. *"A vinder! A nahr mahkt kinder!"*[2]

"Morris! Henry! Stop!" Nettie, Henry and Enid's mother, rushed in from the kitchen. She was a round woman with wide-set features and a kindness in her eyes even her anger with her husband couldn't hide. She looked from husband to son and back again. "Henry, he's upset because he doesn't want anything to happen to you. Morris, you should know better. Can't you see he's afraid?" When her husband continued reading, she raised her voice until, whether from sadness or sheer volume, it broke.

"Mitzn kop kegn di vant—muz men dokh hobn a vant!"[3] A pained look crossed her face. She closed her eyes for a moment, then went to her son and tried to cradle his head to her chest.

"Henry, it'll be okay."

Henry's lips tightened. He pulled away and turned to look out the window.

"Promise you'll write me every day." She paused. "Promise me, Henry."

He swallowed. "I promise, Ma."

"I'll send you packages, Henry. Food, newspapers, anything you need. Wherever you are, it'll help you feel like home."

"Thanks, ma." He turned from the window and hugged her for a long moment. "Now go on in the dining room, Ma. It's getting late and Jack Benny'll be on soon. You know how you hate to miss him."

"Henry, you're really something." Nettie patted him on the head and did as he suggested.

Morris unfolded his newspaper and cleared his throat. *"A toyte beveynt men zibn teg, a nar dos gantze lebn."*[4]

Only Enid stayed near her brother, continuing to watch him. "Well, Daddy. Maybe soon you'll have both."

Morris raised a scolding finger, sighed, shook his head, and went back to his newspaper.

Enid turned to her brother. "Are you going to say goodbye to Frances?"

"I don't know, Eenie." He got up and went to his room, closed the door, and for the rest of the evening, the only sound was the high pitched tinkle of the toy piano he had taught himself to play.

*   *   *   *

"Boo-wee-bo-doh-wee-boh-boo-we-doh!" He couldn't get that melody out of his head. It was a jumping jazz tune, but a different, boppier, more up-tempo sort of jazz than the swing he was used to. He watched New York flash by through the window of the elevated train car, trying to imprint each face and building permanently into his memory. Tomorrow at this time he'd be in Biloxi. In the Army! Everything was changing so fast. New York, his life, even jazz.

"Boo-wee-bo-doh-wee-doh...!"

When Frances opened the door, she stepped back into the apartment, fingertips at her lips.

"Henry, I hadn't expected...the drugstore boy didn't say there was a phone call."

"I know I should have called, Frances, but I'm leaving tomorrow and I had to see you first."

She nodded slowly. "Well, you saw me. I hope it was worth the trip."

He stared at her, blinking. "So that's it?"

She shrugged and bit her lip. "What did you expect, Henry?"

"I don't know. I wanted you to say, to say—"

She stepped forward and put her arms around his waist, laying her head on his chest. "Shhh. I can't."

He closed his eyes, imprinting the Rose of Sharon smell of her hair into his memory. When he opened his eyes, he held her at arm's length. "I think you can. I know you feel what I feel."

"What good does it do us? Certain things really are important to me. Values. Caring about people..."

"Less fortunate than us. Yeah, I know. The unions, the conditions at sweatshops, et cetera, and so forth. Are you sure it's not because my father owns a dress factory?"

"That's not fair, Henry." Her lips hardened and a spark lit in her eyes. "The fact that you say that shows me you don't understand.

Caring about people—poor, hardworking people—is as important to my family as, as going to synagogue on Saturday is to your father."

A mischievous spark lit in his eye. "You know…he misses a Saturday now and then." When she didn't react, he looked upwards and sighed. "Frances, I didn't mean it that way. Doesn't the way we feel about each other count for anything?" He reached for her with his palm, wanting to feel the vulnerability of her delicate features in his hand.

She stepped back, and his hand brushed the side of her head. Her barrette clattered to the floor. She nodded. "It does, but not for everything."

"So you won't wait for me." It was a statement rather than a question. He bent to pick up the barrette, but when he straightened, she had turned away.

Frances didn't answer. She was crying and didn't want him to see.

Henry took a step back from the doorway. "Goodbye, Frances." He walked away, leaving her in the open doorway. It was only when he stepped out into the bright sunlight, that he realized that the smooth, wooden barrette was still clenched in his sweating fist.

*   *   *   *

THE GIs

Several months later, Henry lay on the ship's deck with dozens of other recruits. It had been days since they'd left New York Harbor bound for India, and he was long used to the gentle rocking of the ship. Others weren't so lucky. Many lay moaning in their bunks, below deck. A few gripped the iron railings, gasping at the sea air or refusing to budge from a single spot.

The training at Biloxi had been a blur, perhaps because of the nagging ache that started at the base of his throat and worked down to the pit of his stomach. He had read in one of the manuals that he was expected to report any physical difficulty to his superior officer or the appropriate medical personnel. He would have been reluctant to report, particularly for the record, that he was suffering from the acute effects of a broken heart.

He kept Frances's barrette in his right pants pocket. In the mornings, as soon as he fastened his pants, he would take out the barrette and look at it for a few moments, imagining it had just come from Frances's hair and that it still smelled of the Rose of Sharon trees in Inwood Park. Sometimes, he would close his fist around the barrette so no one could see what was in his hand, then hold it up to his nose and let his mind revel in and expand on the faint but dizzying blend of New York City fauna, finely sanded wood, and his beloved Frances.

Only one moment stood out at Biloxi: when they had told him his assignment. *China.* The Asian Theatre of War. Why didn't they just send him to the moon? He wanted to go to war! To help fight that madman in Europe. What in God's name was he going to do in China? The war in Asia was a secondary war, the backroom game. Frances would be unimpressed.

On the ship to India, he daydreamed in the grim Atlantic sun, escaping the fact that he couldn't even get his enlistment right, and that the woman he loved wouldn't wait for him. Sometimes his mind fled the ship and delivered him to Orchard Beach, where he'd spent so many summer afternoons with Frances, her hair flying in the wind. He thought of Inwood Park, across the river from her family's apartment, where an enormous tulip tree towered over fields of wildflowers overlooking the Hudson. He and

Frances walked, hand in hand, picking raspberries and blueberries on either side of the tree, buying fresh vegetables at the farm down the road. Afterwards, they dressed up and went dancing at the packed Audubon Ballroom on 160th Street.

Once, a voice cut through his daydream and he opened his eyes to see a burly man whose green fatigues were rolled up high on his forearms talking to a lean redhaired recruit, who was smoking with his back against a painted wood compartment. "Oh, India's not so bad. You can buy nice trinkets there for a song, sell 'em back home, make yourself a nice little piece of change."

"I don't know," said the redhead. "Those Indians look a whole lot like niggers to me." He dragged on the cigarette.

A card game was going on about twenty feet towards the stern of the ship and one of the players, a short man with a long, thin face, stood up and walked over to the redhaired recruit. "What did you say?"

"You got a hearin' problem? I said the Indians look like niggers." He grinned at the man he'd been talking to. "What's this guy, passin'?"

The short man hit him with a quick right cross to the side of the face. The cigarette flew from the redhead's mouth and he crumpled to the ground, clutching his bleeding jaw. "Hey, whatcha go and do that for?"

"You don't like niggers? I don't like bigots."

The redhead was about to say something else, but the short man had rejoined his game. After a moment, Henry got up, steadied himself, as he had learned to do when standing up on the ship, and walked over to watch the card game.

"Wanna play?" The short man asked.

Henry sat down. "I really don't play much besides pinochle."

"Spoken like a real sharp. So you'll learn."

"No, really."

The short man showed a toothy grin that with his long face made him look a little like Bogart, a little like Henry's own father, he thought.

"I'm Jake," the card player said, "and these're Maurice, Danko and Benny. It's a friendly game, so don't worry."

As they played, Jake talked about having gone to City College in New York, where he and Maurice had protested the Spanish Civil War. He had met his wife, Blanche, in the American Student Union. She joined him at those and other protests.

"You guys'd get along fine with my fiancé, um, my girlfriend," Henry said. "She has a real political conscience. Says I have none at all."

Jake rolled a toothpick around his mouth with his tongue. "Politics is what you read about in the newspapers. This stuff's life. Look at what's been happening in Europe, even before the war. Fascism spreading like the plague. Germany, to Italy, then Spain. Hell, there's a fascist party in England." He shook his head; the toothpick in his mouth rolled to the other side. "Can't just let that go on."

Maurice nodded. "You don't get involved in it, it'll all go to shit before you know it."

Benny raised an eyebrow. "I don't know. I can't get involved. Too easy to make enemies."

Henry felt the same way, but kept his opinion to himself.

2

The men bounced in the backs of green trucks over dirt roads towards their destination: the 14th Army Air Corps, soon to be called the Army Air Force, The Flying Tigers.

"Kunming," the driver called over his shoulder, "is the City of Eternal Spring."

Henry peered between the green flaps covering the back of the truck, and saw that there were indeed beautiful flowers and trees lining the sides of the road, and the climate was as temperate and comfortable as a spring morning in Inwood Park. But amidst the natural beauty, the squalor of life in war torn China was even more apparent. Low buildings of mud and bamboo stood unsteadily, their doors and windows open to the wind. Anyone wealthy enough rode a bicycle, while most walked or rode ox carts or donkeys, their ragged clothes gray from the road's dust. The injured, sick, and unspeakably poor were everywhere. Bony children, their faces covered with the same layer of grime that lay over the unpaved roads, took it all in with huge eyes that had seen too much in too short a time. Men with limbs missing, wounds barely covered with red tatters, hobbled along, sometimes trying to catch up with more able-bodied family, other times alone, trying only to catch up with something better than their lot this day.

And along the roadsides marched lines of Central Government troops.

"Those're our allies," the driver yelled, over the grinding of the truck's gears. He laughed. "You guys got your work cut out for you if the Army thinks you guys'll be training them to fight!"

Gangs of grimy boys hurried out of the tramping Chinese soldiers' path, hiding in huts and behind trees. "What's with the kids running away?" one of the men asked.

"They'll get grabbed into the Army if the soldiers see 'em. No draft here. They just grab 'em by the neck, and drag 'em along with the unit."

And Henry did see, at the rear of one of the long lines of soldiers, several boys with the lost adolescent look boys get when they are out in the world for the first time without their mothers. He closed his eyes, and reached without thinking into his right pants pocket for the smooth security of the wooden barrette.

In the low, flat area at the outskirts of the city, barely a dozen *li* from Kunming Center, the American Army had constructed the 14th Army Air Force base. Its runways and hangars housed everything from monster aircraft bringing in supplies, to Superfortress bombers, to quick fighters designed to engage Japanese Zeroes and protect Allied ground forces. From the air, the fields between planes might have appeared a shifting olive color, so filled were they with servicemen tending to the aircraft and loading and unloading equipment and supplies.

"Guess you know that ten or fifteen percent of that stuff'll get sold," the driver said.

"What're you talking about?" Jake demanded. "That equipment's for fighting the war and training Chinese GIs."

The driver laughed, started to explain, and laughed again. "First of all, don't call them GIs, we might have an accident, okay? You guys are GIs. Them? Well, anyway, didn't anyone ever tell you about The Squeeze?"

"The Squeeze? Sure, it's a dance..."

"A dance!" The driver started laughing again and the truck swerved violently to the left.

"The Squeeze," he said, taking a few deep breaths, "is the take, the pocket. Everything here is for sale. Anything you get downtown, you send home, and your wife or buddies sell it for you. Some guys have little businesses going. The equipment gets sold too, when guys think they can get away with it."

Jake looked around. "Who would buy—?"

"Think about who needs it, Einstein. The Chinese, us, everyone."

"But don't we share equipment with them anyway?"

"Oh, we share, but only for them to use to fight the enemy. The Chinese got other enemies—like other Chinese."

Jake frowned, sucking air through the gap between his teeth.

Henry watched the scenery. Gradually, the crowds thinned and the lush greens and yellows of the Kunming countryside became more apparent, only to fade to the mauve of runways, hangars, and supply areas, and the tent green of the Rec Hall, PX and Mess areas. Beyond these lay the technical work units, such as Photo Intelligence and Statistical Control, which was Henry's unit. The enlisted men's barracks and the slightly larger officers' quarters were just past these, after which, finally, was the spreading country estate formerly belonging to a local landlord, now inhabited by the austere airman known as the Old Man—General Claire Chennault.

As soon as they arrived at the Statistical Control barracks, a long building of unpainted wood, Henry sat down on his bunk to write his mother. He wrote about the smell of wood, oil and sweat. He did not detail the poverty he had seen, but mentioned only that the streets were like something out of a Charles Dickens novel. Not exactly a lie; more of a misdirection.

Around him, men were putting up cheesecake pinups of models and movie stars, wearing little besides shorts and come hither smiles.

After lunch, Henry finished the letter. This second page was about food. He had taken his mother's cooking for granted.

Major Drum, who was three hundred pounds and so white in hair and moustache that he looked to Henry like an overweight polar bear, rounded the unit up for a briefing with Colonel Root, who was the day-to-day commanding officer below the Old Man.

Colonel Root paced behind an unstained pine desk, small hands clasped behind his back. His face was red with energy or, perhaps, rage, and he gave off a scent of witch hazel, like the barbershops Henry remembered from down on the Avenue in Brooklyn.

"Welcome to the Flying Tigers, men, and to the 24th Statistical Control Unit in particular." The Colonel's mouth moved in what passed for a smile. "Your job here is to collect facts and compile reports."

"On what, sir?" asked one of the men.

"Oh, on everything: missions flown, not just by our Air Corps but by everyone. On planes in the air, planes on the ground, planes shot down, planes repaired. And I want to know the results of the missions: what's been hit, what's been missed. It'll all be coded and sent back Stateside."

The men shifted in their seats.

The Colonel had been pacing back and forth. Now, he picked up the pace. "I want you all to remember why we're here, to remember who our friends and enemies are. For those of you who don't know the difference," he took out two photographs and passed the first around, "this is the enemy."

Someone snickered.

"You see something funny, soldier?" The Colonel walked up to the grinning GI, his face inches from the soldier's.

"No, sir."

"Okay, Drum, pass out the second one. That one's a friend. A Chinese Central Government soldier under the command of Chiang Kaishek."

"Chancre Jack,"[5] someone whispered.

"He's our friend, here, pally. We're here to make him a fighting man and the job of this unit is to keep him supplied and to keep our ship's stores in order. You men were probably accountants and mathematicians and such as civilians. Well, that'll come in handy here." The Colonel made a popping sound with his lips. "Do a good job, and that friend in that picture will be a better soldier, faster, and you know what that'll mean. Anybody?"

Henry put up his hand.

"You're not in school, soldier."

"It'll mean we'll all go home faster, sir?" Henry said, a picture of Frances in his mind.

"That's right," he peered at Henry. "It'll mean these Chinese soldiers will be able to fight their own battles." He turned to walk to the front of the room.

"And we'll be able to get back to the real war, sir?"

The colonel spun. "Who said that? What's your name?"

"McPhee," said a tall, sandy haired GI with sleepy blue eyes.

"Well, McPhee," the colonel's eyes widened. "For your information there are some awfully brave pilots flying supplies over the Hump to feed your skinny butt. Boys over here are going to die, same as they are in Europe. Care to tell their mothers this isn't a real war?"

McPhee winced. "No, sir."

Root nodded. "You men just stay on the same page and remember, these Chinese are allies. I don't want to hear that Chancre

Jack crap. And, oh, that reminds me." His eyes narrowed and he scrutinized the men. "Listen to me very carefully. I don't want you men discussing the internal politics of China. Not at all. Not a word. Not with the Chinese, not even among yourselves. Got that?"

Henry and Jake looked at one another. Jake gave a silent whistle.

The Colonel went on, pacing again. "Major Drum will hand out a list of restaurants you men are to stay away from. These are decent places and no one wants to see them wrecked by any of you on your time off. Okay then. Dismissed."

Major Drum stood at the door as the men shuffled past. "You men meet me at the Rec Hall in ten minutes."

A dark-eyed GI who looked vaguely familiar put out a hand. "Paul Danko. I remember you from the ship. I was one of the guys playing cards when Benny Leonard Junior over there put out that cracker's lights."

Henry glanced at Jake Singer, then grinned. "Henry Neiberg. What do you suppose he meant by us not discussing Chinese politics?"

Danko shrugged. "What do I care about politics? I guess I see what he means about staying out of the restaurants, though. We're not here to break the place up."

Jake looked thoughtful. "I'd like to know what was behind that other thing."

Danko looked at Henry. "You're from Brooklyn?"

"How can you tell?"

Danko laughed as they left the building, the light screen door slamming behind them. "You might as well be wearing a sign. I'm from Wisconsin. Racine."

They walked together to the Rec Hall, a cavernous hangar-like building with a large locked area set aside towards the rear for the PX, a food and supply store for the men. An old radio sat at one end and to its right was an even older upright piano. Round tables and wooden chairs filled about half the hall, with the other end remaining open, as if for a dance floor, though Henry could not imagine with whom one might dance.

Henry pointed to the counter. "Think they have eggcreams there?"

Danko frowned. "What's an eggcream?"

"What's an eggcream?" Henry shook his head. "Never mind, even if they have 'em here, there isn't any way the Army would know how to make a good eggcream."

They sat down at one of the tables, exchanging nods with Jake and two other men. "Jake," Henry said, "ever been to Fineman's Candystore under the El?"

Singer leaned forward. "I've been there. They make the best eggcreams in the city. And for an extra nickel, they'll add a little syrup."

Henry nodded. "And for a nickel less you get 'em plain—no milk. Used to take Frances there. There's a kid with bad skin who works there in the afternoons—"

"Pinky Lash. Yeah, makes an eggcream like nobody's business!" Henry sat back, his chair up on two legs.

"So, what's an eggcream," Danko wanted to know.

"Soda, milk and chocolate syrup," Jake explained, pretending to swoon.

"No eggs?"

"I don't know," said Henry, "the girl who's there on Friday nights can make an eggcream that's as near to perfect as—"

"Have you guys seen any Red Cross nurses?" Danko interrupted. "I heard..."

"Gentlemen!" Major Drum had waddled to the front of the room and was trying to pull himself up on the low, shelflike stage. After a few tries, he gave up and took a corncob pipe from his shirt pocket and held a match over it, puffing a few times. "I'm here to tell you that while everything the colonel just told you is true, the Chinese we're here to help are no bargain. They're as filthy and disgusting as the rest of this country of theirs."

Danko looked at his fingers. "Nothing like selling us on the job."

Drum continued. "But the colonel's right about this: the sooner we get the job done, the sooner we'll be outta here. And that means working together." He pointed in Danko's direction. "And not screwing around. You men do as you're told, stay out of the pilots' way and toe the line around here. My line. Now we have some time before you have to get back to work and I have some paperwork to do, so you guys have the Rec Hall for an hour. But remember, this is your Rec Hall, and there's only one radio, so find a way to work that out. This godforsaken country isn't a democracy, but you guys know how to work things out democratically. Okay, then." He puffed a few times for emphasis and waddled out of the hall.

A few GIs, including Danko and Jake Singer, went back to the barracks for a game of cards. In the corner, a reed-thin, balding GI snapped open a squarish leather case, and fitted three sections of black tubing together. Seconds later, flowery jazz riffed from the clarinet, the sound at times quick and thin, at others mellow and slow. After showing off arpeggios and trills, the soldier settled into a steady swing, dropping down to provide its own rhythm and bass, and jumping up again to fill the spaces with flourishes of melody and embellishment.

The men stopped their conversation, fingers began snapping, feet tapping. Heads bobbed and chins jutted to a constant, distant chorus of low flying bombers and P-42s screaming on takeoff. One of the men, pretending to look shy, stood up and danced around his chair with an invisible partner, kissing and mugging for attention. Henry walked over, opened the piano and began filling in with simple chords, as surprised as anyone when they fit. Men began drifting over, bringing their beer bottles, whistling.

A tall, well-built GI with deep-set eyes pushed to the front. "I hate to break it up," he said in a loud voice, "but it's time for *The Lone Ranger.*" He pointed to the radio.

Some of the men stopped their tapping and whistling, as though they knew this soldier.

"Everyone's having a good time fella," said Henry, not looking up as he wanted to make sure his fingers remained on the right keys. "Can't you miss it this once?"

The soldier shrugged. "The men listen to *The Lone Ranger* all the time. I'd hate to disappoint them. Besides, you can always play later. With *The Lone Ranger* we don't have that choice. Come on, pal, we're all on the same team."

Henry nodded slowly. "Riiight." He closed the piano cover over the keys. "We're real democratic around here," he mumbled.

"It's okay," said Stan, holding up a hand to Henry. "Some of the politicians from my home town practice exactly that kind of democracy." He saluted the soldier, who had joined another, shorter soldier at a table near the radio. "We can play later. Hi-ho, Silver."

He put out a hand. "Stan Freilich."

Henry nodded. "Henry Neiberg. Who are those guys?"

"That's Marlowe, and his friend over there is Mannion. They're pilots. Keep to themselves mostly. And with their ground crews."

"What's that they're wearing around their necks?"

"Medallions," Stan said. "All kinds. Crosses, Stars of David, but usually St. Christophers. They're good luck. When they go out on missions, they put 'em under their pillows and don't make their beds. I guess it's kind of for good luck. Like they'll have to come back if their beds're waiting for them." He overpronounced the letter t, Henry noticed.

"Ohh." Henry had started developing a dislike for Marlowe, but it leveled off to a cool ambivalence.

They found Danko, Jake Singer, McPhee and Maurice playing poker when they arrived back at the barracks. Chung, one of the Chinese houseboys who cleaned the barracks, came in, carrying a broom. He had started sweeping at the far end of the room and was working his way towards the doorway, through which he swept whatever dust and dirt he had collected. The men ignored him.

Within a few minutes Sergeant Larry Curley arrived with the mail, and Henry lay back on his bunk to read a letter from his mother. A package had accompanied the letter, but first he wanted to scan what she'd written for any word of Frances.

He mumbled as he read. "Dum, da dum, da dum, da dum, da neighbors. Dum da dum, da dum, da dum, da Eenie. Dum da dum, da dum, da dum, da Pop. Dum da, dum da, dum da, dum da, dum da Rabbi. Hmmm." His eyes reached the end of the letter and then closed for a moment. "Not a word about Frances." He took the barrette from his pocket and looked at it for a long moment. Then he took a deep breath and opened the package. Instantly, a special combination of soap and kitchen smells filled the area around his bunk. For a moment, his mother might have been in the room instead of on the other side of the world. He took another deep breath to keep the tears from spilling out onto his face, tore the paper off the box and stared at its contents.

He ran his hand over the top item, his parents' wedding picture, then gingerly lifted it from the plain brown wrapping, and hung it high on his locker.

"Ho! That's some catch." Henry nearly jumped off his bunk. The sound of the box being torn open had drawn Stan to watch over his shoulder. "Boxes of candy, canned fruit, nuts and…ohmygod am I dreamin'? A bottle of goddam scotch! That must've cost four bucks! Mind if I have a little taste? Just a taste, I've got my own cup."

Henry stared at him. "Nice of you to ask, *schnorrer*."

At the open end of the barracks, Danko cleared his throat. "Let's fold the game a minute." The men got up to look over Henry's package. He opened some of its contents, including the scotch, and doled portions out to the men. The chocolates he put in a wooden cabinet.

Chung, the houseboy, shook his head. "Don't put in there. Rats eat."

Henry laughed. "How can rats get into a chest of drawers? Reach up and open it?"

Chung pointed to the chest. "No good. Rats eat," he repeated.

Henry waved him away. "Don't worry, Chung. It'll be safe in here."

Stan let out a moan. He was sitting on his bunk, his scotch in one hand, a piece of paper in the other. On his lap was a torn envelope. He swilled the rest of his scotch. "My girl just dumped me," he said, to no one in particular. "Irma's gone. Thank God for your package."

"Sorry to hear it," said Jake.

"I know how you feel," said Henry.

Stan held up his cup. "Say, Neiberg, you got any more of this?"

"I guess, for such a special occasion." He poured Stan some more scotch, which was promptly swallowed.

"But you know what, guys? It's okay." Stan nodded. "I can take rejection. Look what happened at the Rec."

"What happened there?" Danko asked.

Henry shrugged. "Bunch of guys didn't want us to play music, 'cause they wanted to listen to the radio. Let's just say they weren't real *menschen* about it."

Danko shrugged. "We're in this together. We've got to figure that stuff out."

"That's right," said Stan. "I got rejected back in Cleveland, I can get rejected here. I'll bet I'm the first GI to be rejected on both sides of the puddle!" He laughed. "More scotch?"

Henry shook his head. "I think I'll save it for later."

Danko perked up. "I know what we can do, and it'll take Stan's mind off his girl. We can go downtown."

"I'm all for that," said Jake, "except I really should answer Blanche's letter. She doesn't say it, but I can tell she's lonely."

"I can't go, either," said Maurice.

"Me, neither," said McPhee. "I think I ate something bad. Or maybe it's the water. I think I'll go over and see the nurse."

"You've been over there a lot, I notice," Danko grinned.

McPhee nodded. "Well, the water here is a little..." he tilted his hand to both sides.

Danko laughed. "I'll bet."

"I'm planning for the birth of our baby," said Louis Stabler, who'd been quiet until that point.

Henry looked at him. There was something odd about him. He couldn't pinpoint what it might be, but every time he spoke, something struck a wrong note in the back of Henry's mind. He shrugged, looking at Jake and Stabler.

"You guys can always go next time. I'm going to go with Paul here and Stan. I could use getting out of here, even for an hour or two."

3

Henry watched the rise and fall of the countryside through the opening in the back of the truck, wondering how such a beautiful country could be in such a predicament. He had watched a Chinese unit taking rifle practice in an open field two days earlier and had been astonished by how few soldiers knew how to use a rifle properly. Even worse had been the condition of their uniforms and their response, or lack thereof, to their commanding officer. They certainly needed help, especially given the stories he had heard about the singleminded brutality of the enemy.

He looked at Danko, who was also gazing out the back of the truck. Stan Freilich was humming, eyes closed.

Deep green fields were dotted with brown and tan trees and clusters of flowers under the bluest of skies. Henry knew they were approaching the center of Kunming because he could smell food and cigarettes mixed with the musty odor of donkeys and oxen. Soon a blend of voices and vehicles arose, a hum of busy noise.

Danko cleared his throat. "Whatdya think a whore costs around here?"

Henry raised his eyebrows and looked back at him. "I have no idea."

Stanley opened his eyes. "I hear the liquor's real firewater. Rice liquor."

"Rice wine, I think," said Danko.

"No," Stan shook his head. "I think there's a rice liquor, too. Powerful stuff. This truck's running on it, I think."

"The truck's...?"

"Never mind," Stan waved him away. "I was kidding."

Henry shook his head. The truck slowed and he heard the rise and fall of Chinese cadence, with the occasional deeper, drawn out monotone of American English. A donkey brayed and the truck lurched to one side as they pulled onto a side road and parked.

"Got a letter from my sister, Ruth," Danko was saying. "She met some kid, a 4F, I think."

"How old is she?" Henry asked.

"Seventeen. I don't think she ever kissed a guy." Danko looked sheepish. "I kind of wanted to be available when it happened. Just in case..."

"I know," Henry nodded. "I have a sister. Mine's younger too. What about you, Stan?"

"Sister? Me? No. I'm an only child. After me, you could stick a fork in my parents. They were done." Stan laughed; no one else did.

"Everybody out," said the lieutenant with whom they had hitched the ride.

They walked down the main road of Kunming Center, which was flanked by shops and vendors, each bringing their wares as close to the men as they could. Food, familiar and exotic, lay in rows or under makeshift awnings that protected them from the afternoon sun.

Stan bought a pack of cigarettes and a small bottle of some kind of Chinese liquor he claimed was the rice variety. He drank it as he walked, turning to leer at women. None of them would meet his eyes.

Henry thought again of the desperate poverty he'd read about in the works of Charles Dickens. He thought of the movie *The Grapes of Wrath,* which he had seen only a few years earlier, and had a fleeting impulse to meet some of these people, a feeling which reminded him of his mother's kindness and empathy. But when he tried to catch their eyes and smile, they averted their gaze, looked at the ground, or stepped out of his way.

"You guys want to go to a tea house?" Stan asked. No one disagreed, so they went into one of the open front shops, which was crowded with people and smoke. Three other GIs sat in the far corner. One of them waved. The other two were discussing a piece of paper on the table between them. Henry ordered a cup of tea and waited at the counter. Stan waited with him.

"I'm going to ask those guys where to find a woman," Danko said, already walking in their direction. In a moment he was back.

"I'll be back in an hour, guys," he said, winking. "Any takers? No? Okay, then." He left the shop.

Stan chuckled. "Give him ten minutes." He lifted his bottle to his lips and tilted his head back, then lit a cigarette. "You don't know how much I miss Irma."

"Oh, I think I do," said Henry.

Stan shook his head. "We used to just walk, you know? Around Cleveland. That gal loved to walk. Well, she walked right the hell out of my life. What'd she want to dump me for?"

Henry shook his head. "Hard to understand sometimes. Especially now. Maybe she didn't know what to expect when we get back."

"If," Stan corrected.

"Geez." Henry closed his eyes. "Let me try a little of that, willya?" He took the bottle from Stan and took a tentative sip, welcoming its burn. "That's no wine. More like gasoline."

"Well, *gambei*." Stan nodded.

"What's that mean?"

"Bottom's up, more or less. Like a toast."

"You an Indians fan?"

Stan nodded. "Yeah. Guess you're a Yankee fan."

Henry shook his head. "Dodgers."

"Poor guy."

"Whatdya mean, they won the pennant."

"Yeah, but then they got the Yankees and got beat 4–1 in the Series."

"Well," Henry shrugged. "You can't have everything."

Stan nodded. "Not with the Yankees around. They're inevitable, like this damn war." He took another drink. "I just wish Irma—"

"Will you stop about Irma. There's nothing you can do about it. You hear me going on about Frances? You think I don't miss her like crazy?"

They stood in the middle of the noisy tea shop, Stan drinking and Henry trying to ward off persistent thoughts and memories— afternoons on the lower east side of Manhattan, window shopping and chatting as he and Frances passed shops different but not so different from the ones on these city streets. He sighed and blinked against tears he attributed to the smoke.

"Let's get out of here."

"We're supposed to wait for Danko."

But Henry was already walking towards the front of the shop. As they squinted against the sudden sunlight, Danko staggered up.

"Have a good time?" Henry asked.

"Oh, a regular shopping spree." Danko stepped towards Henry, then backed up a few feet, into a table of middle-aged

Chinese men smoking and playing cards. The men fell silent and looked up at Danko, who gave no sign he noticed them. "This town, this marketplace is a regular F.J. Woolworth's."

Henry thought a moment. "I don't think it's F.J., I think—"

"Can't you see what I'm saying?"

"Well, I'd have to hear what—"

Danko rolled his eyes and Henry thought of the performer Eddie Cantor who did the same thing in an exaggerated way. "Harry, these damn Chinks have—"

Now it was Henry's turn to roll his eyes. "Paul, the name's Henry and they're not Chinks." He looked inadvertently at the card playing men. "They're our allies."

"I need a drink," said Danko.

Stan, who'd been watching with an amused smile on his face, pulled out his bottle and handed it to Danko.

"Thanks," said Danko.

"You think he needs that?" Henry asked.

"He said he does," said Stan.

"Who are they to have all those American cigarettes, food, blankets and so on? All made Stateside. We don't even have that stuff. Hell!" Danko waved the flask and turned to the card playing men. "Hell, I don't even have half that stuff at home and you bastards have it here!"

Henry started gently guiding Danko towards the sunlight that spilled through the entrance. "Don't you think some GIs just sold it to em?"

He waved the flask, bellowing. "Our money went to make those things. And some of our boys had to risk their necks flying it over the Hump. Between the damn Himalayas and the Japs, our fellas were lucky to get here with those supplies at all. Those're for us, because we're the ones over here defending these Chinese, and now I come downtown and see them running around with it all while we're stuck in their country, living like the poorest of them." He spat and Henry had to wipe the spray from the side of his face. "We're eating crap and living like animals, and we're doing it for them and they don't care a bit..." His voice trailed off to a mumble.

As they exited the crowded tea house, Henry holding one of his arms, Stan the other, Stan craned his neck back to catch Henry's eye behind Danko. "Speak Yiddish?"

Henry smiled sheepishly. "*A bisl.*"[6]

"*A shicor. Vas auf de ling is auf de tsing.*"[7]

It was as though his speaking Yiddish were a package from home for Henry, a piece of the pavement from the corner of East Ninth and Avenue J. Stan Freilich became more than a skinny Jewish eighteen-year-old from Cleveland who played a little jazz and felt sorry for himself. He became a whole person, a Brooklynite, despite being from Cleveland. But the metamorphosis went beyond Stan. It was as though a black and white photograph began to have subtle hues of color. China began slowly to come alive—gasping, coughing, and still more than a little threatening—but alive nonetheless.

A boy at the side of the road was playing marbles, and Henry squatted beside him and watched. The boy barely glanced at him.

"I used to play marbles, son. Whatcha got?" Henry watched him shoot one marble into another with his thumb.

"Come on, let's get going," Stan said.

Henry nodded and they started walking again.

As they stumbled towards the truck, they passed a Chinese man carrying two buckets on either end of a long pole carried over his shoulders.

Danko lit up. "Hey, I've always wanted to play that. Quick, let's get in the truck."

"Play what?" Stan asked.

"Spin the Slopey. You just drive towards one end..."

"Yeah, never mind." Henry pushed him towards the truck which, he quickly realized, was unoccupied. He turned the trio around and started down the road towards the base. "Follow the yellow brick road," he mumbled.

They approached the body of a Chinese man of perhaps forty at the side of the road. Flies buzzed around the man's ear but otherwise, no notice was taken by anyone besides the three GIs.

No one spoke and as they edged past, Stan said, "Wait, give me a minute." He went back to the body while Henry propped Danko's arm over his shoulder. Faintly, Henry could hear the familiar syllables. "*Yidgadaal, veeyidgadaash…*"

When Stan came back and helped with Danko, Henry stared at him. "You said the mourner's *Kaddish* for that man? You don't know who he is, what kind of life he lived…nothing."

Stan shrugged. "He's a man. He's dead in the street. He's got nothing, no one. Maybe now he's got a little dignity."

After they'd walked about ten minutes, a long low limousine approached. Stan jumped out in front of it, waving his arms. The window rolled down and Stan had a short interchange with the driver, after which he opened one of the rear doors and motioned Henry and Danko inside.

"They're going to the base, too."

Within seconds, Danko was asleep and Henry was able to relax. Besides the driver, the only people in the car were an old Chinese man, who smiled and nodded continually, and a very young, very beautiful girl, perhaps twelve years old. Henry smiled back and the man leaned towards him, speaking in broken English.

"My daughter spend weekend with American GI officer!" he grinned and nodded emphatically.

"But she's…she's a child," Henry blurted out.

The man continued to nod and smile.

Henry and Stan had barely gotten Danko into his bunk, when Larry Curley, who worked at the PX and delivered mail, peeked into the barracks and pointed a finger at Henry. "Major wants to see you."

Drum was smoking his pipe, his eyes half closed, in his office when Henry knocked and was invited in.

"Neiberg. Neiberg. I understand you've come into a little... inheritance."

Henry squinted. "What do you mean?"

"A little," he rubbed his fingers together, "you know."

"I don't know what you...oh, you mean the stuff my mother sent? Hah. So this is the Squeeze I've heard so much about."

Drum shrugged and puffed, still not looking Henry in the eye. "I know the other men are jealous, and things could go badly for you with them." He shook his head, then began to cough from somewhere deep in his lungs. His face reddened and he choked and coughed and tried to clear his throat. Henry wondered if he ought to pat him on the back. Finally, the major calmed down.

"I can help you with those fellas. I can make sure they stay off your back, and only for, say, a cut of half."

"You want half of my packages? You want half of what my mother sends?"

"You're right. Maybe that's a little high. Perhaps I can be persuaded to settle for a bit less. A third then."

"Ah, major. I have to get back to work."

"Fine, fine." The major waved. "You go on back and think about it."

       *   *   *   *

Numbers swam together before his eyes. He had been working
for seven hours, comparing columns of numbers with lists of
Army issue equipment, and he was beginning to feel as though he
were on a merry-go-round. The wooden room kept in and magni-
fied the heat; his uniform was wet against his back. Behind him,
Jake Singer was whistling through the gap in his teeth. In front of
him, Stan Freilich sighed, probably obsessing over Irma. The work
was the sort that led to daydreaming, which was never good. One
did not daydream about Army life. Frances intruded, and not just
her image but her voice, phrases she used and the dry touch of her
hand on a cool autumn afternoon. Thinking about her added up
about as much as the numbers on the ledger on the raw pine desk
in front of him.

He looked at the numbers, his eyebrows knitting together as he
concentrated, trying to see what was wrong. Something didn't
make sense. The equipment tracked as going out to the Chinese
Central Army did not jibe with what they seemed to actually have.
They appeared more undersupplied than they ought to have been.

Henry bit the inside of his cheek, thinking about what he ought
to do about the discrepancy. Frances's voice spoke into one of his
ears; he could all but see her pointing to the sheet.

He found Major Drum at a corner table at the PX chewing on
some kind of sandwich consisting of brown meat covered with
what looked like ketchup.

"Okay," he said, through a mouthful of sandwich, after Henry
had explained what he'd found.

"What do you want me to do about it, sir?"

"I want you to get back to work."

"I understand, sir. But I'd like to know what to do about the
discrepancy." Henry shifted from one foot to the other, thinking
about sitting down but hesitating, as he had not been invited.

"Leave it alone."

"Sir?"

"I said, leave it alone. It's close, right?"

"Sort of. But it's wrong. Come on, I'll show you, sir."

"Never mind. I know it's close so that's good enough for me."

"You know...?"

Drum looked up at Henry. For a long moment he said nothing. When he did speak, it was slowly, carefully. "You did your duty, Neiberg. I'll make a note of your request and it'll get taken care of. Now get back—say, when're you going to stop by the office with my ration?"

"Your what?"

"You know, from your package."

"*Chutzpah*," Henry muttered, shaking his head.

"Excuse me? What did you say?"

"Oh, ah, one of the foods my mother sent, a Jewish-ah delicacy. Chutzpah with matzoh balls—real balls. You know, the good heavy kind." Henry smiled, showing his teeth and holding his hands in front of him, fingers spread.

"Kutz pie? Sure, bring it on." Drum looked down at his tray, which was nearly empty. "Oh, by the way. There's a small library, you know where it is?"

Henry nodded.

"Good. Why don't you bring it there tomorrow after your shift. I like to read. War books, mostly, like *Red Badge of Courage*. McPhee goes sometimes, too. He reads detective novels. You know, the hardboiled kind."

"Really!" Henry couldn't believe it. "I thought McPhee'd be out chasing Red Cross nurses every second he could get."

"He does that too," Drum agreed. "Anyway, I could use a little snack before dinner."

Henry cleared his throat. "I'll make a note of your request." He turned and walked away.

"Neiberg! I didn't say 'dismissed'."

Henry nodded over his shoulder and heard the major's voice following him.

"Dismissed!"

As he left the PX, he noticed a flock of grimy boys hovering around the back door. One appeared to be acting as lookout while the rest rooted through the garbage.

"Get away from there!" Henry took a step towards them and made a shooing motion, and the boys ran twenty yards into the nearest field, turned, and looked at him.

Larry Curley's head poked out of the back door. "Henry, leave 'em alone. They don't mean no harm."

"It's garbage. They'll get sick..."

"It's also head and shoulders better than any food they get anywhere else. I save scraps and give 'em out and they take it back to to their families. Let 'em take what they can find. Trust me. Our garbage is their Thanksgiving."

*   *   *   *

An hour later Henry lay on his bunk, having finished another letter to his mother. He had not mentioned Major Drum or the discrepancy in the statistics he had found. Nor had he mentioned the fact that Frances had not yet written.

"Stabler, you like chocolate? I have some stashed away."

"Of course." Stabler appeared next to Henry's bunk. "Where?"

Henry pointed to the chest of drawers, got up and pulled the drawer open, then stepped back. The drawer was empty, except for torn bits of paper and some brown smears. "That bastard sure can move fast, despite his weight!"

Stabler looked from the drawer to Henry. "Who?"

"Who? Drum. He tried to blackmail me into giving him a third of my package; then when I said no, he took it."

Stabler shook his head. "You said no? You got real *cajones*."

"Real, excuse me?"

Stabler shook his head. "Never mind. But I wouldn't say no to Drum. He's the sort of guy to make trouble for you if you do. Besides, it wasn't him."

Henry squinted. "What do you mean?"

"I mean he'd just take it, not break in through the back of the drawer."

Henry pulled the drawer wider and peered inside. "Oh, my God. There's a hole ripped right through the back of the dresser." He took a step back. "Chung told me about the rats, but what kind of rats could've...they're like something out of a Faye Wray movie!"

*　　　*　　　*　　　*

The next day several of the men made a trip downtown to find mousetraps and came back with huge, spring loaded metal power-houses which they began baiting with bits of cheese sent from home. Drum, in particular, seemed to have an endless supply of cheese, though he was only convinced to part with it by the sheer numbers of men involved in the baiting project.

On the morning after the first night of baiting, the traps remained untouched. The second night was no different. Early on the third morning, Jake asked Chung why the traps had failed.

"Rats won't eat cheese," the boy said.

"Why not, Chung? Where we come from rats love cheese."

"They've never seen it before. We have no cheese here."

"Why? Don't you have milk?" Jake scratched the side of his head. "Come to think of it, I don't remember seeing any cows. Only water buffalo."

Chung shook his head. "No cows."

The GIs took Chung's suggestion to bait the traps with chocolate and within a week the base was rid of its rat problem.

*   *   *   *

That night the men ate candy until well into the night, and played cards on two foot lockers pushed together. Just after two thirty, Henry felt suddenly sick to his stomach and stumbled out of the barracks. When he returned, he heard a low rumbling that grew steadily louder. He and Jake looked at each other and Jake's eyes widened and suddenly it was raining candy and the air was thick with dust. A thunderclap sounded and men were yelling and running in all directions.

Instantly everything in sight was covered with debris, and there was a ringing in Henry's ears that no amount of head shaking would dissipate. Everyone, whatever his opinions or habits, was suddenly a close buddy as they raced together towards trenches around the outskirts of the base. The bombing seemed endless.

"Guess this is what my brothers go through every day."

Henry looked up from under his helmet, grateful for the distraction of McPhee's words.

"Where're your brothers stationed?"

"Got me. Europe somewhere. But knowing Bill 'n Charlie, they're in the thick of it. Lieutenants, both of 'em. Born leaders." His loopy grin looked absurd to Henry.

He tried to think of things to say, anything to keep his mind and stomach off of this roaring, whistling horror.

"My mother's afraid they'll bomb the states," Henry muttered, fighting to keep his voice even. "She figures it'll be the west coast first, though."

"You kidding?" Danko said. "It'll be my home town, Racine, Wisconsin. My baby sister works in a factory, building planes. You know, when we get outta here, I think I'm gonna build one myself, outta wood. I used to build models, you know."

"I don't know," said McPhee. "We've got Pratt and Whitney in East Hartford. Their airplane production is pretty—" A screaming whine, followed by a jarring roar, cut him off.

Henry felt the explosion on his skin and in his ears, which were sore deep inside. He kept his face buried in the trench, and for the next few hours got lost in examining the bugs that crawled in and out of sight, their lives apparently undisturbed by the insanity around them.

For days after the Japanese bombed the base, the men slept in trenches. And afterwards, Henry refused at first to return to the barracks. The trenches were fine, he claimed, the dirt perfectly acceptable.

Henry asked the Quartermaster for a blanket, but was told that the only Army issue blankets in China were for sale on the side of the road, downtown. While cursing the black market, he breathed into fists that gripped Frances's barrette. He confided to the barrette that he had never been so terrified.

He was not able to write his mother for a week.

Jake Singer dreamed that the burning smell that refused to dissipate was his grandmother's baking in Philadelphia. His grandfather was out in the yard, building a *succah*, a small house of branches and leaves, and little Jacob and his friends climbed first on grandfather then up and onto the *succah*, using it as a clubhouse. Before long, Grandma Singer called the boys into the house for treats. Though they were poor, his grandmother encouraged his friends to eat as much—often more—than they wanted, and when it was time for everyone to go home, she refused to put away the leftovers, stuffing the little cakes into his friends' pockets.

The men were allowed back in the barracks once the four foot hole in the wall and most of the roof were repaired. That evening, a Saturday, Henry ran into Louis, who was carrying a broom handle and a rolled up pair of socks, on his way to the Rec.

"What're you doing tomorrow night?" Louis wanted to know. His mouth opened in an enormous smile showing even, white teeth.

"Gee, I dunno," Henry shrugged, "I was planning to visit a cousin on Long Island."

Louis laughed. "Wiseguy! Well, if you can break away, why don't you meet me at the Rec? I'm having a party for my pals. Strictly champagne and cigars."

Henry shook Louie's hand. "Is the occasion what I think it is?"

Louis threw the balled up socks up into the air and batted them with the broom handle. "I've got a good reason now to practice my swing." He trotted off, calling over his shoulder, "Kid doesn't want his own old man to look bad!"

"His old man already looks bad," Henry called over his shoulder. "See you tomorrow night!"

4

Henry smoothed the front of his uniform as he and Jake approached the Rec Hall.

"Got a date?" Jake laughed.

"I was over at the pilots' quarters this afternoon, looking for Marlowe."

"Oh?" Jake was surprised. "What did you want with that guy?"

Henry shrugged. "Get to know him, maybe. We didn't hit it off too well, and I thought maybe I'd say hello. You know, get back on the right track."

The throaty growl of planes taking off made him pause. He grabbed Jake's forearm, stopping him as they got to the Rec Hall door. Above them a v-formation of planes had flown over, followed by another, and another. The planes took off in waves, joined their formations and flew off to the west, gathering speed as they disappeared in the distance, then reappeared at their cruising altitude, in full formation, flying en masse towards their destination.

"God help them," Jake muttered.

"I didn't think you were much more religious than I am," Henry said, smiling.

"Give me time," said Jake. "Place like this'll make you religious."

"Anyway," Henry dropped his eyes. "I got to their barracks and their beds were unmade." He nodded knowingly, then raised his eyes to the sky.

"That's their mission just went out, huh?"

"And if I hadn't seen their beds, I could've probably figured it out from the way the rest of the guys over there were acting. You know the ground crews act awfully funny when their guys're out on missions. Some're depressed, others're ready to pick a fight."

"I don't blame them. If you were over there…" Jake didn't finish the sentence, but looked up after the disappearing v-formations. "I'm glad you're on the ground, Hank."

"Thanks," said Henry. "Anyway, it's kind of hard to dislike a guy who may not come back, you know?"

*   *   *   *

A mellifluous baritone crooned over the hum of voices in the Rec Hall. Henry and Jake stopped in the doorway and watched the goings on inside. A handful of men from Photo Intelligence were playing cards in the near corner. Drum and McPhee faced one another over a checkerboard, while in the far corner four men appeared to be taking turns pushing, boxing and wrestling. The General's houseboys were serving from several bottles they'd brought from the wine shop they ran in the afternoons.

Just inside the front door and to one side, a Chinese man and woman stood behind a small card table, serving something from a steaming container onto plates.

"What do you suppose that is?" Henry asked.

"Only one way to find out." Jake walked over to the table, where the man was talking to Larry Curley. "So far, we've sold only six or seven. I'm not sure the men want to try anything unfamiliar," the man was saying. The woman saw Henry and Jake approaching and nudged the man with her elbow. His wide smile showed white, even teeth. "Good evening, corporal, sergeant. Care for a dumpling?"

Jake looked at Henry, then back at the man. "Your English is excellent."

The dumpling salesman shrugged. "I was educated at a missionary school. I speak several languages, English among them." He smiled. "Thank you."

Jake put out his hand. "Sergeant Jake Singer, and this is Corporal Henry Neiberg."

The dumpling salesman put out a hand. "Ai Wenti, and this is my wife, Huida."

Jake shook each of their hands, as did Henry. "Nice to meet you, Mr. Wenti," Henry said.

"In China, the family name is first," the man said. "Mine is Ai. So I would be Mr. Ai, but please don't call me that. Call me Wenti."

"You're a dumpling maker?" Jake asked.

Mr. Ai handed him a plate. "You be the judge."

"Delicious!" Jake exclaimed, motioning for Henry to try one.

"Mmm," said Henry, after obliging.

"You don't play cards, or dance with chairs?" Mr. Ai looked around the room.

Henry shook his head. "That stuff's not for us."

Jake agreed. "We're more interested in reading our letters." He patted the top pocket of his uniform. "That's why I came down here."

"Right," said Henry. "Or talking to people like you."

Mr. Ai looked confused. "But most Americans do not care to talk to us. In fact," he leaned close to Henry, "some find my English difficult to understand. Too well-educated." He nodded eagerly. "It's interesting to talk to a soldier with a different perspective."

Jake gave a booming laugh, causing Huida to jump back. "Ha! Very good." He sighed. "My grandmother taught me to be inquisitive, so we have that in common, I suppose. Growing up, I always did a lot of reading, learning about other cultures."

Henry agreed. "And my mother was rather like Jake's grandmother. She also taught me not to be too loud, to be easy-going, and so forth. That's why we're not wrestling, or swilling alcohol."

Mrs. Ai laughed. She was so thin that one could see the outlines of her bones and veins beneath her skin. Her laugh was sharp and quick, like her hand movements. A few faces turned. Mr. Ai touched her arm, calming her. She leaned towards her husband and said a few words in Chinese.

"Mrs. Ai says you have a classical Chinese education. Very well schooled in philosophy of Kung-Fu-Tzu."

"Oh," said Henry. "Well, I don't think so. I don't even know who that is."

"He's the man you call Confucius. His teachings contain the basis of all proper behavior. But it seems you know that already." He laughed, and his wife joined him. This time Huida's laugh was softer. She looked around self-consciously.

Jake took another dumpling and put one on a plate for Henry. "If being respectful, polite and so forth is what Confucius taught, then that's my grandmother. When I was a boy, you know, we were the poorest of the poor, yet she put away money in a little *pushke* box on the wall. And when anyone needing charity came around, she always gave."

Henry nodded. "Sounds like Mama. And, to tell you the truth, sounds like Frances."

"Who is Frances?" Mr. Ai wanted to know. "Sister?"

"No, my sister is Enid. She's a sweetheart, too. Frances is, well, I had hoped she would be my fiancé, but it didn't work out."

Mrs. Ai started to say something, but Mr. Ai cut her off with four quick words.

"Well, it was great talking to you," Jake said, passing the empty plates back to Mr. Ai. "Thanks for the dumplings. They were delicious."

"Hope you come here again," said Henry.

"To tell you the truth," Jake said, "I'd like to learn more about China."

Mr. Ai smiled and nodded. "Perhaps you will."

They sat down at a corner table and Jake took an envelope from his pocket. The way Henry knew the letter was from Blanche was that a light perfume hung in the air where the letter had been.

Jake quickly read the letter and stuffed it back.

"Everything okay?" Henry asked.

"Fine," said Jake, shrugging. "No big deal."

"You know, you don't have to play down your letters just because Frances doesn't write me. You can read the whole thing, you know."

"I did read it. I don't know what you're talking about." Jake took a toothpick from his pocket and began twirling it in the space between his front teeth.

*   *   *   *

Two days later, Henry brought a piece of paper into the barracks and showed it to Jake. "Look what I found tacked up at the Rec."

Jake scanned the sheet. "A tea? A tea for American Servicemen at a dumpling shop tomorrow night...I never heard of such a thing. Think it's...?"

"The same guy? How many dumpling shops could there be in Kunming?"

Henry threw up his hands. "I don't know! Maybe it's like grocery stores, and there're dozens."

Jake looked at him. "Why don't we go? We told the guy we'd like to get to know more about this place. So here's an opportunity."

"You said that, not me."

"No, you said it, too, or something like it."

Henry shook his head. "I don't remember saying any such thing. I think you have a pretty selective memory. I'm not so sure I want to see any more of China than I have to."

"Look," said Jake, "we'll be here a while. You're not going to get your chance with Frances until after the war. You think she's coming here any time soon? So why don't we go?"

"I don't know..."

Jake nodded slowly. "Yeah, I guess there is an awful lot going on around here. How could you possibly leave, even for a couple of hours?"

Henry smiled. "Well, I guess. And Stan'll probably come. He's so bored and down about his girl he doesn't know what to do with himself."

Jake looked hard at Henry. "Yeah, how could a guy get so wound up about a girl back home? I don't get that!"

Henry pointed a finger at Jake. "You know, I was starting to think you were okay..."

"So, talk to Stan and meet me right here at five o'clock tomorrow afternoon."

*   *   *   *

For weeks after the base was bombed, Henry had trouble sleeping. He lay awake, his body rigid until three or four in the morning, his eyes darting around the barracks at every sound or motion. He made nervous, shuffling trips to the latrine. His bladder was even more frightened than the rest of him. He wished he could tell Frances how frightened he was; she was so matter-of-fact, so filled with the wisdom of day-to-day life, so like the Bronx itself. Her quick wit and flashing eyes would be the perfect sleeping tonic, even if they had to be culled from words in a letter.

Sudden sounds made him jump. The clatter of forks and knives at meals, the slam of the barracks door, the quick crack of a staff car's backfire. All of these made his muscles lurch, his stomach heave, and his conscious connection to reality recede to a far corner of his mind while the fight or flight—mostly flight—instinct reigned over the rest.

At first he was ashamed, assuming for some self-centered reason that he was the only one who was afraid, but a week after the bombing he was tossing and turning and hearing his father's voice pleading with him to let him use his influence to find him a desk job, when a truck started suddenly and a sound like a small animal in pain, a puppy perhaps, came from one of the iron bunks across the room. Henry struck a match and heard a rustling of blankets as the flame whooshed and caught. In the glow, Henry looked at the spot where the sound had seemed to come from and saw Danko, eyes shut unnaturally tight, shoulders trembling.

It was funny how things changed, and then changed back again. He had started this hitch thinking Danko would be his friend, but had come to see Danko as a very different sort of man, not one who considers the other man's point of view. And he had begun to suspect that such a man was not really his friend. More recently, because of Marlowe's unmade bed, and now Danko's sleepless fear, he was beginning to feel a part of something more inclusive, more forgiving of political, social, even moral differences. Friend or no, they were in this together.

He wondered if the fact that Danko was not Jewish affected their potential friendship, relegating him to the status of comrade in arms, keeping him at that safe, faceless distance. All his life, his friends had been Jewish, though it was a fact he never noticed. While his father sometimes went to synagogue on Saturdays and the family observed most Jewish holidays, Henry did not think of his Jewishness first. His father was culturally observant rather than strictly Orthodox, and Henry did not think of himself as religious at all. He saw himself as a Jewish American rather than an American Jew, and had never consciously considered religion when he was choosing friends.

Yet who were his closest friends here? Jake Singer and Stan Freilich, both Jewish. And he heard himself or thought he heard himself sounding more Jewish, whether that meant using a Yiddish expression or phrase, or simply identifying himself as a Jew. Perhaps it was the way he was perceived by others. They thought he was a Jew, so he became one. In Biloxi, two men had circled him warily one evening, pretending to inspect the top of his head for horns. Was his reaction to bigotry to become more Jewish? Or perhaps it was a reaction to his fear of being in such a strange place, a way of circling the wagons.

*   *   *   *

The dumpling store was just off the main road in the center of Kunming. People in faded, loose-fitting clothing came out with little packages, and were instantly accosted by clusters of stick-figure children, grasping and cajoling. Like the shops around it, the store had no windows and was of plain wood with a slanted bamboo roof. Dough and prepared dumplings were sold over a counter that separated the front buying area from the back preparation room.

It was late afternoon when Henry, Jake and Stan entered. Immediately, two women who were shopping inside rushed out. The dirt floor crunched under Henry's boots. Jake pointed to the white sheet draped over the counter. It read "Welcome American GIs."

Mr. Ai appeared and enthusiastically waved them inside. "Come in, my friends! We've been waiting!"

The GIs took a few steps inside. The only other people in the room were four Chinese teenagers, two boys and two girls, who were seated on corrugated boxes that lined the sides of the room. The dirt floor was littered with what appeared to be a mixture of straw and flour. From behind the counter peered the faces of a woman and little boy. All stared at the GIs as motion in the room stopped and the sounds of voices, animals and trucks intruded from outside.

Henry closed his eyes and inhaled the warm bakery smell. It reminded him of Avenue J on a Saturday morning but with a subtly different flavor.

"Will we be interrupting your business?" he asked.

"Business closed for the day," Mr. Ai clapped his bony hands. "Let's make our guests welcome! Huida, tea!" A large wooden tray that appeared to have its own thin, bowed legs made its way into the room. Huida's bright, darting eyes were barely visible over the steaming black porcelain cups. She stood in front of the soldiers until each took one.

Mr. Ai placed the tips of the fingers of one hand to his chest. "I am Ai Wenti and this is my wife, Huida." He spoke primarily to Stan.

Jake stepped forward. "This is Stanley Freilich."

Now it was Mr. Ai's turn. "And this is Neil Ku Nuli."

A slight wisp of a boy stood up and shyly put out a hand. "A pleasure to meet you," he said, in English.

"Does everyone around here speak perfect English?" said Jake, taking his hand.

"I went to missionary school. Thank you."

"Why are you thanking him?" Stan looked uneasy, his hands on his hips.

"For fighting in Chinese war," Neil Ku replied.

Henry looked at Stan. "Well, what have you got to say to that?"

"I've never heard of a Chinese saying thank you." Stan turned to Neil Ku. "You're welcome."

"Actually," Jake said, taking a cup of tea and sipping it. "Ooh, hot. Actually, we're accountants more than fighting soldiers."

Mr. Ai shook his head. "All part of Army. All part of war. Neil Ku is right to thank you. Huida!" He barked in Chinese, his eyes flickering to the back room and back again. His wife uttered a few fierce syllables in return, then turned and went towards the back room.

"This is Ju Shiyan, whom we call Jane; Cha Wulin, whom we call Mary; and Chong Lingxiu, whom we sometimes call Anton." Mr. Ai smiled, showing tall, even teeth. "But he prefers his given name, I think."

Everyone shook hands. Ju Shiyan was a thin girl with flowing black hair and an angular, pretty face. Cha Wulin was both bigger-boned and taller. Her hair was short and her features wider and flatter. She looked to Henry as though she had participated in sports, or perhaps, he decided after a moment's thought, manual labor.

Chong Lingxiu stood out from the group because he did not have the look of a student. He was older, more mature in both demeanor and carriage, and his round spectacles gave him a learned appearance. When he greeted the GIs in Chinese, his *"Ni how"* was uttered in the deep tone of a confident, grown man.

For a moment after the introductions everyone stood looking at one another, not knowing what else to say. Then, Jake cleared his throat.

"Ahem. Just as you thank us for helping you, we thank you for having us in your country and we sympathize with your circumstances. We've heard about the atrocities at Nanking and Shanghai and, well, we hope we can do some small part in the war to put an end to that kind of suffering."

Mr. Ai began to applaud. Mrs. Ai, who had appeared from behind the counter with another tray, this one full of some sort of bread or cake, put down the tray and joined her husband. The students joined in.

"Some of us," Mr. Ai put his arm around Neil Ku's shoulder, as Neil looked at the floor, "have had personal losses at these places. What happened at Nanking and Shanghai was unspeakable. We hoped to let you know more about what we're doing, what some other Chinese are doing in, well, an unofficial war effort."

"Unofficial war effort?" said Jake. "I'd like to hear more."

Chong glanced at Mr. Ai, and said a few words. Mr. Ai paused, then nodded slowly. "Perhaps," he said to Jake, "another time."

Stan had taken three cakes from Mrs. Ai's tray.

"Stanley," Henry said, "have some manners."

Stan looked at Henry, then at the cakes, then at Mrs. Ai. "I'm sorry." He began to put them back.

"Take, take, rice bread!" Mrs. Ai nodded and grinned, showing a missing front tooth. Stan shrugged and kept what he'd taken.

"I always said you take the cake," Henry said, wagging a finger. *"Schnorrer!"*

Stan cleared his throat. "I'd like to hear more about this unofficial war effort. We've heard nothing good about the Chinese Army's war efforts."

"Be polite, Freilich," said Jake.

"Quite alright," said Mr. Ai. "But best discussed another time. When we visited your base, you spoke of traditions in your home. Your grandmother, Sergeant Singer…"

"Jake, please."

"She gave to charity, though she was poor. You seem to pay much attention to social issues. We have not met many GIs here who think that way. Why is that?"

"I've been wondering about that," Henry said. "I suspect part of it is, as we said last time, we have family who are socially conscious. Jake's grandmother and my mother are both the kind of people who cannot ignore seeing people treated poorly. And," he spoke slowly, "it may be that being raised in a Jewish home has something to do with it. Though I was never observant, there is a Jewish tradition of reading, studying, that goes back centuries. There are values, too, that go along with that."

"Very similar to Chinese way of growing up," said Chong Lingxiu.

Mr. Ai nodded. "I told them last time about Chinese classics. They understood right away."

"At missionary school," said Neil Ku, in a voice so soft the GIs had to lean forward to hear him, "we learned similar values. So my education fit with what I learned from my father, growing up."

Jake cleared his throat. "You know, I went to City College, in New York. And while there, I was a member of the American Student Union, the ASU, and we protested against, well, a variety of things. Fascism, for one. The Spanish Civil War."

"Franco," said Mr. Ai, exchanging looks with the students. "How so?"

"Well, we felt that the authoritarian way Spain was run was really just a precursor for Hitler. It seemed to be part of a trend."

Mr. Ai was nodding, smiling, and raising his eyebrows towards Chong, who was shaking his head.

"Doesn't Mr. Chong agree?" Jake wanted to know.

"He does agree," said Mr. Ai. "I think he sees an interesting comparison. Better for another time. Tell me, what else did you protest?"

Jake thought about the question. "Oh, there were all sorts of issues. There was something called the Rapp Coudert Committee. They were a local political committee who went after teachers thought to be Communists. Quite a few good teachers were fired as a result of pressure Rapp Coudert brought to bear." He shook his head. "Terrible thing."

"And you protested against this Committee?" Chong Lingxiu asked.

Jake nodded. "It's how I met my wife, Blanche. She was also in the ASU, and I tutored her in accounting. We're all basically accountants you know."

"It's how we account for ourselves," Stanley said, laughing. No one else laughed. On either side of him, Jake and Henry turned slowly to look at him.

Before the soldiers left, Mr. Ai invited everyone back for a visit two days later and graciously accepted Henry's offer to supply refreshments.

*   *   *   *

"What do you think of these American GIs?" Mr. Ai stood in front of the students. As usual, the two girls, Cha Wulin and Ju Shiyan, looked into their laps.

"You were right," said Neil Ku. "They do seem different. Not so loud. Almost Confucian in their attitudes. Why not tell them about the Liberated Areas? Once they find out that a Chinese Army has been successful against the Japanese, they'll go back and spread the news. It might be a good way of letting the American Army know more about what's going on in the North. It doesn't seem they'll ever hear about it from their own Army officers."

Mr. Ai laughed. "As usual, you're thinking ahead."

Chong Lingxiu disagreed. "Think about what you're saying, Nuli. Whatever else they may appear to be, these men are soldiers in what is essentially the Kuomintang airforce! Their leader, Chennault, is a personal friend of Chiang Kaishek! At least get to know them more."

Neil Ku Nuli considered this. "Your years in prison made you cautious."

"Don't forget, I've lost a lot. My wife is dead. I haven't seen my son in many years. You have yet to lose anything." Chong waved a finger; his voice rose. "We need to guard against suffering more losses. I only want to be sure."

Huida was in the corner, playing with their toddler son, Ai Wei. She had filled a sock with beans and was trying to show him how to keep it in the air by kicking it. Ai Wei found the sight of his mother kicking a sack of beans hilarious, collapsing with laughter each time it bounced into the air.

Mr. Ai looked at each of the students, and at the two girls, who were their guests. "Have either of you anything to add?"

Cha Wulin shook her head.

Ju Shiyan said, "The soldiers downtown say things that aren't nice to me when I walk past. These soldiers do seem different, although one of them stared at me directly."

Not to be outdone, Cha Wulin added, "And they seem progressive, interested in political causes."

Mr. Ai had made his decision. "Well, one is, anyway. As Neil Ku suggests, these soldiers can help spread the word about the war effort against the Japanese in the North. We can also learn a lot from them—about daily life and politics in America, for instance. Perhaps we might even publish some of that information here, for Lianda students."

A murmur of agreement went up around the room, from everyone but Chong Lingxiu. Now, Mr. Ai turned to him.

"But I agree with Lingxiu in that we must be cautious. We are lucky to have Governor Lung's autonomous way of doing things. If he didn't run his province his way, we wouldn't be sitting here having this conversation at all. We'd all probably be in jail, so let's not push our luck."

Huida let out a yell and clapped her hands. Ai Wei had kicked the sock himself for the first time, sending it high into the air.

*   *   *   *

Henry, Jake and Stanley sat quietly in the back of the truck on the way to their next visit, leaning against boxes, avoiding the back section of the truck's bed, which was lined with airplane parts.

"What's in the bag?" Stan wanted to know.

Henry brightened. "Cheese, some candy, a stuffed toy for the little boy."

"They'll like that."

Jake didn't answer. After a while, his thoughts came together. "I don't think most of the men have any opinion on who our friends are. Maybe they think it's a little strange that we're not out drinking and finding prostitutes, but I don't think too many would see anything wrong with it."

"Some people have to belittle anything different," Henry said, quietly. "Makes them feel better about what they lack."

Stan didn't say anything. The conversation had reminded him of Irma and brought him back, as all thoughts of Irma did, to why she had left him. "I could use a drink," he said, to no one in particular.

* * * *

Mr. Ai was waiting in front of his shop when the truck pulled up.

"Come in, my friends!" He grinned and beckoned, gripping them each by the arm as they stepped down from the back of the truck.

"Thanks, Larry," Henry called to the driver, Larry Curley.

The dumpling shop was neater than when they had last been there. The floor had been swept, and the burlap sacks and boxes were stacked neatly along the side walls, rather than strewn around haphazardly. A strong smell of tea hung in the air. The students had already arrived.

Neil Ku stepped forward, formally offering his hand to each of them.

"It's a pleasure to see you again, my friends," he said, stepping from Henry, to Jake, and finally to Stan.

Chong Lingxiu waved and nodded, but did not get up from his seat on one of the boxes in the far corner of the store. "I don't think he likes us," muttered Stan.

Jake cleared his throat. "Are these two young ladies students, too?"

Mr. Ai spoke to the girls in Chinese. The thinner one with the longer hair answered.

"I asked their permission to tell you about them," Mr. Ai explained. "They agreed. Cha Wulin is a farmer's daughter. Her father, Cha Siansheng—Siansheng is the same as saying sir or elder in English—arranged for her to marry Pei Han, the fish seller's son."

Henry raised a hand. "May I ask a question? Her father arranged with the fish seller's mother for them to marry?"

"Exactly," said Mr. Ai.

Henry shook his head. "Arranged marriages," he muttered.

"At least they have each other," said Stan.

"Cha Wulin felt as Henry does. She did not wish to marry Pei Han, so she ran away. She knows a professor at Lianda University—"

Jake interrupted. "That's where you fellows go to school?"

Mr. Ai nodded. "Ju Shiyan is Wulin's best friend. Cha Siansheng is a farmer and he delivers to Ju Shiyan's father's noodle shop, as well as to me. So you see, we all know each other." He smiled, his perfect teeth showing.

Stan was looking at Cha Wulin. "So she ran away because she didn't want to marry this guy? How did she know the people at the University? How did she get in with this crowd? In fact, how did all these students come to be so friendly with a dumpling maker? Everything we've seen in China seems so separated. The rich are here, the poor there, the educated over here..."

Mr. Ai smiled and looked at the floor. Neil Ku answered. "We all like good dumplings, and Mr. Ai makes the best dumplings in Kunming. We became friends after coming many times. We have many things in common."

"Some of the professors from Lianda come into the store regularly, and as you can see I am very outgoing." He laughed, "so we became good friends after chatting frequently."

From the back room came Mrs. Ai's rising and falling intonations. "My wife, Huida," said Mr. Ai, "says I am more educated than many storekeepers. I am not so sure. Anyway, I became friendly with a professor who eventually helped Cha Wulin and Ju Shiyan. Our friendship developed in much the same way as ours has with you."

Huida came out of the back room carrying a tray of tea and wearing a big smile. She made a point of saying "welcome" to each of them by name. Henry could see she had practiced.

Jake opened the bag he had brought and called to little Ai Wei, who was hiding behind his mother's leg. "I brought you something, son." Jake waved the brown bear, stroking its fur. Huida patted her son on the head, said something softly to him, and nudged him gently on the back.

Unable to take his eyes from the toy, the child came forward and took it back to his mother. After gentle prodding, he turned to Jake. "*Sheh, sheh.*"

"Thank you," his mother translated.

Ai Wei rubbed the bear against his face and exclaimed in Chinese, then ran to his parents, the students and the two girls, rubbing each of their faces against the bear.

"He says it's very soft." Mr. Ai smiled.

"I also brought candy," Jake said, spilling the contents of the bag on the floor. "This is called taffy. You have to hit it against something hard to break it up. Like so." He slammed the taffy against the floor, then opened its wrapper, and gave out the contents. Everyone oohed and aahed.

Huida gave out the tea.

Mr. Ai cleared his throat. "We are very interested in learning more about you, and about American life in general."

"Well, we'd be happy to oblige," Henry said. "Ask us any questions."

"I have an idea," said Jake. "I might be able to have Blanche, that's my wife, send magazine or newspaper articles from home."

Neil Ku nodded. "That would be an education all by itself."

Stan looked at Jake. "You don't think that'll cause a problem, you know, for Larry or the censors?"

"What for? Newspaper articles? Nah!"

"You know," Mr. Ai said, "we've been talking here about how much we have in common with you, and how uncommon you three are, if you don't mind my saying so. What I mean is, you seem to have family experiences that make you different. Your, um, values, seem to make you more concerned about people, the right way to treat people. This is very much like what you would call Confucianism. It is the basic Chinese way of living. Let me explain. Many Chinese children grow up learning particular virtues including trustworthiness, sincerity, respect for elders, and modesty. This philosophy is hundreds of years old."

"Moderation," Neil Ku added.

"Yes, moderation. And it seems that you American soldiers somehow learned the same or similar values through your families."

"That's correct," said Henry. "I remember we spoke about that last time, and you're right. We are lucky to have been raised by good people with good values. Now it's our turn to ask why you are so different from most of the Chinese people we have met and heard about so far."

He cleared his throat. "You know, not all Chinese people are so interested in fighting the war against the Japanese. We've heard, in fact, that quite a bit of the equipment we give the Army here gets socked away to fight the Communists. Our jobs, by the way, are to catalogue that equipment, so we are in a unique position to know these things."

Mr. Ai nodded. "I have no doubt what you say is true. Neil, would you like to explain about Lianda?"

Neil Ku took a long sip of tea. "Well," he said, then paused. "Well," he began again, "when the Japanese invasion came, the Chinese people, including Universities, had to move to the west. Lianda is a wartime conglomerate of three great Chinese Universities."

"I see," said Henry.

"I don't understand," said Stan, putting his teacup on the floor between his legs. "Why is it that you folks are so different from the other Chinese we've heard about? Sure, you all have these values, this Confucius stuff, but there's more to it than that."

Chong Lingxiu said a few quick words. Mr. Ai answered him.

"Lianda is a unique place," said Neil, his voice barely a whisper. He spoke slowly, choosing his words carefully. "It is a progressive place. Ideas flow here more freely than in most places."

"Why is that?" Stan asked.

"One part has to do with the Governor. He has had disagreements with Chiang Kaishek in the past, so he does not enforce such strict adherence to Chiang's politics. Different ideas are tolerated, at least to some degree, at Lianda."

"Do you mind if I ask what would happen if you exceeded that tolerance?" Jake asked.

"We would be arrested," Neil answered.

"This tolerance is unofficial," Mr. Ai explained. "Anyone can be arrested at any time. Progressive ideas, democratic ideas,

Communist ideas—none are officially tolerated. All can bring...
big trouble."

＊   ＊   ＊   ＊

On their next visit, two days later, Jake handed out shaving
equipment and packages of cheese that had arrived in a box from
Blanche. "We thought you fellas could use these."

The students stared at the bounty. "It's too much, but thank
you," said Neil Qu.

Chong Lingxiu pointed to the supplies. "Please forgive my
curiosity. Would your officers agree with these gifts being brought
to us?"

Stan laughed. "The Colonel? That little rooster would probably
have us tarred and feathered."

Chong looked taken aback. "Tar and...feather? I had thought
the American Army was..."

"It's an expression," Henry explained. "He just means the
Colonel would probably not like it very much, if only because he
didn't expressly order it. I don't know that I agree. More likely
he'd be upset we didn't make you pay a lot of money for the stuff.
That's what the Squeeze is, you know. Selling everything that's not
tied down is okay, long as you get enough for it."

Chong nodded. "We have plenty of corruption too!"

Jake looked at Henry. "We've heard rumors that there is something going on in the North. Some different way of fighting the
war. The sort of thing we've overheard in tea shops, and at the
PX. Unofficial stuff, you know? Do you fellows know anything
about that?"

Stan put a hand on Jake's shoulder. "We've been talking an
awful lot about internal Chinese politics. If you remember what

the Colonel said when we got here, we were specifically told to stay away from that subject."

Jake turned. "Did he say anything about talking to local store-keepers and students? He said discussing, right? Am I discussing? No. I'm asking. Besides, the subject isn't even Chinese politics, it's the war itself, and how it's going in another part of China."

Henry wagged a finger at his friend and bunkmate. "Were you on the debating team at City College?"

While Chong Lingxiu shifted in his seat and appeared uncomfortable with the subject, Neil Ku looked at Mr. Ai, who nodded.

A convoy of trucks rumbled past the front of the shop. Neil waited until they were gone, closing his eyes for a moment against the dust that blew in through the open doorway. "In the North," he began, "there are areas of successful resistance, a different kind of fighting. We call them the Liberated Areas."

The GIs looked at one another. "So, these are not connected to the Central Government's Army?"

Neither the students nor Mr. Ai answered.

"Not Chiang Kaishek?" Henry asked.

"No, no!" Neil answered right away. "These are people in the countryside organizing, fighting, winning in those areas. Even the Japanese Imperial Army cannot defeat the people in their own homes when they're mobilized, organized."

"You guys're Communists?" Stan held a piece of rice bread halfway to his mouth.

"A generalization," said Mr. Ai.

"Communication has been established in some areas in a kind of makeshift way," Neil Ku continued. "And there is an organized war effort that reflects a mixture of different groups: some Communist, some democrat," he shrugged, "all patriots who want to save our country. And it's working." He looked Stan in the eye. "The only successful Chinese war effort against the Japanese is this one I'm describing. We thought you should know about it—and we hoped you'd tell other American servicemen."

Jake thought a moment. "Maybe you guys could tell them yourselves." He looked at Henry. "They could come to the base. We could have forums. You know," he waved a finger. "I have an idea. There's some literature gathering dust, I&E, uh, the Information and Education Literature. Interesting stuff, really, about fascism."

Henry looked skeptical. "You think Drum'd go for it?"

"We could go over his head."

Stan laughed. "You wouldn't have far to go."

"You think Colonel Root'd go for it?"

Jake shrugged, then grinned. "Depends how we presented the idea. Have a look at some of the I&E literature and present it like that—like an Army thing, a um, patriotic thing. These guys," his arm swept, open palmed, over their hosts, "represent people who're fighting the war with success. Think of all we've heard about the Chinese war effort, not just incompetent, but—"

"Indifferent," Henry nodded, turning to Mr. Ai. "Yeah, what we've heard about the Chinese Army isn't good. They haven't been all that motivated to fight."

"They prefer to fight internal war," said Neil, after a Chinese sentence from Chong.

Henry looked at Stan, who was staring at Ju Shiyan, then he nudged Jake, who slapped Stan on the back of the head. "Wake up."

Neil Ku turned to Mr. Ai and then to Chong, and spoke a few syllables in Chinese. Chong answered, Neil Ku translated.

"Lingxiu asks that you please be seated and we will explain." Everyone sat down on boxes, with Chong and Neil Ku remaining standing in the middle. Mr. Ai retreated with his wife to the back of the room. As he disappeared behind the counter, Ai Wei peeked his head out, "Aiya ya ya!" he giggled, then disappeared. A moment later, the bear appeared, dancing from side to side.

"Hello, little bear!" Henry called. The bear waggled back.

Jake sighed at some memory, then turned his attention back to their hosts.

"We told you a little about Lianda already. Our university is a poor place with not enough food or places to live. We borrow from the local high schools." Neil stopped while Chong spoke a stream of animated syllables.

"But we do have some of China's great poets and teachers. A school is more than its buildings."

Jake nodded. "We agree there."

"We are dedicated to winning China back and letting everyone know how pitiful the government's war effort is. Incidentally, if this American Army literature you're thinking of discussing with your friends is about fascism, we suggest you take a good look at some of China's politics today."

"I had that thought exactly," said Jake.

Henry looked excited. "This is the first we've heard about any successful Chinese war effort."

Jake smiled to himself. Henry looked more animated than Jake had seen him since their arrival in Kunming.

Mr. Ai had returned. "Huida has prepared some tea. Please help yourselves." He waved a hand toward the counter where Mrs. Ai was placing a stack of cups next to a black porcelain bowl.

"We are all very curious about America," Mr. Ai continued. "Would you mind if we asked a few questions about daily life, your jobs, your families, President Roosevelt?"

"Not at all," Jake said, standing up and moving towards Mr. Ai, who was in the center of the shop. "We're happy to help you."

"We really have so little information," Mr. Ai said. "What you suggested before about articles from magazines or newspapers would be a big help. America is a fascinating place."

As Jake answered questions, Henry looked around the room. The two girls had remained seated, averting their eyes when he looked their way. Chong Lingxiu stood tall, chin up. Soldierlike, Henry thought, remembering that no one had directly answered the question about their political affiliation. Neil Ku was more bent at the backbone, as though he were too thin to stand straight.

He leaned towards Jake. "Look at Stan," he whispered. Jake turned and they both watched as Stan, two cups in hand, approached Cha Wulin, extending one cup to her, smiling and saying something inaudible. She was trying to turn away, but her back was to the wall.

Henry was about to stop him, but Mr. Ai's question so startled him that he forgot about Stan.

"Do you have a wife or girlfriend waiting for you at home?"

Henry swallowed. "I have a, well, not exactly. My girlfriend didn't want to wait for me."

"Ah yes," Mr. Ai remembered. "You mentioned her when we first met. Frances."

Henry nodded, misery plain on his face. "She didn't think I was sympathetic enough to poor people and she has a sort of, I don't know what you'd call it, unionist maybe, point of view and—" Part of his mind watched, amused, while his mouth continued on, sharing personal details of his life with strangers who he was certain had no point of reference for what he was saying. Could that be why he was saying it? He needed to say these things and these people were safe because they couldn't possibly understand.

"Ah," said Mr. Ai, who was nearly crowded aside by his wife, who had suddenly taken an interest in the discussions. "I understand perfectly."

"How can we hear more about these Liberated Areas?" Jake wanted to know.

"You come back to dinner," Mr. Ai said. "Sunday afternoon. We talk about everything." He listened as his wife said something, then smiled at Henry. "She said you tell us about your girlfriend, but don't worry. Not important."

Henry raised his eyebrows and looked at Jake to see what he thought, but Jake was looking across the room.

"Well, I'll be damned," he said.

There, on Mr. Ai's torn green couch, Stanley Freilich was leaning over one of the Chinese girls, trying to kiss her. Her hands were in front of her face, which was turned away.

Mr. Ai had also seen. The skin on his face tightened, his cheeks shone and he clapped his hands and called out, "Truck driver is ready to return to base! Party is over! Thank you! See you all again, soon."

5

THE STUDENTS

After this most recent visit with the Americans, the students climbed onto their bicycles and rode back to the old huts and decrepit buildings that comprised Lianda University. While Neil Ku and Chong Lingxiu chattered about how much more sensitive these American soldiers appeared to be than others they had met, best friends Mary Cha and Jane Shiyan rode silently side by side.

Cha Wulin's arrival at Lianda had not been of her own design. Such big changes: her arranged marriage, her flight from the only home she had ever known, and the very inappropriate disrespect she had shown her beloved father, Cha Siansheng. They had not been her doing. In this case, Shiyan had been behind the move, and it had all happened so fast.

They had been playing with puppets made from their fathers' shirts one morning when Shiyan noticed that her best friend was quieter than normal. Guessing that the problem was connected to the arrangement Wulin's father had made with the Tiger Lady, who was the mother of Pei Han the fish seller, the girls had commiserated about life under the weight of such a marriage.

When Wulin did not respond to Shiyan's jokes and puppetry, Shiyan deduced that the problem was something more, and within minutes had elicited from Wulin that she felt a terrible dread about marrying the smelly fish seller and joining the Tiger Lady's household.

This situation had one positive side: for the first time in her life, Wulin felt she was the more worldly of the two, more experienced than her Kunming city girlfriend. She liked that. And now she had another point of superiority.

They rode in silence. Shiyan had not spoken since the American GI had tried to kiss her. She had not even looked at her. Wulin smiled to herself. The American had pointed to himself and said "Stan. American. Stan." Then American Stan had pointed to her and she had said, "Cha," her family name, and then, "Mary," the anglicized name her Lianda University friends had given her.

He had said, "Tea?" The Mandarin Chinese word for "tea" was indeed "Cha" but that was not the meaning of her name. She did not explain this, however, since speaking to this American GI would have been inappropriate, to say the least.

So he had gone on believing her to be, in English, Mary Tea, his pointed American face smiling and repeating, "Mary Tea, Mary Tea," and then he had leaned forward with his lips and closed his eyes.

An open-backed truck filled with raucous American soldiers passed the other way, and there was whistling and hooting in Shiyan's direction.

Wulin steered around one of the larger stones in the road.

Shiyan had warned her about GIs, just as she had about the Tiger Lady, just as she had about everything! Shiyan was the worldly one, the city girl, while she, Cha Wulin, was merely the farmhand. Become ice in winter if the GIs talk to you, whether you are in the Lianda Bookstore or in a tea shop or on the street. Do not look at them or talk to them. They are dangerous!

Well, she had shown Shiyan who was worldly now. She was no shirt puppet!

Mary Cha Wulin suppressed a smile, keeping her eyes on the front wheel of her bicycle.

*   *   *   *

Far ahead Neil Ku and Chong Lingxiu were pedaling at a furious pace, leaning far over the handlebars and talking breathlessly.

"You'll write the article tonight, Neil, and we'll have the posters made in the morning." Lingxiu could not keep the excitement out of his voice. "You have what a great journalist needs—a knack for being there for the great story. This is the most important quality a journalist can have."

Neil Ku nodded, unable for a moment, to answer. Because he was smaller than Chong Lingxiu, he was having trouble keeping up. He was also working out the headline for the wall newspaper in his mind.

Wall newspapers were the new media on Lianda Campus. With innocuous, academic-sounding names like *Read* and *Study*, they were ways for the furiously competitive political factions to compete for the attention and political mind of the majority of the University, which was politically middle-of-the road. Most students were neither Kuomintang affiliated nor Communists. Many, such as Neil Ku, were leaning a particular way, but as yet were unaffiliated officially.

So ideas, editorials and commentary were carefully written on tall sheets of paper, which were tacked up conspicuously around campus and Kunming. Gangs of students from competing groups were sent to tear posters down or cover them with their own. Originally, Neil Ku had been one of the students chosen to put up posters because he was innocent, not known to be affiliated with a particular group, and because he could run very fast. But this had changed once his journalistic bent was discovered, and he was well on his way to becoming the writer he had long dreamed of becoming.

"Liberation Areas get the word out to American GIs." Neil panted and pedalled to catch up to Lingxiu. He grinned. "That's my headline."

"The headline's just the beginning," said Chong Lingxiu. "We need the rest of the story and maybe some information about America, the war effort and other, social things. We can show that *Read* is the wall newspaper to watch for. We're the ones who know. You've found an excellent source. First rate information!"

*   *   *   *

Kunming was a place of green hills and flowers, where the grasses grew tall and rustled in the light breeze. The clouds had an edge defined by soft sunlight and the greens of Kunming's vegetation were lush from rains that were hard but not harsh, the drops small and evenly scattered. And after the rain there was a cool, fresh smell that was the flowers and plants accepting the moisture.

While its surroundings were beautiful, the Lianda campus was poverty stricken. Vacant buildings became makeshift classrooms, with supplies borrowed from townspeople or built as needed. But what it lacked in decor, Lianda made up for in academic tradition and renown—some said infamy. The university was not grounded in its campus but in its teachers, some of whom were China's finest poets and writers. And the atmosphere of flight only increased their enthusiasm for teaching and deepened their convictions.

The students sat in a circle in one of the fields outside the mess hall. The broken bricks and rotted wood contrasted with the yellow and red flowers that dotted the grass around them. A light easterly breeze blew over them from between the buildings.

Students were posted as lookouts twenty yards in each direction, with instructions to whistle a particular way if authorities. Unfriendly students or faculty approached. Chong was about to explain the strategy for writing the next day's issue of *Read* when Professor Shin appeared, his hand on the shoulder of a new student.

The boy's hair was of equal length all the way around his head, as though a bowl had been placed over his hair as a guide for cutting. The students shifted in the grass until Chong Lingxiu quieted them.

"This is Tong Xie," said the professor. "But that is not his real name, as you will soon understand. He's new to Lianda and I was hoping that you would welcome him, introduce yourselves, make him feel at home."

Everyone nodded and smiled, and Tong Xie inclined his head forward and looked at the ground. Professor Shin extended his hand. "These two young ladies are Mary Cha and Jane Shiyan, not students, but best friends from right here in Kunming. They are..." he paused, "visiting."

Tong Xie smiled. Wulin and Shiyan refused to look at one another. "Best friends?" he asked.

Neil Ku smiled. A boy with an assumed name could be trusted. "They're hiding from Wulin's arranged marriage."

The boy nodded.

The professor continued. "And this young woman is Lin Teu. We think of her as our movie star."

Lin, sitting with Sung Hongai, her supposedly secret boyfriend, smiled.

"And that's Sung, who wants to leave Lianda as soon as possible to live on a houseboat."

Sung Hongai shook his head and smiled to himself. "Not until the war's over," he countered.

"And that's Neil Ku, our young journalist, and Chong Lingxiu," he paused, not sure of how much to say about Chong's affiliations, which stretched beyond Lianda to more politically murky areas.

Neil Ku slapped Chong on the back. "He's our big brother." Neil laughed, and Chong smiled, the tension broken.

"I am honored to meet you all," said Tong, and he crossed his legs beneath him and sat down.

"Oh, and over there at the edge of the group," Professor Shin pointed to a dark boy who sat alone, his knees drawn up close to his chest. "That's Chen Liduo. You'd best not bother him too much."

"Why not?"

Neil Ku leaned close to the new boy. "Nanking."

"Oh," said Tong, understanding immediately. "Nanking."

Chen's dark eyes opened wide and stared at Tong. "You could not possibly know about Nanking unless you were there."

The students drew back. They had never heard Chen speak out loud about his experiences at Nanking. Even Professor Shin was taken aback.

Chen continued, standing up. "Nanking was a beautiful, sacred city, filled with ancient places and surrounded by mountains and the Yangtze, both of which we thought would protect us." He laughed and scratched a thin white scar on his cheek before continuing. The students shifted in the grass.

"There were pavilions, temples, monuments—old, important places. And lotus blossoms, green edged lakes. But it was a modern city with paved roads and electric lamps and running water. And children, everywhere you looked were children running, running—" He stopped and looked at his feet, bent down and picked up a blade of grass and chewed on one end of it. "We had heard about the Battle of Shanghai. It had gone on for so long and was so hard fought. It lasted months! So we thought the invaders might be tired, or perhaps they'd focus on the soldiers and even if they captured Nanking, what attention would they pay to its citizens? Certainly they'd leave us alone."

Lin Teu was whispering in Sung's ear. Chen Liduo shot her a stare so harsh her eyebrows went up as though pulled by strings. She looked into her lap.

"The troops may have been tired," Chen continued, "but more than that, they were angry." He paused. "We knew they were coming and most of our neighbors left the city days before the Japanese arrived. My mother, sisters and grandfather were all ready to leave. My father is in the KMT Army. I still don't know where he is or even if he is alive. But the rest of us were ready to go. But then my grandfather fell out of bed, and something went wrong with his hip and he couldn't walk. So we had to stay. We hoped that Nanking would hold or that the soldiers would be tired or merciful." Chen began to laugh, softly at first and then louder, until uncontrollable gales rolled from deep within his stomach.

"I, I just cannot imagine the word mercy, in any way, in any way..." He licked his lips, wiped his eye with a finger and went on. "We stayed with friends very close to the water, thinking that we would have another escape route, since they had a small boat. Well, the city was surrounded, bridges burned and thousands of soldiers were trapped inside. There were more soldiers trapped in the city, in fact, than there were enemy soldiers holding them there. If our trapped soldiers were somehow coordinated, everything might have ended differently, but no one was organized; everyone, the soldiers included, was terrified. They were promised fair treatment if they surrendered, and so they did. And the army was divided up into smaller groups, taken out and shot. I suppose this was the fair treatment. Everyone was shot equally. And after being shot, like all corpses, everywhere in Nanking, the soldiers were bayoneted."

Chen's voice dropped to a near whisper. "The Yangtze ran red, its banks rising up as it was filled with the dead. And as soon as they were finished with the soldiers, they turned on the citizens. Young, old, everyone was beaten, then mutilated, then shot. There was no resistance, no need for fighting, but the slaughter went on just the same. Decapitating, bellies ripped open. And the raping..."

He took a deep breath, glanced at the girls and bit his lip. "Women, no matter what their age, were forced to pose in pornographic ways, then were raped by dozens of men in succession. Afterwards they were told they could go free, and as they ran away, naked, they were shot in the back."

"Liduo," Professor Shin started to say.

"Don't..." Chen held up a hand. "Some of the women were made sex slaves and not killed right away. When the soldiers arrived at our friend's house, I ran into some bushes along the riverbank and waited while they rounded up my mother and sisters and dragged my grandfather from his bed. I thought if I waited, maybe there would be a chance to do something. I waited while they took turns raping my sisters; I waited while they raped and beat my mother; and finally I waited while they beat my grandfather's head in with a rifle butt when he ordered them to stop." He swallowed, tears spilling from the corners of his eyes. "But there was always one soldier who stood to the side, who was guarding them. There was never a moment, never a moment." He brought his hands to his face, covering his eyes with his palms. His shoulders shook. After a few minutes he regained his composure.

"So I started crawling through the brush towards the house when I heard the three loud cracks. I knew my mother and sisters were dead. A fourth crack and my grandfather was out of his misery."

He stopped and looked over the faces of the students and professor. "I did not stay to watch the bayonetting, but cut myself with a sharp stick, being as quiet as I could, then smeared the blood on my chest and face and rolled into the river with all the other bodies."

"Pleased to meet you, Tong, or whatever your name is." He nodded towards the professor and sat down.

For quite some time no one spoke and when he did, Professor Shin's voice was barely audible. "It's nearly one o'clock. Perhaps we should continue our introductions in the mess hall. I understand if no one feels like eating, but let's stay together." He stood up and everyone quietly followed him along the dirt path towards the low shack used for communal eating. Chong Lingxiu put his arm on Chen Liduo's shoulder, but Chen shrugged it off.

Sung Hongai, who was long legged and lean, with long black bangs extending over his eyes, let the tips of his fingers brush Lin Teu's waist so that no one would notice. If Lin Teu objected, he could claim the touch was an accident, though of course, they both knew it was not. She was a petite, dark young woman, smaller than Wulin and even Shiyan. Her eyes had an energy; they moved from person to person, analyzing, evaluating, as she planned her life with her future husband. She had long ago decided that their marriage would be exemplary of the New China that was soon to come. Whether they lived on Hongai's houseboat and followed his fishing dream was unimportant. This group of students, led by Chong Lingxiu and Mr. Ai was the right choice. Together they would fight for the birth of what they all knew was coming, whether with weapons, wall newspapers or words. She leaned her head on Hongai's arm. And she would have her experienced Hongai next to her all the way!

It was time for lunch, so they brushed themselves off and walked together to the mess hall, waiting on line for a bit of rice at the bottom of a bowl. The rice was not clean, and one had to pick out inedible bits of this or that from the bottom of the bowl with one's chopsticks before commencing to eat. They sat as a group around a round wooden table.

Shiyan finally broke the silence with her best friend. "So, you think you know what you're doing?"

Wulin didn't answer.

"I'll tell you what I think."

Wulin lifted her eyes, and Shiyan was startled to see none of the deference that had been Wulin's most charming, to Shiyan at least, asset. "I knew you'd get around to telling me what you think. Now's as good a time as any."

"I think you're doing this to spite me."

"Doing what?" Wulin looked into her rice bowl as though she had lost something.

"Exactly the opposite of what I told you to do! I said when the American soldiers look at you or talk to you, become ice in winter. Ignore them. But you talk to them and, and—well, look at what you did!"

Wulin was fascinated with a particular piece of rice, keeping her bowl in front of her mouth to hide her smile. She had waited all her life for this moment. "I did nothing."

"That's right. You did not send the American GI away when he approached you. You did nothing."

"I did not encourage him." She was now the city girl, wasn't she? The worldly Shiyan was the country bumpkin! A magic trick performed by the new Mary Cha Wulin!

"I liked him," she said, with all the nonchalance she could muster. She nodded towards Professor Shin, who was approaching the table with his own lunch. She did not tell Shiyan how awful she felt about leaving her beloved father, Cha Siansheng, how disrespectful such a thing was. Shiyan should have known that and sympathized!

"Now that he's had a chance to get to know who we are," said the professor, "perhaps we ought to give our new friend, Tong Xie, a chance to tell us all about himself."

Shiyan leaned close to Wulin's ear. "He thinks you're a whore!"

Wulin feigned surprise, glancing at Tong Xie. "Why we've never met!"

"You know who I mean. The American!" Shiyan hissed, and Wulin closed her eyes, feeling she might faint from enjoying the moment too much.

Tong Xie cleared his throat. His voice was unexpectedly deep, like Chong Lingxiu's, but without the experienced timbre of their group leader. Neil Ku was deep in conversation with Chen Liduo. Sung Hongai was whispering into Lin Teu's ear, his fingers dangerously close to her arm.

Professor Shin spoke up in a loud voice. "Tong is from Shensi Province."

Immediately the talk stopped. Shensi was the birthplace of the revolution, Mao's home.

"He has just returned from the 25,000 Li."

The table fell silent. Even Sung pulled his hand away from Lin Teu, who looked up, startled, appraising the new boy with respect bordering on reverence. The 25,000 Li was the Long March.

Tong Xie smiled faintly and flipped his bangs out of his eyes. "So you see why I cannot use my name." He looked around, making sure guards had been posted, protecting the conversation. "I was brought up in a wealthy family not far from Shensi, the middle of three boys." The students shifted in their seats, putting their bowls on the table in front of them. Chong Lingxiu shushed them.

"When I was quite young, in middle school, perhaps younger, I was fat from eating rich foods. My father brought home candy and treats and gave them out each afternoon, but when the cooperatives were formed my father was smart enough to see what was coming and he joined up while his business associate refused and was eventually put out of business. I think my father understood all along that his wealth would be seen as a detriment because he seemed so happy after joining. He never looked back, as far as I could tell."

"Tell us about the 25,000 Li." Lin Teu's eyes sparkled with anticipation.

"Well…" Tong shook his head and took a deep breath, which came out as a sigh. "You know the saying 'Revolution is not a tea party.' It's the truth. We spent days packing machinery and all sorts of household goods on the backs of animals, most of which spilled off as we walked. It was my father, my oldest brother, who was twelve then, and myself." Tong looked out over his audience. "My mother and sisters stayed behind. I have not seen or heard from them since." He said it as though it were a bit of food or an old toy he had left behind, rather than his own flesh and blood.

"I was nine or ten at the beginning of the 25,000 Li. We had trouble at first because we went in straight lines, and Chiang Kaishek was able to keep his armies on top of us. But after a while we began using diversions, so it looked to them like we were going in several directions at once." He took a deep breath. "Early on, my brother was caught and shot through the back of the neck."

Tong put his forefinger to the side of his own neck. "Often we marched at night to avoid bombing." He closed his eyes and on the other side of the table, Lin Teu strained forward to hear.

Tong regained his composure. "But we recruited along the way. Once they heard who we were, many joined us." He smiled. "Spreading a rich merchant's land among poor peasants can be very popular."

Lin Teu nodded. "They saw you were an army," she said, and Hongai turned to stare at her. What was she doing?

"But no one was intimidated," Tong replied. "We were welcomed, not feared."

"An army worth joining," Lin said. "The thought of an army as anything but oppressive must have been new for those you met along the march."

"Quite a few did join us—but we lost more. We saw mountains higher and more treacherous than I ever imagined existed. I have always been afraid of falling. I used to ride my father's shoulders and even that frightened me. But I learned to ignore that fear. There were much worse ones."

Chong Lingxiu sat alongside Tong, rocking slowly forward and back. "Tell them about the Lolos," he urged.

Tong smiled. "The Lolos, you know, are a minority that's particularly difficult—an independent people, but we turned that to our advantage. You see, they had always been oppressed by armies, but as the young woman says, not by our army." He smiled and Lin Teu blushed. Sung Hongai looked at her with amazement. As his fingertips approached her leg, she slapped his hand away as if it were a mosquito.

"The way to approach Lolos is to examine their circumstance and find a way to agree with them. We promised them independence and to side with them when the Civil War comes. The Lolos

became allies when Liu Po-Ch'eng joined the Lolo chief in drinking the blood of a chicken."

"What about the bridge," Neil Ku called out from one side.
"The chains across the bridge, the hundreds running from the
few."

"Right," agreed Hongai, anxious for Lin Teu's sake to show his
enthusiasm.

"The Liu Ting Bridge!" a few others called out.

Tong nodded. "That's my favorite part of the march to talk
about, though I'm sure you all know the story."

"Personally," Neil Ku called, "I've forgotten it." Everyone
laughed, since no one would ever forget the heroes of Tatu Ho.

"The Government tried to destroy the bridge and had left only
the support chains stretching across the Tatu River. We had to get
across but the wood had been burned away; there was nothing left
to walk on and we had no choice but to cross on the chains—the
only part of the bridge left. Meanwhile, they were shooting at us
and the first across the bridge would face almost certain death."
He paused. "And that was what happened. Men swung across the
bridge and quite a few were shot and fell into the river. But some,
a few, managed to throw grenades at the soldiers as they got near
the far side. They were the heroes. Quite a few of the enemy were
killed and the rest ran."

"But after crossing, we faced our most determined enemy—the
weather. Most of us were from the south and we had never experienced cold like that before. Many died while walking barefoot
over the ice. The mountains seemed to go on forever. But we made
friends and organized villages all along the way, collecting food
and money from the landlords and distributing it among the peasants. We abolished taxes and found that when we arrived at a
place, the people there had been expecting us."

"What about the Mantzu?" Chong prodded.

"The Mantzu people were more difficult than the Lolos in that they hate all Chinese; they took food from places before we arrived and shot at us from trees. Any Mantzu who aided us was threatened with being boiled alive. My father was one of many to die fighting for food and the only good to come out of this part of the Long March was that no one would follow us through the Mantzu area." He closed his eyes, which were partially covered by his long bangs.

"I'll have to tell about the rest of the Long March some other time. Thank you for welcoming me to Lianda. I thought you might like to hear one of the songs of the Long March." Softly at first, he began to sing and Chong Lingxiu, who knew the song, joined him. The voices grew stronger and louder, no one caring who heard.

Hongai looked at Lin Teu and was startled by her eyes. He had never seen them so rapt, so focused as they were now on Tong Xie, the new boy from Shensi.

6

Professor Shin leaned close to Wulin and whispered a question. She glanced up, smiling.

"Yes, better, thank you. I miss my father and, well, I'm not a university student."

"I made sure a message got through to your family," the professor said. "We made sure they knew that you and Shiyan are safe and staying somewhere nearby. For them to know more details might be dangerous."

She looked at him. "Dangerous? For them?"

"For you. Pei Han has been traveling all over, looking for you. He has the money and connections to execute a pretty thorough search." He saw her draw back. "Of course, we have resources, too."

Mary Cha Wulin set her lower lip. "I will not run away from Pei Han any more."

"Listen," the professor pointed, "it's Neil's turn."

Neil Ku Nuli bowed his head. "I grew up on the cobblestone streets of Chengdu. My father made chops—artist's stamps—but was also a high school teacher. But that's not what I remember most; I remember the twenty years of taxes he had to prepay. I remember the tall iron gates in front of warlords' houses and the music that used to float out their windows while I ran through the rain-soaked streets on some errand for my mother."

Professor Shin took his hand from the back of Wulin's chair and raised it, as though he were a student. Neil Ku smiled and pointed to him.

"Tell us what you want to do after college."

Neil Ku lowered his eyes. "Well, I've always wanted to be a journalist."

The professor stood up and turned to look at the teenagers around him. "Can't you tell from his descriptions? Neil is one of the leaders of our Wall Newspaper Association." He looked at Tong. "Our paper is called *Read*."

"I've seen it around," Tong nodded.

"My friend Ai Wenti," the professor continued, "feels Neil Ku will be instrumental in our war effort against the Japanese because, you see, he is so well spoken, so self effacing." Neil Ku shook his head and looked at the ground, embarrassed.

"It was Mr. Ai who suggested Neil Ku talk to the Americans about the Liberated Areas once we learned we could trust them."

"Americans?" Tong Xie looked from Professor Shin to Neil Ku and back again.

Chong Lingxiu adjusted his spectacles. "We met three very interesting American soldiers. They did their own political protesting in the United States against government oppression and the Spanish Civil War."

"I did not realize there was government oppression in the United States."

"They seem open minded, interested, not the headstrong bullies we usually meet."

The rest of the students nodded.

Professor Shin agreed, "we were delighted. And some of us were a little too delighted." He gave a pointed look towards Mary

Cha, who met his eyes, and it was he who was forced to look away. Shiyan watched, amazed.

"So now we're hoping to invite ourselves to the base to talk more about the Liberated Areas and point out that the Nationalists are hoarding equipment to use in a civil war." The professor shrugged. "We plan to open some eyes. If Americans, not just these three, but others, can be made to understand that the KMT is more interested in fighting the Communists than the Japanese, maybe their government or military leaders might change their allegiance."

"Or at least put more pressure on the KMT to negotiate," the professor added.

"There's something special about these GIs," said Neil Ku.

"Better be careful about that kind of sentimentality." It was Chen Liduo.

"What do you mean by that? Why?" Neil Ku wanted to know, but Liduo waved him away.

"Can these new Americans help somehow with the wall newspaper?" Tong asked.

Chong chose his words carefully. "They can teach us which way the wind is blowing in America. What we get from radio broadcasts and from our usual sources is one thing, but information from a trustworthy American source, well, this would be tremendously useful! Maybe we can keep the government a little off balance. Shouldn't we learn everything we can about President Roosevelt and American society in general? I'm interested in their labor unions, and Neil here wants to know more about what they call the 'soft wind' they use to bring new soldiers into the Army."

"It's called a draft," said the professor.

"Just be careful," Chen warned, his eyes suddenly lit. "These are Americans. They have long puffy faces and round eyes. Don't trust them so easily."

*   *   *   *

At the same moment, a half dozen *li* away, another meeting was taking place.

The building looked exactly like the stores it was attached to; it had at one time been a store. Its front was dirty white and none of the window frames contained any glass. Much of the building was empty but at the moment, a dozen young men and two women were seated on the floor in one bare room on the second floor. They sat in a crescent shape, facing two older men, one in reasonably well cut clothes, the other in a Central Government military officer's uniform.

"Bai and Xiang will point out which students we're looking for," the officer was saying to the other senior member of the group, a graying university professor. He looked from the professor, whose name was Wu, out over his young audience. "Xiang is in the unique position of being accepted by various student groups. These groups, the ones we're discussing here, may not tell him everything, but on the other hand, they do not chase him away."

"They are not the sort of students to chase anyone away," Xiang called out.

The officer ignored the interruption. "Bai has managed to gather information about their meetings and the way they spread their information. Bai?"

"I followed them all week using the quiet techniques you taught us," the dark-eyed student coughed into his hand, a wracking cough that persisted in the back of his throat for nearly a minute. Several times he was about to speak, but the cough got the better of him. "I don't think they knew I was there or, if they did, they were only vaguely aware. I was not seen. They meet in Room 44 of the freshman dormitory. Chong Lingxiu goes there each evening. They post guards to protect their conversations."

The soldier interrupted. "You all read the sheet I gave you on Chong Lingxiu's background?" He nodded curtly at the eager assent on each face. Two of the listeners had asked that the sheet be read to them, as they were illiterate.

Bai looked at his feet. "Once they may have seen me looking into the room as Chong Lingxiu went in. I saw one of the youngest, Chu Nuli."

"No," said Xiang, standing and waving a cigarette. "It's Ku. Neil Ku Nuli. He is the thin one who speaks well. He helps them put up the wall newspapers and now, I understand, he has begun writing them."

"Ku. He's right," said Bai, and he paused to cough, then smiled to show his own teeth, of which he was very proud. A friend of his father's had paid a debt by giving him two very large false teeth in the front of his mouth. "Anyway, that was two days ago, and they've gone from meeting in the dumpling shop to the field behind the dormitories—even yesterday, in the rain. It's safer there."

The soldier paced the front of the room. "Hmm. These radical students are friendly with Ai Wenti, the noodle maker, and Ai is friendly with more than a few American officers."

Xiang laughed. "Ai is friendly with everyone! He smiles and his wife smiles and even his baby smiles. They are the friendliest family in Kunming." His expression turned suddenly savage. "And if you believe that, you'll believe the rice in the Lianda dining room is the highest grade!"

Doctor Wu scratched his thinning hair and sat in one of the two armchairs at the front of the room. He seemed to consider pouring a cup of tea from a pitcher on the long table that was the only furniture other than the chairs in the room, but decided against it. "You need not tell us about Ai Wenti. We know him well. A clever man and not one to be underestimated."

"Another veteran," the soldier went on, "is Sung Hongai. He's done a lot of political work, along with Chong Lingxiu. Isn't that right, Xiang?" The soldier grinned at Xiang.

Xiang, who had been falling asleep, jerked awake and nodded blankly. "Yes, sir."

Bai raised a hand and coughed. "They had wives, according to your information, but I've seen no wives with them in Kunming."

"You are right, in part, Bai. I'm glad you brought that up." Doctor Wu raised an eyebrow and the soldier nodded. "Hongai was never married but he spends time with Lin Teu, another radical, the small, dark woman, younger than he. Remember that; it may be useful. And Chong Lingxiu was indeed married. His wife was in prison. She herself was killed there, but she had a son." He paused, but only briefly. "He believes his son was killed as well, but we know him to be alive and living with a farmer, a Mr. Gong, and his family—we know where they are and we're keeping our eyes on them. They may also be of use to us."

"I don't understand," said one of the two women. "How can students who were once well off, sons of merchants, write what their newspaper associations are writing? Their backgrounds are like ours, so why do they care so much about peasants and so much else that shouldn't concern them?"

"They listen to poets and peasants." Xiang shook his head.

"They should be grateful for their wealth!" said another student.

Wu chuckled. "These students are young. Their parents may have loved Sun Yatsen as much as Colonel Yin here and I did.

Now they say we ought to give up all we've worked for so that everyone will be better off." He shook his head. "Will they really give up everything they worked so hard for when the time comes?" The professor poured himself a cup of tea and lit a cigarette. "I think not."

Automatically, three of the students lit cigarettes.

Wu became serious. "None of them realize they're in for chaos. A government cannot be run by peasants and laborers any more than a university may be taught by students."

Colonel Yin cleared his throat and began pacing again. His remarks took on the clipped tone of a man getting down to business. "Now, this is what we'll do. We'll put up our own wall newspapers, covering theirs. The first issue will say…"

Xiang's hand shot up. "One of these students was asking about ways of getting revenge…"

"Revenge?" The soldier's eyes narrowed. He pivoted and looked hard at Xiang so that Xiang shrank in his chair. "One of these students? How well do you know him?"

"Well, sir, I've been cultivating his friendship. The student's name is Chen Liduo, and he is from Nanking. His family was, well you know how it was there. And now he can think only of what happened to them. He's blinded by rage, wants only revenge. I think he could be valuable to us—to the Generalissimo. We spent an afternoon together. I shared some western cigarettes with him and oh, I offered to teach him to use a knife the way you showed us. He's a natural—quick on his feet with fast hands. You should see him!"

"Oh, I'll see him. Tell me, does he spend time with Chong Lingxiu? Does he believe…?"

"Yes but he's cynical. Ideology is too rational for him. He is not as interested as the rest, not in academics, nor in revolution. Only in revenge." Xiang shuddered in spite of himself. "I brought him to my new place," he sighed at the thought of his new room, "and he was very interested in my victrola...and my knife, as I said."

The soldier nodded. "Get to know him better. Spend more time with him. Ask about his friends and, above all, be careful of a trap."

The group broke up and the colonel asked that Xiang remain behind. They watched as the students and the professor left. "Just a word of advice, Xiang. We think you are doing a fine job, but all these objects you keep in your room. They are too ostentatious."

Xiang looked as though he had been slapped in the face. "Yes, sir," he said.

"If you focus more on our objectives and less on your own whims, we'll all be better off."

"My thoughts exactly, sir."

＊　　　　＊　　　　＊　　　　＊

Henry's feet were up on the metal railing at the foot of his bunk; his hands were behind his head. He couldn't see Stan from that position, but he thought he could imagine the look on his face.

"So, is she going to convert, Stanley?"

"Wulin Freilich," Jake added. "Has a nice ring to it. A real *balabusta,* she'll make. Quite the Jewish homemaker!" He roared, laughing so hard he hit his head on the iron support bar of the bunk over his head.

"Hey who said anything about marriage? So I tried to kiss some girl. Big deal. She didn't let me, did she?"

Louis Stabler, who was writing a letter to his wife, said something inaudible under his breath.

Stan looked at him. "Come on, we'll toast your new son. Louis Junior, right?"

"The third."

"The third, then."

"Go to hell."

Jake glanced at Henry, biting his lip. "We stood him up," Jake said. "Jeez, I just remembered. He's got a right to be angry. Louis, we're sorry. I know we were supposed to celebrate with you, but we got caught up in…" His voice trailed off.

Louis didn't answer.

"How is your son?" Henry asked.

"He's okay. Doing just fine."

"And his mother?"

"She's okay, too." He looked back at the paper in front of him. "Thanks so much for thinking of her."

Henry poured out the three shots and handed one to each of his friends. "To our new friends and…who knows, maybe a girl-friend." He raised his glass. Stan shook his head but did the same. Each of them drank.

"Ahhh. You know?" Jake held up his glass for emphasis, "what these Chinese kids told us about those areas in the North is impor-tant stuff and, as far as I know, no one in the army knows about it but us."

"Knows about what?" McPhee had come in, with Danko and Mickey Warren, a wiry, balding man who walked with his elbows out at nearly right angles.

"We met some local people downtown," said Henry. "Interesting folks."

"Oh?" said McPhee, sitting down next to Henry on his bunk. "How so?"

"First of all, they were friendly. And they want to fight the war."

"And they're doing something about it," Stan added.

"What would that be?" McPhee asked.

"They told us about another part of the Chinese war effort," Jake explained. "In the North."

"They said it's been successful," Henry added.

"Bet Drum and Root don't know about that." Stan raised up on his toes, and back down again. He was jittery, nervous.

"Listen, Barrymore," said Mickey Warren, looking at McPhee. "I'm going to get some of those carrot seeds my mother sent and try planting them out by the trenches. You guys'll be here until we go back to work?" He sniffled, and wiped his nose on his sleeve.

"Yeah, make that about fifteen minutes. I told this Red Cross Nurse, Robin, I'd be—"

"Right, Valentino. Be back soon." Warren waved to Henry and Jake, ignored Stan, and left the barracks.

Jake watched the door slap shut behind him, then turned back to his friends. "You know, I have an idea. I've been reading the Information and Education Literature over at the Rec. A lot of it's about fascism. It's pretty good stuff. Talks about the last ten years and what's been going on in Europe, and how fascism's been spreading...even to places you wouldn't think of. And I've been taking a good look at the way the Central Government here runs things, and, well, maybe we could have some kind of talk with the guys about it. And at that talk maybe we could mention these Liberated Areas." His eyes brightened. "You know, our new friends're really fighting fascism, as well as the Japanese. They're doing it any which way they can and they're succeeding and no one on our side knows a damn thing about it. It's important."

Stan had overheard. "Think the brass'll take to our alluding to our allies as fascists?"

McPhee pointed a finger. "Better talk to Drum about it first."

Danko scratched his cheek with a dirty fingernail. "Why the interest in the locals?"

"Sounds like they have something to offer," said Jake.

"At first, I wasn't interested either," Henry added. "But, well, I liked them. They reminded me of my family."

"Your family?" McPhee was incredulous.

"I know what he means," said Stan. "They welcomed us. They chatted, small talk, you know? Like my mother small talks."

"Exactly," said Henry. "And their kid's cute."

McPhee started for the door. "Knock yourselves out, guys. I need a nurse."

"Oh?" Jake said. "Something hurt?"

"My heart. It's breakin'. But I'll be back. I've got to write letters to both my brothers. I send 'em to my mom, who sends 'em to Bill and Charlie."

"Where're they?" asked Henry.

"Got me. Givin' 'em hell somewhere. Bill's in the infantry in Europe. Charlie's in the Navy, probably closer to here than home. Probably doing magic tricks for his shipmates right now. He always was a whiz with slight of hand. Bill, on the other hand, had a way of making a bottle of whiskey disappear."

Danko nodded. "I'd better go write my sister. Last letter I got, her boyfriend was having her over to listen to records."

Henry leaned forward. "To his apartment? No chaperone? You'd better go write her."

*   *   *   *

Major Drum was sitting behind his wide pine desk when Henry and Jake knocked on the door.

"Come in. What can I do for you boys?"

"How are you, major?" Henry asked.

"Kids okay?" Jake sat down on a wooden bench opposite the major.

"Susan and John are fine, thanks." The major's eyes twinkled. "Nice that you think of them."

"Mrs. Drum teaching up a storm at school?" Henry continued.

"Actually, Ella's been asked on as a drill press operator downtown. Had to give up teaching, for the moment, anyway. But I'm sure she'll get her reading done, same as I get to read my war books here. Sounds like you two are gentlemen with an agenda."

"Nothing big," said Jake. "Just wondering if we might get a few interested fellas together to talk about that Information and Education literature that's gathering dust down at the Rec."

Drum frowned. "What for?"

"Talk about fascism." Jake sat up straighter; his voice rose eagerly. "We don't think the men really know the scope of it. And we happened to pick up some of the sheets and look 'em over, and they're pretty good, you know?"

Drum nodded. "Guess there are a lot of distractions around here. Take your mind off what we're here for." He lit his pipe and puffed a few times. "'Course some distractions can be good. Can't blame the men entirely for taking an interest in a woman or a fight. I saw one of our boys hit a fella—hardest damn shot since the Brown Bomber hit old Maxie Schmeling, Hitler's finest, on June the twenty second, 'thirty eight." Drum sighed, and blew a stream of smoke into Henry's and Jake's faces. "Yup, Joe Louis."

Henry rolled his eyes. "Sports could be part of it, sir. You could come in as a guest, talk about the fight, in fact. Great for morale."

Major Drum squinted through the smoke. "Don't snow me, boys."

Henry cleared his throat. "Jake and I met a few Chinese fellas downtown who might be interesting to listen to. Fellas who want to help the war effort. Sir—"

Jake flashed him a warning look, but the major didn't react.

"Well—" He took a dirty toothpick out of his top pocket and picked at the space between his front teeth, his pipe still in his other hand. "I guess it wouldn't be the worst trouble you could get into around here."

"Thank you, sir." Singer saluted. "Just trying to do our part, sir."

"Carry on, son."

* * * *

The Ais' home, which was in the back of the dumpling store, had a warm smell Henry could not place, hot tea and bodies per-haps—homey like his mother's kitchen, yet different. Perhaps the difference between the back and front of the store was in their odors. The front contained street smells: animals and gasoline, while the back of the store had the lived-in smell of a family at home.

The walls and floors were unadorned wood, the roof was bam-boo tied together by twine and cemented with mud. The din of ani-mals and voices drifted through the open doorway. Henry and Jake sat on two old chairs while Mr. and Mrs. Ai sat on sacks of what Henry assumed were flour or grain. A wooden bed, scattered toys and a kite made of thin, white fabric sat in the rear corner.

Every few minutes, the bear Blanche had sent slid into view from behind the bed, accompanied by an exclamation, a giggle and a small pair of curious eyes which quickly disappeared.

"...and ever since they bombed the base," Henry was saying, once tea was poured, "Jake's been sleeping two, maybe three hours, and having nightmares the rest of the night."

Jake threw his hands up. "Why'd you have to tell them that? Besides, what're you, Teddy Roosevelt? C'mon, Henry! You hear a truck backfire and you jump half out of your skin!"

"Where is your friend?" Huida had entered from the tiny kitchen, carrying a tray and four bowls.

"I suggested," Jake explained, "that until Stan could come for the right reasons, maybe he ought to stay away."

Henry looked hopefully at the tray, then at Mrs. Ai. "Duck?"

Jake shrugged, still stung by Henry's betrayal. "I hope so."

Huida gave each of them a bowl. "You tell your family at home about nightmares. Here you talk to us."

Mr. Ai smiled affectionately at his wife. "Now it's official. You have two families."

"Well," Jake said, quietly, "wouldn't it be crazier not to have nightmares?" He fumbled with his chopsticks and managed to bring a piece of meat to his lips.

Huida tilted her bowl toward her, using the chopsticks as shovels rather than tongs. "My husband has nightmares about Shanghai massacre all the time." The chopsticks moved in a circular motion, down into the food, towards her mouth, up and away again.

Mr. Ai stared at her.

Huida gasped; her chopsticks clattered to the wood table. "Forgot to serve tea." She hurried into the kitchen, leaving behind the tea pitcher.

Mr. Ai nodded sadly. "It's true." He sighed and looked at Jake. "I have nightmares every week—used to be every day. People killed, raped, houses burned, terrible things." His eyes welled with tears.

Jake was respectfully silent. "Guess I shouldn't be so upset, huh?" he said, after a full minute.

Henry nodded, lost in thought.

Huida returned without the tea.

Mr. Ai motioned for them to relax. "No, it's understandable to be upset. It's the human condition. Each of us has only our own experience." He smiled as his son came into the room and lay his dark head in his father's lap, humming to himself. "Many of the feelings, the insides, are the same. We are," he stretched his hands straight out to either side, "so far apart, but so close." He brought his hands together. Ai Wei laughed and clapped and touched his father's fingers.

Henry reached forward to touch the boy's hand, which drew back. "It's okay, son."

"His name is Ai Wei," said Mr. Ai.

"Hello, Ai Wei," said Henry, reaching out again. The boy did not meet Henry's hand with his own but he smiled and Henry smiled back. "Gee, I'd love to have kids someday."

"You will," said Huida.

Mr. Ai looked sternly at his wife, the skin on his neck tightening. "Not polite, Huida."

But Mrs. Ai ignored her husband. "They are family. You take my word. You have children. I know."

"It's okay," Henry said. "If you say I'll have children, that's fine by me. The point is, you are two of the nicest people we've met here." He smiled at Huida. "I get the picture."

Huida looked at her husband. "What picture?" She reached for the tea pitcher. "More tea?"

"We brought you some magazine articles." Jake reached into one of his jacket's deep side pockets, took out two envelopes and handed one to Mr. Ai. "Now you can learn more about us."

"Thank you," said Mr. Ai. "Any information you can get us about American society, politics, habits—anything—we appreciate very much." He put the envelope aside and looked squarely at Henry. "You receive letters from girlfriend?"

Henry did not meet his host's eyes. "Ex-girlfriend." He returned the remaining envelope to his pocket. "It's okay. I guess I don't mind your asking. Anyway, one. But it was everyday stuff. This one's from my mother."

"Why you don't write girlfriend more serious note?" Huida demanded to know. "Tell her about China! Tell her feelings. She like to hear." She leaned forward, eyes sparkling, her tone emphatic. "Get picture?"

Henry looked at her, surprised. Then he looked into his lap. "Thank you, Mrs. Ai." He was embarrassed at her mention of Frances, but he was beginning to feel more comfortable with Mrs. Ai's boldly personal inquiries. They were oddly refreshing, diminishing his shame and fear of rejection by exposing those feelings to light and air. He changed the subject. "This duck is delicious, Mrs. Ai."

Ai Huida and Ai Wenti looked at one another. "Duck?" they asked together.

But Henry didn't notice. He was leaning back in an old creaky chair, surrounded by friends and a homey aroma, more relaxed than he'd been since he'd last seen his family on Brooklyn's East Ninth Street.

7

Because it was Cha Wulin that Pei Han was looking for, Ju Shiyan was able to travel back and forth from her father's market to Lianda daily. It was in the dusty street in front of the market that Cha Siansheng shuffled over to her and raised his shaking finger. Neil Ku, who had accompanied her, waited with their bicycles.

More than a few of the old man's neighbors had seen his daughter around Kunming with her University friends. When word reached him, he was at once relieved that his daughter was alive but mortified that she was involved with such a political band of students.

Shiyan saw all this on his face before he uttered a word. She sighed and looked beyond him at a wispy formation of cotton clouds. One of the larger planes, a bomber, was descending slowly towards the American base. A lonely old man's only daughter's marriage to a respected family was now publicly ruined. The furious jilted groom scoured the countryside for his bride-to-be. The old man's back was bowed from all that weight.

Her pity getting the best of her, Shiyan smiled and greeted Cha Siansheng cheerfully. The smell of fried dough from the shop behind them mingled with a thousand odors of the marketplace.

"If you see Wulin—" He swallowed and his eyes grew small. "Tell her that Pei Han has gone to find her. He has suffered terrible loss of face."

Shiyan saw that he was pointing out his own loss of face. Cha Siansheng hobbled closer. Inadvertently, she stepped back.

"I convinced him to wait," the old man continued, "I told him that I would find her and bring her back. He knows she will listen to me."

Shiyan touched the sleeve of his jacket, within which his frail forearm shuddered with a multitude of age-related conditions; tears filled her eyes as she walked the old man back to the side of the road and promised to tell Wulin everything he said if she happened to see her. She had known Cha Siansheng all her life and thought of him as a quiet man, busy with his farm, who barely noticed his only daughter. Perhaps he saw her as a reminder of his own inability to produce a son. Now she saw the grief in his eyes. "How could I know where Wulin is?" she forced herself to say.

She squatted on her heels and watched the cart recede into the dust.

A flock of boys chased one another through the street, weaving among the wagons and bicycles, their laughter echoing loud enough to drown out the wails of the street beggars just beyond the market.

*   *   *   *

The Flying Tigers' library was a small, unadorned room behind the PX containing two standing shelves of books that had been donated from various places, primarily from the men themselves, and two long unstained pine tables surrounded by chairs. Men brought coffee in from the PX, picked out a book and sat; others, having found the noise in the barracks or the Rec too much for their concentration, wrote letters or played checkers.

As they entered the nearly empty library one afternoon after their SCU shift was over, Henry held two cups of coffee while Jake carried the I&E literature. As they sat down at the far end of the room, they nodded to Major Drum and McPhee, who were playing checkers near the door.

Jake waved. "And how are you gentlemen this lovely day?"

"I see you found your fascism literature," said Drum.

"Yes, we did, thank you. We were just going over it before we invited the men in to talk about it. What about you, Kenny? Will you join us for a little Information and Education?"

McPhee smiled down at his hands; he tapped one red checker against the top of another. "I don't think that's for me."

Henry sipped his coffee. "Ooh, hot. It's really for everyone, Ken. We'd love to have you."

"You'll have to excuse Sergeant McPhee," Drum smiled and reached across the table, slapping McPhee's shoulder. "He's pining away for Lady."

Henry leaned back in his chair. "But from what I've seen, Ken's got the whole nursing staff chasing after him. What's one lady...?"

"Lady's my pooch," McPhee growled. "And she's more loyal than any girl ever was. Boy, that dog's a better friend than...ahh, why do I want to explain it to you? What'd you have to tell them for, major? They're bookheads. They'll never understand."

"Why don't you put Lady's picture up on your locker?" Henry asked.

"And why don't you keep your opinions to..." He saw that Henry was wide-eyed and serious. "Yeah, that's not a bad idea."

"Major," Jake asked. "Will you be joining us?"

Drum nodded. "Sure. I'm ready to learn something new...or old, as the case may be. Don't look at me like that, McPhee. Those of us who're not lady killers have to find something to do with our time."

"I guess," McPhee shrugged, then he pointed, glaring. "And bad choice of words."

Drum cringed, shading his eyes.

Marlowe's head appeared at the door. "Anyone up for cards? We're two short."

McPhee and Drum shook their heads. Marlowe looked at Henry and Jake. "I should know better than to ask you guys."

"Marlowe," Henry looked at the pilot.

"Yeah?"

Henry smiled. "Good to see you."

Marlowe looked confused for a moment, then grinned crookedly. "Yeah. Good to be seen."

Jake opened the first of the faded Army pamphlets. "Okay, Hank. Time to get to work."

*   *   *   *

The same time the following afternoon, twelve men sat around the same two tables in the library. Many had turned their chairs around and were sitting with their arms crossed over the chair backs, cups of coffee in their fists.

Jake stood up, rubbed his palms together, and picked up the sheaf of papers. "Henry and I thought you fellas might find it interesting and informative to talk about some of this literature, Information and Education, they call it. You've probably seen it lying around; the Army puts it out."

"That's all well and good," said Danko, "but what's it to us?"

"A good question," Jake replied. "You know, before joining the service, I remember reading the papers and becoming more and more afraid of fascism. Of course, we all know about Hitler and Mussolini, but did you know that there's a British Union of Fascists that was founded in 1932? You didn't, did you?"

Mickey Warren sniffled. "So here we are in China. Should we be worried about some bunch of guys in England who may not even be around anymore?"

"It's really the bigger picture that concerns us, as it does the Army. There's fascist parties all over the world. I guess you know about Franco, in Spain. Pretty brutal little war they've had over there. Mussolini and Hitler joined right in. They could do that anywhere."

"That's right," said Henry. "There are fascists in Belgium, and..."

"How'd this whole fascist thing get started?" The question was from Major Drum. "Was it an international conspiracy? What?"

"Well," Jake said, holding the papers with one hand, scratching the stubble on his chin with the other. He waited while a plane took off, rumbling overhead. "In a way yes, in a way, no. The successful ones want to get stronger. So you have Hitler and Mussolini, and even the Japanese willing to pitch in and help the smaller ones, so they'll have influence in those places."

"Belgium," Henry added. "And France."

"France..." Drum tapped a finger to his lips.

"There's a pretty healthy fascist party in France, from what we've learned. And, as Henry says, Belgium." Jake picked up his coffee, took a slurpy sip, and put it down. "Now you all know about the Depression. Well, it affected much of the world, and as a result, just like in Germany, people got pretty desperate for a way out of their poverty. And often, the thing that looked to them like an answer was a strong person or party willing to throw away their constitution or laws to make things seem healthier. Cleaning up crime, taking over the economy, taking money from certain groups, giving it to other groups. These are things a fascist party might do."

Mickey Warren chuckled. "Doesn't sound all that bad, in a way."

"And at first, it might not seem to be." Jake sucked in his cheeks, thinking. "Next thing you know, you or your kid's dragged into the army, your business is confiscated, and before long you've got the Third Reich. Nice little things like the Bill of Rights go out the window." He spun the papers he'd been holding into the air.

"What about here?" someone called out.

Henry watched Major Drum, who was looking around at the men's faces.

"Well, we're just learning about China's history," Jake said. "And it has that same sort of pattern to it. Everyone was pretty bad off for a long time. That creates an opening for a strong, tough leader to come in and run the show his way. Then he might get a call one day from Adolph or Benny, offering a helping hand."

"Or wallet," Henry added.

Danko had been leaning back in his chair; now he let it slam forward. "You guys seem to think Chiang Kaishek is that kind of guy. But he's our ally."

Jake nodded. "He is today. But I've heard he threatens to switch sides if he doesn't get the arms or cash he wants."

"You fellas read that in there?" Major Drum pointed to the I&E literature, which Jake had retrieved from across the room.

Jake shrugged. "Some is interpreted from what we've read here."

"Interpreted..."

"Some is from observation, looking around Kunming. Forced conscription, for one thing. The bit about Chiang threatening to switch sides is something I read in newspapers my wife sent from back home."

"Really? An opinion column or news?"

"Don't remember, but I'll check it out and get back to you. My impression is that's just the way he does business."

"We've made some new friends, downtown," Henry began. "A group of young Chinese students, some of their friends, a shop-keeper, all of whom have interesting opinions about the war, about Chiang…"

"What do you mean?" Drum had folded his hands in front of him and was listening, his white-topped head cocked slightly to one side.

Jake held an open palm out to Henry as if to say "take it away; you started this."

"Well," Henry took a deep breath, "they didn't have much that was nice to say about Chiang Kaishek. Man's out for himself, they told us. To keep the arms we give him to fight his enemies here." Henry looked around at all the eyes on him. His voice lowered, and trailed off altogether.

Jake came to his aid. "They also told us about a group of Chinese, friends of theirs, in the northern part of China, who have had success fighting the Japanese. We'd never heard that before. And we thought it was important."

Henry's voice regained its confidence. "They're just different. You guys meet 'em and you'll see. They don't look away. They're friendly, confident. They want to win this war as much as we do. They're good people." He hit the table with his fist.

"Major," Jake said, putting down the papers. "We'd like to bring them to the base to talk to the men, if you'll allow it. What they have to say about what's going on up north, well it seems pretty relevant."

Drum didn't answer at first. Then he took his pipe from his top pocket, lit it, and puffed a few times.

"Chiang's our ally, like Danko said," Mickey Warren unwrapped a stick of gum and stuffed it into his mouth.

"Doesn't mean we shouldn't keep an eye on him," said Henry. "And keep an open mind."

Jake shrugged. "What if he's a fair weather ally? Like we've heard."

"Let me talk to the Colonel, see what I can do," Drum said finally. He slapped the table, pushing his bulk away and up, groaning softly with the effort. It was the signal that the meeting was over.

"There you are!" Stan rushed through the doorway and sat down in front of Henry and Jake. "I'm glad I found you guys. I need your advice. I'm not interrupting, am I?" He continued without waiting for an answer. Sweat stood out on his forehead. "I've been thinking quite a lot about this local girl—Mary Tea, her name is—Cha, in Chinese. That means 'tea,' did you know that? She doesn't have the—what would you call it—preconceptions, the women stateside have. We really hit it off and, you know, spending time with her, well it made me forget about the war—a little, anyway. You can understand that, can't you?"

Jake's expression softened. He and Henry exchanged glances. "Yeah, we can understand that, except you've been with her about thirty seconds, and she didn't seem particularly interested in—"

Henry stared. "Yeah, I can understand, if by hit it off, you mean she didn't run away screaming."

Stan ignored him. "I've been turning it over in my mind and I figured I might never see her again and what if she's the one...you know...for me?"

Henry's mind was instantly half a world away; his fingers caressed the smooth wood of the barrette in his pocket.

"You've got some imagination," Jake whistled.

"So, I went over to her school to ask around."

Jake shook his head. "You should have asked the major."

"That took guts," said Henry. "And a dose of stupidity."

"I don't care." Stan shrugged, then his expression changed. "Only when I found one of her friends, he said she was gone. No one has seen her in more than 24 hours."

"Maybe they were just telling you that to..."

"No. Henry, it wasn't like that." Stan held up a finger, and Henry noticed that his friend's hand was shaking. "They were scared, they were upset. It wasn't natural, they said. These people don't go off on their own like we do; they're always together." His voice went up a notch. "Except when they say the wrong thing. Then they—" He snapped his fingers. "They vanish. She's missing, I'm telling you. First I lose Irma, now Mary. Jake, you're friends with these Chinese. You gotta help me—help her!"

*   *   *   *

The meeting was set for the following Sunday. A truck would pick up the students and bring them to the Rec Hall where they would address what was expected to be a small group of enlisted men. At the appointed time, however, the audience had swelled to nearly forty, half of whom were officers. As Mr. Ai, Neil Ku, Chong Lingxiu and Chen Liduo walked into the Rec Hall, an Army photographer stepped forward.

"How about posing for some pics for the Army paper?"

Mr. Ai held up his hand. His manner was formal, his English clipped and precise. "Please, no photographs. This is only an informal discussion. Not of importance to your newspaper." He sounded embarrassed. "Please."

Major Drum, puffing on his pipe in a rear corner, called out, "Would you gentlemen mind introducing yourselves?"

Jake Singer was standing next to Henry in front of and to one side of the dance floor, where the students would be speaking. He took a breath, intending to introduce his friends, but Ai looked quickly at him, then looked the crowd over with the same warm smile he had worn when he had first met Henry and Jake.

"I am Ai Wenti, Chairman of the Welcome 14th Airforce Committee."

"Army Air Corps," yelled Stanley.

"Yes, welcome," said Mr. Ai. "And these are my neighbors." He held a hand out to the students. "My friends are Neil, Anton and Chip."

Neil Ku coughed. "Ahem. One of ah, the topics our friends," he bowed his head toward Jake and Henry, "asked us to discuss, was the abilities of other Chinese soldiers in other areas to fight the war."

A GI raised his hand.

"Yes?"

"Sergeant Weiss, sir."

Mr. Ai chuckled at the "sir" and Neil Ku blushed but no one else seemed to notice.

"Excuse me for saying so," Weiss continued, "but we haven't seen much evidence of Chinese success in fighting the war."

"Exactly," said Neil Ku.

"Or even of Chinese interest in fighting the war," someone else called out. There was a stirring among the officers along the rear wall.

"The situation in the North is different." Neil Ku stood up straighter, his hands clasped in front of him. "Fifteen or twenty areas the Japanese claim are under their control in the North are really liberated. They have their own elections and have established communications. There is a standing army of over a million men." He nodded at the dubious commotion around him.

"It's true. This is an army that has and will fight hard against the Japanese."

A low muttering from the back of the room was followed by one of the colonels standing up. "Young man. What did you say your name was?"

"Neil."

"Neil. Yes. You say there are elections in the North? Free elections?"

Neil Ku nodded and the colonel drummed his fingers on the back of his chair. "Tell us about these elections."

"Well, the candidates for office sit down in a row, with their backs facing the people—usually in the Square or a large outdoor area. Everyone is given a small bead."

"A bee?"

"A bead. Small, round—"

"Bead. Yes. Go on."

"And behind each candidate's back is a small bowl on the ground, and the people walk behind the candidates and drop their beads into the bowl of their candidate."

The colonel remained standing and stared at Neil Ku, even after another soldier asked a question and the discussion moved on.

After the supply truck drove the Chinese back to Lianda, Henry and Jake stayed in the hall to clean up the coffee cups and put away chairs.

Louis Stabler came over and shook Henry's hand. "Those're some new friends you made. I think they were a hit."

"So you're talking to me again," said Henry. Stabler shrugged.

"Excuse me." The colonel who had asked Neil Ku about the elections stepped between Henry and Jake.

"See you guys later," said Louis. The colonel turned to Henry, while Jake went back to folding chairs, but he stayed nearby, listening.

"Like the man said, interesting friends you boys have." The colonel tilted his head back and his eyes widened.

"Thank you, sir."

"Some of the brass might like to hear more of what they have to say. Think you could get 'em back for a return engagement?"

"Well, they're pretty busy with their studying, sir."

"Guess they're mostly students."

"Uh, that's right. I mean, I guess. I had to bug them to get them to come even this once."

"And what do they have against being photographed?"

Henry shrugged. "I don't think it's that big a deal, sir." He clasped his hands behind his back and met the colonel's gaze. "They're modest and don't want a big to-do about an informal chat. They're just some Chinese kids who want to win the war, like we do...sir." His hands were wet with sweat.

The colonel looked Henry in the eye. "That so?" After a long moment, he turned on his heels and walked out the door. Henry and Jake looked at each other.

Jake grinned nervously. "Looks like we really stirred things up around here."

"Just what we need," Henry said.

"That was some talk, gentlemen." Major Drum had been standing behind them. He was swaying forward, up on his toes, then back on his heels. "I was looking forward to hearing what you had to say about our I&E Literature, seeing as how we had such a nice discussion the other day in the library. I understood that was the topic." His moustache twitched like a metronome. "I told the officers it was the topic, too."

Henry was unable to speak. Jake looked hurt. "That was what was talked about, sir. How to fight fascism."

"Funny, I don't remember hearing the I&E material mentioned even once."

"Not by name, but we did hear about some Chinese folks who've been doing things along the same lines. It was sort of the Chinese version of the I&E. I'm sorry if we didn't make the connection clearer. A few of us ran into these guys and figured maybe the Army'd like to know, too. It seemed to fit in with what was in the I&E."

"Umhmm," said Drum, nodding. "Umhmm."

*   *   *   *

Four days later, Larry Curley was walking across one of the dirt fields that bordered the airstrip. From a distance he saw Henry go into the SCU barracks and took off after him.

"Henry!" he called breathlessly, as he entered the barracks. He looked around, friendly concern plain on his face. No one else was inside. "I'm glad I caught you. There's a problem with your mail."

"What? I suppose it's held up on the other side of the Hump again because..."

"No! You're on The List. What the hell'd you do, anyway?"

"Larry, calm down. What're you talking about?"

"Your mail. Double censor. Even what's okayed by the censor officer has to be passed to specialists for another once over—twice over, in fact." He shook his head. "They're going through your stuff with a fine tooth comb. I don't know what you're involved in, but you'd better watch your ass."

Henry looked at the mail carrier. "I'm not involved in anything. It must be some kind of mistake." He stood up. "But thanks, Larry. I appreciate your telling me." He started for the door, and paused. "Any idea where Sergeant Singer is?"

* * * *

Neil Ku Nuli was leaving his Russian studies class when his professor called him back.

"Stay for a moment, Ku. I have something to discuss."

Neil Ku sat at a desk until the rest of the students were gone. The professor looked grave. "You know Doctor Wu, don't you?"

"Of course."

"Well, he came to speak to me this morning, to ask what I knew of certain students who went to the American Army Base with Ai Wenti, who runs the noodle shop downtown. He said this group of students and citizens informed the GIs of the superiority of the Reds to the Central Government. Wu has been pressured about this himself, I'm told, and is anxious to determine who is spreading what he called vicious propaganda."

Neil Ku tried not to let the anger in his chest show on his face. "Why ask me?"

The professor smiled. "He calls this propaganda detrimental to our war effort against the Japanese invaders."

Ku Nuli liked this professor; they had often discussed literature and politics. But he forced his face to become a mask. "How can the truth be detrimental?"

"Ah." The professor laughed.

"Did Wu mention any names?"

"Oh, yes." The professor did not appear to notice the sudden tension betrayed by Neil Ku's eyes. "Besides Ai, he mentioned Anton, Chip and," he grinned, "someone named Neil."

Neil Ku shrugged. "I know of no such people."

The professor nodded. "Mm, I thought not."

Fifteen minutes later, Neil Ku Nuli was downtown at Mr. Ai's noodle shop, leaning his bicycle against the pile of crates outside and rushing around a family of ducks that splashed in a puddle outside the store.

Mr. Ai looked unfazed when Neil Ku finished explaining what he had heard. "It's the sort of thing we've been expecting." He laughed, his black eyes shining. "You did such a magnificent job. Perhaps the faculty would like you to join them to teach public speaking."

Huida came into the room. Ai turned to her. "Neil Ku spoke so eloquently and effectively to the soldiers, he has drawn the attention of the authorities. He's our golden boy."

She laughed, showing the gap in her teeth. "Such a gift for speaking is a valuable commodity."

Ku Nuli shrugged. "I never thought they would listen to a Chinese student; with American soldiers, the relationship is usually reversed. We listen to them."

"If Ai says you were wonderful," said Huida, "you must have spoken very well." She grinned at her husband. "He has high standards in all things."

"But the rest of us used our Anglicized names," Neil Ku pointed out. "Yours was the only real name they knew."

Mr. Ai shrugged. "Whatever will happen, will happen. Do you think they will shoot me? I make dumplings. Perhaps someone may come and speak with me to ask about students I have never met except for this one time and will certainly never meet again— students who forced me to accompany them." He looked at his wife and they both laughed.

*   *   *   *

"My uncle coughed until he couldn't breathe and his spit was thick and mixed with blood." Chen Liduo's eyes welled up but he did not cry. His high, dark forehead wrinkled with the effort of holding back his emotion. He was grateful they were in the dorm-room rather than out in public.

With his free hand, Sung Hongai clapped Liduo on the shoulder. "Come on, let's put up some newspapers." They went outside, the cuffs of their loose white shirts and black trousers rippling in the stiff breeze. Heavy gray clouds rushed overhead. The wall newspapers, which were poster-sized and inked on thin paper, tried to blow out of Liduo's arms as he held on while his friend navigated the bicycle through the crowded streets.

"My aunt, who was pregnant, died of the same thing," Sung said, as they stopped and Liduo held the bicycle and the newspapers while Sung climbed up on the seat and tacked a newspaper over a Government slogan. Once he was down, they moved on.

"But the worst was what they did to my best friend…"

Sung stopped and held the bicycle motionless. "You shouldn't think about it that way. If you think of it as personal, you'll drive yourself crazy. Do you know how many people were beaten, raped or killed in Nanking?"

Liduo kept his eyes on the bike's front tire. "I only know those I saw. It's easy for you to say that—you weren't there, watching, hearing them scream and beg for their lives." He looked up as a huge transport plane thundered just below thick blue clouds.

"After the war you can remember what they died for. The Japanese didn't look for your family in particular."

"I don't care," said Liduo, and he started walking again. They passed a row of abandoned buildings and Liduo seemed to stumble and his leg struck one of the doors. He laughed at his clumsiness.

Once they were around the building's corner, the door Liduo kicked swung open and Xiang emerged, along with Bai, who sported a new shirt that stood out against his dirty pants and scuffed shoes. Xiang nodded in the direction of the poster Liduo and Sung Hongai had put up and Bai held up a poster of his own.

Xiang leaned over. A glob of spittle inched down a corner of his lip, hung a long time and fell, leaving a long strand behind it, which Xiang wiped on the back of his arm. They stood at the base of the wall, reading the poster they were about to cover, which was about Professor Shin, a philosopher and friend of the controversial poet, Wen Yiduo's.

Bai coughed a few times and clasped his hands to make a foothold for Xiang. He leaned away from the wall, trying to keep his new shirt clean.

As he walked on ahead, Liduo was trying to ignore Sung's explanation of one of Mao Zedong's poems. He was remembering Xiang's words, instead. He had not been sure, still wasn't sure, but he could not afford to wait to see if the choice he made was correct. Xiang's entreaties to him had made so much sense. He was the first person in Kunming who had agreed to the necessity for revenge and presented him with a plan. He had to act. His grandfather, mother and sisters were looking over his shoulder.

*   *   *   *

Neil Ku let the young woman push the bicycle while he carried the load of posters; she walked slightly ahead of him, but he did not mind. There was no hiding it—he was exhausted. Three hours of studying his class assignments, another two of reading texts assigned by Chong Lingxiu, and several more translating articles from newspapers their American friends had brought, had taken every ounce of his energy.

This last had been an emotional roller coaster. He was at once buoyed by the knowledge that General Stilwell was in favor of supplying the Communists, but depressed that General Chennault disagreed. He could barely walk and it was only the thought of his dead little cousins, Mai and Pui, that inspired him on. The green and beige fields merged and melted into one another as the early morning sun hurt his tired eyes.

The young woman talked incessantly. "We have dozens of papers to put up—don't slow down now." She stopped and waited for him. "I know about all the other work you do, but if you're too tired, you shouldn't have volunteered." Why didn't she tire? With all the chatter whooshing in and out of her it was amazing there was any breath left for walking!

He climbed the bicycle as she steadied it. "I'm sorry," he breathed. "You're right."

She looked at him and there was a flash of something between curiosity and sympathy in her eyes before she said, "Liduo and Hongai are probably finished by now—let's hurry. We can get back and study awhile before meeting with Lingxiu. If we study beforehand, you see, we might have time to look at more of the American newspapers afterwards. Don't you agree?"

He had stopped thinking of her as Bing Po and begun thinking of her as "the-girl-who-talks-too-much too-early-in-the-morning." He sighed and struggled to catch up.

8

Unlike her best friend, Jane Ju Shiyan rarely slept at Lianda, instead returning home most evenings to help care for her younger brother, Weima, while her parents prepared produce for their market, cleaned the store, brought items to and from the roadside, argued with farmers—including Wulin's father—and prepared meals. Shiyan's parents were more modern than Cha Siansheng; they were aware of the changes occurring in China and that, as much as they were frightened for her, their daughter was irrevocably caught up in those changes.

One particularly cool afternoon, Ju Shiyan went into a tea shop while her father and Weima waited in the wagon. Weima was singing a child's song, yelling the tagline out to passersby, most of whom were too busy, tired or important to notice.

Shiyan was annoyed for two reasons. Her "little sister" was at it again! Hiding unobtrusively from Pei Han was one thing, but turning that into a superior quality was disrespectful to the highest degree!

Shiyan shuddered as she ordered and paid for her father's rice bread and tea. Her thoughts strayed to Pei Han, and she was struck by a pang of sympathy for her friend. Lucky that marriage had been averted! Imagine marriage to Pei Han! She thought of his hands, oily from the fish in his father's market, and she shuddered again. Little sister had a whole year's worth of luck in one day when she'd escaped that life!

"Look who it is! My long lost cousin!"

Her tongue grew thick, her feet heavy. Pei Han had come into the store with his mother, a squat woman with a heavy chin, who squinted at her. It was the Tiger Lady herself!

"It's Ju Shiyan, mother. Wulin's best friend. They call each other big sister and little sister."

The Tiger Lady folded her arms; though very short, she was powerful, ready to pounce at any moment. "Why did your friend not wish to marry my son?"

Shiyan felt faint. "Sick," she managed to say.

"She's sick? Why was I not told? We know doctors. We could have helped. Where is she now?"

"Yes." Pei Han, whose chin matched his mother's, reached for her sleeve. His hand looked huge and animal-like to Shiyan; it seemed to shine with fish oil. "Where is Wulin? Why don't you take us to her?"

Her father was calling from the wagon for his tea and bread. Little Weima echoed him.

"Now we'll find out, mother, whether I saw what I saw!" Pei Han grabbed her arm and pulled her to him. The fish stench was overpowering. "Wasn't Cha Wulin with the students who put up wall newspapers at Lianda? Doesn't she live with activists and troublemakers?" He noticed her look of alarm and mistook it for one of guilty fear. "Ah, you didn't think we knew that, did you?"

Mrs. Pei tried to look sympathetic. "We're only thinking of her," she said. "If she takes up with people like that, what can her future possibly bring?"

"Where is she?" Pei Han demanded, his features distorted with rage.

Someone was tugging at her other arm. It was little brother, Weima. She had never been so glad to see him.

"Papa says to come out, now. We're late."

"This is my darling brother. Ju Weima," she said, her hand on Weima's shoulder, her nausea temporarily abated. "I'm sorry, Mrs. Pei, my father's calling—got to go now. Sorry." She kissed her brother and they hurried out, her father's hot tea stinging her hand and Weima looking at her, bewildered at his sister's sudden public show of affection.

*　　　　*　　　　*　　　　*

A family of ducks scattered, clearing a path. As Ju Shiyan pedalled harder, she saw that Professor Shin had slowed to keep pace with her. He called ahead to Neil Ku, who was disappearing over a ridge, brown dust flying behind him.

"Neil! Slow down!"

"Wulin used to tell me about her new friends' sincerity," Shiyan gasped. "And now that I've met you, professor, I see she was right."

Professor Shin nodded without looking at her. As they passed over the ridge, she saw that Neil Ku had slowed and was looking back over his shoulder. "You said Neil Ku is going to be a journalist?" she babbled gratefully.

"If that's what he told you," the professor said, as they drew alongside Neil Ku.

Professor Shin glanced at him. "Shiyan says you want to be a journalist."

Neil Ku began to pedal again. "So much is changing all over the country. It's only the beginning. Someone has to write it all down. Carry the news."

The same three Americans she had met a month before were visiting the Ais again. They smiled as she entered and Shiyan looked shyly at the floor, stopping in the doorway until Mrs. Ai pulled her in by the arm.

The green-eyed American who had tried to kiss Wulin was looking at her.

She had been thinking how grown up her new friends—Mary Cha Wulin's new friends—were, compared with those they had grown up with in Kunming. These new acquaintances were never the least bit competitive, while her old friends—children like Pei Han, often bickered and vied for attention while maintaining an appropriate, Confucian face. She saw the looks on these faces in front of her—not only on those of Mr. Ai and his family, but on the American faces as well. Only then did the possibility occur to her that little-sister-turned-big-sister may not return.

Words poured from her. "Pei Han grabbed me at my parents' market. He must have been waiting for me. He tried to get me to talk about where Wulin is but I didn't." Suddenly, she was crying. "I have heard nothing at all from Mary Cha," she explained, wringing her hands and trying to think of some better news to give her new friends. "Once Pei Han stops looking for her and making threats she might..." Her voice drifted off. "She's never missed New Year's..." She felt the weight of many eyes on her and looked down at her folded hands. Two of the American soldiers began talking very fast, each nodding at the other's remarks and everyone else smiling furiously. The only word that made any sense to her was "Roosevelt."

The third American, the one who had tried to kiss Wulin, was still staring at her. After a moment he began to speak, after which there was an awkward silence.

"Stan would like to speak with you outside," Mr. Ai explained. "Neil, why don't you accompany them."

As she went outside, Shiyan wondered why no one else seemed concerned about Wulin being missing. It was all so confusing.

"You are Mary Cha's friend?" Stan asked, waiting patiently as Neil Ku relayed the question in Chinese.

"Yes."

"She will come back?"

"I don't know." He did not seem happy with this answer.

"I am also her friend," he said. "I hope she comes back so we can become better friends, and talk some more." He smiled at her, and the smile had the feeling of a leer. "Maybe we could have a party, a picnic at Grandview Park." He scuffed his shoe in the dirt, as though embarrassed.

Shiyan closed her mind and sealed her face against this American GI and said, "Yes, what a good idea," giving Neil Ku a look that ended the conversation.

$$*\qquad*\qquad*\qquad*$$

It rained all day the next day, and the SCU barracks floor was tracked with mud.

"Want to take your clarinet and go out in that?" Henry asked Stan.

"Sure," said Stan. "This rain'll provide the beat."

"Those pilots won't give you a hard time?" Jake wanted to know.

Henry shook his head. "I've gotten to be friendly with them. Marlowe especially. Not a bad guy, really. Was a high school wrestling champion."

"Good guy to make friends with," Stan said, as he took his clarinet's black case out of his locker.

"You ought to see the layers those guys wear when they go on a mission," Henry said. "They call the outfit a Mae West, because it..."

"Yeah," Jake nodded. "I can imagine."

"Not a bad guy," Henry repeated. "You've just got to give a guy a chance."

"Come on guys, let's go." Stan was waiting for them at the door.

After the three friends left, Danko, McPhee, Mickey Warren and Louis Stabler sat on their bunks, writing letters home.

"Who you writing to, Louie?" McPhee wanted to know.

"My parents. They're doing good. Working in a dress factory. Used to be a dress factory, anyway. Now it's a parachute factory." He ran his fingers back through his hair. "Pretty good job for them, actually. All kinds of people working there—women, coloreds..."

"Hey," said Warren. "There's a war on, didn't ya hear?"

"You know Neiberg's father owns a dress factory," Danko said.

"Yeah," said McPhee. "I know."

"Who you writing? Your brothers?" Louis asked.

"Yeah," said McPhee. "Well, through my family. They pass the letters along. I don't know about those guys..."

"Your brothers?"

"No, Neiberg and Singer. These new friends of theirs. What's with them?" He looked from Warren to Danko to Louis Stabler. It was Danko who answered.

"I thought they were pretty interesting. I like knowing where all our equipment's going and if it's going to be used for something besides what it was intended for."

McPhee considered this. His sleepy blue eyes nearly closed. "I kind of like going with what the Army tells us. They're brass for a reason."

"How're your brothers doing?" Louis asked.

McPhee brightened. "Great. At least Charlie's great. He learned this new magic trick. Something with making a dime disappear. He uses a magnet somehow. Got a date with a Red Cross nurse with it."

"Maybe you should try it."

"Maybe I don't need it."

"How about Bill?"

McPhee shrugged. His eyes wandered around the room. A drip had formed between two of the ceiling planks. He watched it fatten and finally fall. "He's drinking a lot, and getting into fights." He shrugged. "He's winning 'em, though. What about your brother?"

Louis laughed. "Tony says it's cramped in that tank, but he draws artwork all over the inside. Say, Mick. Curley was in here looking for you. Had a letter for you. I think he said it was from your brother."

"Then it's just as well he didn't find me," Warren said.

No one said anything for several minutes. Finally Danko asked, "Mick, how're those carrots you planted doin'?"

"Good," said Warren, his voice still sullen. "What's really doin' well are the lilacs. And the annuals my mom sent are coming up."

"Just like home, huh?" said McPhee.

"Just like home." Warren looked up. "Your buddy Drum seems to like these new Chinese buddies of theirs." His eyes flickered towards Henry and Jake's bunk.

McPhee sucked saliva over the tip of his tongue, making a "tsk" sound. "He does seem to, doesn't he?"

*   *   *   *

A few days later, when McPhee asked the carefully prepared question, Mr. Ai maintained his smile and shook his head. "No, I am not a Communist. I am a concerned citizen." He took a deep breath and looked around with his eyes, his head remaining stationary.

"My feeling is that the war is more important than politics right now," Mr. Ai said, calmly. "Communists, along with other progressive groups, have, as we explained last time, retaken land in North China and made it self sufficient through the common efforts of the people there. We had hoped you might have verified that information since then. These are not political people, incidentally. These are farmers, villagers, who wanted to survive."

Danko turned to McPhee, whispering. "You know, the man's got a point—I hate to admit it, but if what these slopes're telling us about the North is true, whether we agree with the Communist part or not, the war effort would be..."

"Aw, c'mon," McPhee looked annoyed. "Don't tell me you believe these guys!"

"Do you know anything about Chinese conscription?" Ai was asking, looking over the group. Neil Ku was off to one side, smiling into his lap.

"Well, I know a little about the American draft. Very efficient, very fair. You make allowances for the sick, for those pursuing educations." He shook his head. "Here, it is different. You might be working out in the fields of your father's or uncle's farm, and a regiment happens to pass by." He paused, pressing his lips together. "It doesn't matter that you're not exactly the right age or that you don't want to join the army or that you may not be in perfect physical condition. You're dragged through the dirt and forced to fight. You do not," he looked the group over, "sign up at a desk. You are beaten, starved, warped by scurvy, if not worse."

Mr. Ai spread his arms. "But we are here to talk about all we have in common, not our differences!"

Danko leaned close to McPhee. "Your pals're here," he muttered.

Two unfamiliar majors were pushing towards the front, raising cameras over their heads and clicking away while approaching the podium.

Henry tapped Jake Singer on the shoulder and the two shuffled to a spot just in front of the men. Stan, who had been sitting nearby, suddenly stood up with Henry and Jake, blocking the two majors' view. The three men raised their arms over their heads, applauding.

"Out of our way," one major growled.

Henry made himself as tall as he could. Jake whistled and clapped. Stan waved his fists like tall trees in a stiff wind. "Bravo!" he called.

The applause spread, and in its midst Mr. Ai and Neil Ku made their way out a back door. Henry and Jake looked at one another, at once frightened and laughing.

*   *   *   *

The face of China was changing in Henry's mind. What had been the manifestation of a nightmare had softened, thanks to his new friends. He had discovered a refuge, an element of safety in this hard, war torn place. Dinnertable banter, complete with children's voices, had been resurrected, as if by magic, here on the other side of the world. Even his own mother's well intentioned nosiness, her ability to find and uncover the hurt and to apply the salve of her warm heart, had been returned to him in the form of Mr. and Mrs. Ai, Neil Ku Nuli and the others. And when Henry stopped to consider this, he was amazed and overwhelmed. While he had been ashamed to write Frances, unwilling to broach the wall she had put up, his experiences were too important and private for him to share with anyone else.

So in his free time, after work, before and after meals, and before lights out, he wrote her about his new friends, their shared experience, their innate understanding of his loneliness and homesickness. He wrote of the foods they shared, of their laughter and the surprising ease of communication between them. He wrote of their curiosity about American politics and sociology and of the concern they shared with Jake and himself about life in China and America after the war.

*   *   *   *

Bai and Chen Liduo watched Xiang wave to the leader of the regiment and toss an orange from the nearest fruit stand to him, reminding him about some future appointment. The officer laughed and remarked that he had more important plans, stomping on the orange for emphasis.

Xiang reached into his pocket for a cigarette as the fruit vendor, his white apron flapping, started to say something and thought the better of it.

"Bai, give me a cigarette." Xiang looked down at his thin protegé. "Come on back to my house. Liduo, have a cigarette? Bai, give him one." He put his hand paternally on Liduo's shoulder. "I will explain why these things Chong Lingxiu and Mr. Dumpling have been telling you are lies."

They walked three abreast down the center of the road, moving only for Army vehicles and soldiers, not even looking up at the P-42s coming in to land. Xiang walked slightly in front of the other two, his arms swinging imperially, his stubbly hair, height and fancy clothes setting him apart from other teenagers. Boys pulled rickshaws far to either side, occasionally slipping into the muddy roadside ditch and calling ahead for bicyclists and pedestrians to clear the way lest they suffer a similar indignity.

"Until now you've followed what I've told you for a simple reason. Revenge," Xiang explained, over his shoulder. "And don't get me wrong, it's a good reason. But please understand, Lingxiu is a dreamer. He and Mr. Dumpling are dangerous men. Look at how they've stirred up our city." He stepped over two muddy placards left over from the recent demonstrations.

"Dreamers," echoed Bai, trying to spit in the slow manner Xiang did but succeeding only in soiling the front of his shirt.

"He talks about the future without regard to the present." Xiang shook his head and thrust his jaw forward. Bai jumped to one side, avoiding a second spot on his shirt.

"We, on the other hand, are an Army," Xiang continued, "trained tactically by the world's best to fight against anyone who threatens us. We do not worry about the peasants or land redistribution or any such political nonsense. We defend our country, our families, ourselves. And what we earn, we keep. If we can better ourselves, fine. If not, too bad." He waved his hand at a girl walking behind an oxcart. "If we choose our women to be glamorous, like Madame Chiang, that is our business. We don't bother with anyone else's business."

"And as for the war," Bai said, his voice catching some haughtiness from Xiang, "the Japanese might win one or two battles, but the truth of the matter will soon come out and we'll hear about the Generalissimo's great victories."

"Shut up, Bai." Xiang sniffled, and turned to Chen Liduo. "I know what your experience was, but be that as it may, even more than the Japanese, the bigger threat may be from disloyal Chinese. The fact is, we, in our positions, cannot possibly understand it all.

That is why we are not the leaders. How could Chong Lingxiu understand? He is a student, not a soldier. Colonel Yin, on the other hand, is..."

Chen Liduo found Xiang's theatrics tiresome. "Will I be able to slit the throats of Japanese soldiers? Will I be able to watch them bleed to death in the street?" His eyes grew animated. The hair on his arms bristled. "That's what I want to know. It's what my grandfather's spirit wants to know."

Bai began to cough violently. Xiang sighed in a patronizing way. He did this to cover up his fear and to buy time to think of what to say. While he thought of himself as a Nationalist soldier, a servant of Chiang Kaishek and an admirer of the Generalissimo's beautiful wife, deep in his heart, violence terrified him. He became physically paralyzed when confronted with it directly.

"Of course, in good time," he said, whistling tunelessly.

"No. Not in good time. Now." Liduo's eyes clouded. "My grandfather was my hero; now he is dead, butchered by the Japanese. My mother and sisters were not only raped, but mutilated. If you can show me a road to revenge, that is fine. Otherwise, I'll make my own road."

"A wise man waits to pick his fruit until it is at its ripest," was all Xiang could muster. He remained silent the rest of the way, his eyes down, focused on the road.

They heard the bird before entering Xiang's shack. As the door opened, the finch flew to him and deposited droppings on his shoulder. Xiang screamed and swatted at the bird, which was too quick and flew to its cage and whistled back. Xiang lit a cigarette, spat on the floor, and launched into an angry diatribe directed at the enemies of the Central Government and how they had created a false impression of the war's progress. Lies spread by spies! The real followers of Sun Yatsen would emerge! Their fathers' and grandfathers' ghosts would lead the way, violently redressing these lies, undoing the Unequal Treaties. He put a record on the ancient turntable and took out the worn photograph of the Generalissimo's wife. He took another of Bai's cigarettes and offered one to Liduo, who declined, watching the proceedings with cat's eyes.

Xiang sat back and puffed contentedly. "When the Japanese invaders are defeated and the bandits routed, we will have such beautiful lives."

Bai began to cough.

"Shut up, Bai," Xiang ordered, spitting onto the carpet and grinding his cigarette out with his shoe.

*   *   *   *

How appropriate! The one woman who understood him—who had ever understood him, by his way of thinking—and he had lost her and was left only with her cold fish friend.

The chill ran up Stan's back and out through the clarinet, deepening in feeling and tone and echoing off the walls of the Rec Hall as his fingers skittered over the keys. After the run, he let Henry fill in the original melody on the piano while he poured himself another drink. He knew the Chinese girl understood him. *Her eyes had said: I can't let you do this but I would if I could. If you'll be patient, we can get to know one another.*

At least that had been his interpretation, but now she had disappeared, and he was a loser on both sides of the ocean! *How appropriate.*

Around them, men were whistling, fingers snapping, heads nodding. Whenever they played now, they drew a crowd. The Army had made him a big musical fish in a local pond. In this way, China wasn't so bad.

He had a memory of his father telling him to put down that damn, screeching instrument; *he* was trying to eat. His father had called him "Pockets" because young Stan had walked around with his hands in his pockets. The name was not a compliment. No, in its own way, China was an improvement.

Stanley looked into his drink, proud of his loneliness and the continuity of it all. *How appropriate!*

9

Neil Ku Nuli and Tong Xie leaned against the wall just inside the entrance to Lianda. The sky, clear moments ago, had darkened—thick clouds, with dirty white tops and heavy bottoms thundered like some new kind of airplane. Tong's blue button down shirt was missing two middle buttons; his pants were of a light, thin material with no pockets. He opened the most recent issue of the *Hsinghua Daily* high in front of his face; around it he had wrapped a brown paper-covered edition of *King Lear*, which Neil Ku pretended to read over his shoulder. Jane Shiyan waited a few paces behind, her black hair blowing back over her shoulders. Neil Ku beckoned for her to come up alongside them. She felt uncomfortable, ever the newcomer, afraid because her best friend and younger sister-turned elder sister was still missing. She told herself to welcome this sign of inclusion.

Neil Ku shielded his eyes against the sun. "You know, if the American Vice President Henry Wallace is going to walk through Lianda's entrance tomorrow with the President of the University—"

Tong Xie giggled. "With half the government."

"It would be difficult for them all to avoid seeing a large wall newspaper right up here." He spread his hands outward and upward. Jane Shiyan followed the grand gesture to a tall wide tree quite close to the road, angled so that its upper branches overhung passersby.

Tong smiled. "It's true what they say about you Nuli. You are a disruptive influence!" He looked up at the tree and saw how close to the road the sign would hang. "And imagine if this particular poster were in English!"

Neil Ku continued, mock serious. "And what a shame if such a newspaper mentioned how much everyone around here, with a few very notable exceptions, wants to fight the Japanese."

Tong laughed. "And how corrupt certain officials are!"

Neil Ku clucked. "Now you've gone too far! That might be embarrassing for Mr. Wallace's hosts. What an awful shame that would be!"

Jane Shiyan laughed to herself and the two boys glanced at her. She blushed, but it was less from embarrassment than it was at the strangeness of the sound of her own laughter. She could not remember the last time she had laughed.

These friends with her today and the Americans were more like each other than they were like her! She was at once shy and intimidated, yet attracted and intrigued. She wished she could share this odd feeling with younger sister-turned older sister.

The next day, a procession did pass through the front gate of Lianda, and Vice President Wallace, Owen Lattimore, and a large entourage were flanked by University officials and hand-picked faculty, smiling and waving to the students and residents of Kunming who had flocked on foot and bicycle to the event and seemed, to the relief of their hosts, to be on their best behavior. As they passed through the gate, the Vice President's expression did not change, but his eyes did stray to the boldly lettered poster that hung just off to his left.

His eyes lingered; his forehead wrinkled, and just then a steady rain began. Officials on both sides scrambled to raise umbrellas over their guests' heads. A University official leaned over and spoke to the Vice President, then smiled and pointed in another direction. Other officials glanced at one another. Lianda's president searched the crowd, but if he saw anything at all, it was only the backs of two small figures on a single black bicycle, their dark clothes glistening with rain as they pedalled away as quickly as they could.

*   *   *   *

Though it was mid November, Sunday morning dawned with the kind of soft orange sunrise and fresh green smell that had brought the City of Eternal Spring its nickname. The temperature rose only a few degrees in the afternoon, and when Henry, Jake and Stan climbed down from the truck and up the hill to Grandview Park, the sun was comfortable, not too hot, on the backs of their uniforms. They never saw Ken McPhee watching from behind a Chinese newspaper, fifty yards away. The blond sergeant was silhouetted against Kunming Lake, which glittered in the afternoon sun.

"We shouldn't have to wait too long," said Henry, spreading out the blanket and arranging the items he had carried on it: cigarettes, shaving items, soap and a few newsclippings.

Brooding, Stan said nothing.

"Anyone who'd mind waiting at a park like this on a day like today," Jake lay down and stretched his legs, "well, they'd be out of their minds, is all." He had brought cartons of meat, cheese, candy and canned foods. He sat up. "Here they come. Is that Neil Ku?"

"No," said Stan, "it's Zhou Enlai. Who else would it be?"

"What's the matter with you?" Henry asked, taking out a comb and running it back through his hair which, though curly, was too short to need combing.

"Nothing."

Jake squinted into the sun. "It's Lingxiu, I think." He grimaced, trying to see. "Yeah, a tall guy and a skinny—looks like Neil's behind him, wheeling that bike of his."

Stan snorted, laughing, to himself. "Those modern Chinese."

"What?" Jake glared. Then he turned as the two friends approached. "Lingxiu, Neil, sit down." He motioned them to sit. "Enjoy the beautiful day; have a bite to eat. Oh, here. We've got some more articles from home. These are from the *New York Times* and *PM*."

"Excellent, thank you." As they sat down, Chong Lingxiu smiled at each of them and handed the stack of papers to Neil Ku, who immediately began to read. With equal fervor, Lingxiu began to eat, sampling each of the items on the blanket.

"I got two letters today," Henry said. "A strange one from Frances and another one from my father. He said I'm mistaken about China. Things aren't the way I write in my letters."

Neil Ku looked up from the articles, which were spread out before him like a banquet. "How could you be wrong? You are here. He is in New York."

"Of course," said Henry. "But he reads the *New York Times*."

Stan shook his head, his mouth full of crackers. "Besides, he knows better. All fathers do."

"Read that article I gave you," said Jake. "That's right, the long one. You'd think the Nationalists are a perfectly organized fighting machine."

Henry shook his head. "And winning the war singlehandedly, no less."

"Yeah," said Stan, who was eating a piece of hard candy, "making the world safe for freedom and justice."

They waited as Neil Ku read and then handed the article to Chong Lingxiu, who leaned back on one elbow, shaking his head.

"You know," he said, "General Stilwell sees the way things are."

"Yup," said Jake. "Him and the Dixie Mission. Those boys the government sent over to look at what the Communists did up north seem to have gotten the story straight. But that doesn't mean anyone'll listen to 'em." He made a helpless gesture. "I think our government's already decided which side its bread is buttered on." He shook his head. "I don't see them changing horses midstream."

Chong's eyebrows went up. "Bread and butter? Horses?" He looked at Neil Ku, who responded in rapid Mandarin. "Ahh," said Chong. "You don't think American Government will supply Communist Army, even though they know about success against Japanese, and even though they know about corruption."

Henry shook his head. "I think maybe Chiang Kaishek's threats of changing sides work. He successfully throws a scare into our government."

"I read that Stilwell calls Chiang The Peanut," Stan said. "Because of the shape of his head?"

"I don't know why it is," said Neil Ku, "but Stilwell doesn't respect Chiang. He and your Dixie Mission understand China well. Your Government should listen to what they have to say. After all, that's why they were sent here, right? To investigate."

Henry had stood up and was squinting into the distance, one hand shading his eyes.

"What're you looking at?" Stan asked.

"Nothing. Nothing." But he had seen something. A shadow maybe, but for a moment it had looked like a man in a cap watching them. Something about the shape of the man's head was familiar. Standing about sixty yards down the hill, he had blended in with a clump of bushes. The more he thought about it the more he was sure that the man had been watching them. But he was gone now. Disappeared against the colorful backdrop of countryside.

"What effect do you think our bombing raids are having on the Japanese?" Henry asked Lingxiu, who paused to consider the question, a square of cheese between his fingers.

"The Japanese have taken too much territory," Lingxiu said, adjusting his glasses. "They have advanced too far west, and now they must try to hold and supply these areas. This is where the American planes are most damaging. They attack supply and communication lines just as the Japanese are trying to link their new territories with those in the east. At some point their resources will—what is the word—expire? And they will be forced to fall back."

Neil Ku was sitting with his hands drawn around his knees. "But the Japanese are pushing south as well," he said in a soft voice. "In our direction—we hope they will exhaust themselves before they reach Yunnan."

"Are you sure that's what they're doing, Neil?" Stan asked. He had lapsed back into a comfortable pool of self pity, and mention of the Japanese Army had startled him. "Our officers haven't said anything about that."

Lingxiu shrugged. "Would an officer want his soldiers to think about what may come next week or next month?"

Stan sat up. "Next week? Are you guys nuts?"

Henry was looking from Neil Ku to Lingxiu and back again. "They're pushing south you say? We really hadn't heard...but no, I don't suppose anyone would tell...jeez!"

"Nuts?" Lingxiu scoured the food on the blanket. He changed the subject. "Next week I will be going away for a while."

"Why?" Stan asked, still shaken.

Lingxiu smiled. "Vacation."

Neil laughed nervously.

"The KMT are looking for you, aren't they?" Henry said. He tried to force back the hysteria gathering in his stomach.

Lingxiu nodded. "As the Americans learn of the liberation in the North, there is more pressure. Your Dixie Mission put a lot of pressure on some of us. The fact that your government knows about the success in the north now has thrown a scare into the government here. And that means it's time for a vacation for me." He saw Henry's confused frown.

"The liberation of even those small areas is a powerful, controversial idea." He gestured at the pile of newspaper articles. "...even though your American journalists don't think much of it, and it doesn't seem your government thinks differently. Here," he laughed, "here, there is an impact. People will be looking for me." He smiled. "So I will take a short vacation."

Neil was eyeing a woman twenty yards away. She was holding a large pad of paper and an artist's quill and her body was facing a gnarled tree but her head was turned toward the picnic group. He cleared his throat and nodded toward her.

Lingxiu glanced toward her, then pointed to the tree. The lines in his forehead deepened with the discomfort of his ill fitting wire glasses. "That species of tree is rarely found in warmer climates," he said, his voice overly loud. "It would do better in Manchuria. It's bark is thick and acts as a shield against the cold, so it is out of place here." The smile was gone; he pushed his glasses up on his nose, never taking his eyes from the girl. "Look closely at the branches," he urged, and everyone turned and looked. "*It is not what it seems to be.*" He lowered his voice to a whisper. "She is pretending to be an artist, but she is a government spy." He raised his voice again. "It is rare to see such a tree so far south, in such a hostile environment—dangerous for that tree."

The girl stood up, appeared to put the finishing touches on her sketch, and walked down the hill to the bridge that spanned the lake at its narrowest point. She walked slowly across, pausing to look at the foliage and then quickly back at the picnickers. Midway across the bridge was an enclosure. She disappeared into it.

"She is watching us from the pagoda," said Neil Ku, matter-of-factly.

Lingxiu nodded. "Did you notice her heavy coat? The weather is too warm for such a coat. She is hiding something."

"Field glasses?" Neil Ku asked.

"Jesus," said Stan. "I could use a drink. You fellas got any of that rice wine? How 'bout a little..." he moved his forearm in an arc, "*gambei?*" he said weakly.

Henry folded his portion of food into a napkin. He had lost his appetite. The fear that had appeared with the censoring of his mail was back in full force, joined now by a new fear—for the safety of his new friends.

*　　　*　　　*　　　*

The girl returned to the pagoda's tiny room and sat patiently on the bench until Colonel Yin, Dr. Wu and the others arrived, two hours later. She explained what she had learned while Xiang and her older brother, Bai, told about the Shensi boy who had gone on the Long March.

Before the Colonel could comment, a new, dark complexioned young man stood up. "You will allow me to kill them please," he said, calmly.

Xiang's eyes widened. He lit a cigarette.

"To kill whom?" asked Dr. Wu, smiling just a little.

"The boy from Shensi, Chong Lingxiu, the American soldiers—it doesn't matter. I will do it tomorrow."

"What did you say your name was?" Colonel Yin asked, his eyes narrowing.

"Chen, sir. Chen Liduo."

"Ah, Mr. Chen. We appreciate your enthusiasm. You can be of service to us, but you must leave strategy and tactics to us—to Dr. Wu and myself and to our superiors. That is the appropriate military way. We know you understand." He smiled suddenly, showing his teeth. "Let this young man be an example," he said, looking over the group. "He has devotion and more importantly," he gave a hard look at Xiang and Bai, both of whom looked away, "he has courage."

*   *   *   *

Tong Xie had been eating slowly, methodically, and so diligently that he never noticed Lin Teu beside him until she spoke.

"Could you tell me what it was like?"

He started at the sound of her voice, which squeaked and betrayed her nervousness. "In the mountains, I mean."

Tong Xie looked at the girl through his long bangs and saw that her eyes held more confidence than her tone of voice. She looked him clearly in the eye; he was impressed. "Cold," he replied, biting into a piece of rice bread.

"But you were warm inside, right? Knowing why you were enduring that cold."

He looked at her, emotionless, but Lin Teu thought she saw laughter hiding behind his eyes. "We were cold on the inside and the outside, and tired, but you could never sleep for very long."

"And what about the Lolos—I've heard all kinds of..." She went on as she thought of questions, all the while slowly convincing herself that this man—she could not think of him as a boy despite his appearance; his experiences had made him a man— that this man would be her husband. Well, why not choose for herself? She was a "new woman" of the sort New China would be proud.

"...but if you don't have even a small hut to sleep in night after night, wouldn't you get...?"

"I'm sorry, Lin Teu, I should finish this analysis." He tapped the stack of papers on the table next to his bowl.

"I can come with you, give you ideas. I'll help—"

"I don't think so." Tong Xie smiled, and Lin Teu realized she had gone too far. The skin on her forehead grew warm and she looked away, at the stacks of books and ink bottles beneath the window, but what she was thinking was, "You can't discourage a woman of New China so easily."

*   *   *   *

There were thirteen, perhaps fourteen people there. The poet, Wen Yiduo, who had already spoken, had taken a seat next to Professor Shin in the middle of the floor. Sung Hongai was sitting with his back against the classroom's cold outside wall. He was thinking that Lin Teu was leaning too close to Tong Xie. He watched them closely while pretending not to.

"The participation here among students and in the city among workers is excellent," explained Chong Lingxiu, "and we in this room are best qualified to spread that into the countryside. The poorest farmers who understand only food and their sick babies must learn how we're helping them and why they were never helped before…"

Lin Teu and Tong had moved slightly apart now, but Sung saw that their hands were all but touching, and his insides went cold. This was no physical accident—no coincidence of circumstance. He himself was a master of such subtlety. He forced himself to concentrate on Lingxiu's words.

"I received a letter today from a farm in the countryside. The courier who brought it suggested I wait to open it until we were all together." He unfolded the paper, smiling, and adjusted his glasses. "It is from Mary Cha Wulin. 'My friends: I am on a small farm—where is not important. I and another refugee, Chong Tanshi—'"

Lingxiu's voice pinched at the end of the name and he paused to wipe his glasses. Two whispered words travelled, seemingly under their own power, around the room. The words were "his son."

Lingxiu gathered himself, his voice regained its strength. "'I and another refugee, Chong Tanshi, are awake before dawn to feed the pigs alongside the farmer. I enjoy this since the pigs are so clever. And they are neither dirty nor corrupt.'"

Everyone in the room laughed. Lingxiu swallowed several times before continuing.

"'I want you all to know that I am well and looking forward to the day when I can return and fight or, if I cannot return, when I can go where I can help most. I miss my studies, in the classroom and out. I miss my family, and I miss you all.'"

Chong sat down and the room was silent. Even Jane Shiyan sat quietly in her seat in the back row, trying to imagine spoiled younger sister feeding pigs. She wanted to laugh and scream at once.

"I can no longer risk visiting our American friends," Lingxiu said, folding the paper carefully and wiping each of his eyes with a single fingertip. "The success in the Liberated Areas is making my daily existence here difficult for others—a happy dilemma." He smiled. "So I'll be going away within the next few days. I'll return soon."

He paused, as if for a response, but no one said a word.

"Please look up to Neil Ku Nuli as you would to me. Also to Tong Xie and Mr. Ai. When you need to talk to a friend, they'll be there. They're...experienced." Nodding hurriedly, Chong Lingxiu rose and walked quickly to the door, his blinking eyes looking vaguely down and forward.

He did not explain about his son.

Tong Xie stood up, brushed the hair out of his eyes, and cleared his throat.

"Everyone around town reads the wall newspapers. Important new ideas—and they're important to all of us—are communicated directly to farmers, students and storekeepers. Everyone reads them. Neil Ku, you've been a real journalist; you've given talks at American GI bases. We're all proud of you. You'll be our information liaison and, if we all agree on it, the new editor of our wall newspaper."

Neil Ku blushed. "I only made a very small speech, if you could call it that at all."

"Well, who thinks Neil Ku might make an excellent editor for *Read?*"

Everyone applauded.

Tong Xie looked at Lin Teu. "And anyone who writes well and has," he clenched a fist in front of his chest, "the same desire—"

A young man rushed into the room, hair pulled back in a braid, which jumped this way and that on his collar. He screamed several unintelligible syllables, and from the side pocket of his brown, dusty coat he drew a long, thin fish knife.

Jane Shiyan cried. "It's Pei Han! She isn't here! She's gone away!"

Pei Han looked around, eyes wide. He seemed not to see her. Sung Hongai stood up, thinking of Lin Teu's safety and that here was an opportunity to regain his face, but his body was frozen and would not move in Pei Han's direction.

Pei Han was peering at the crowd, waving his knife and calling, "Wulin! Where is Cha Wulin? I demand to know!" He pointed the knife at Tong Xie, who recoiled, his eyes on its blade. Sung Hongai watched Tong recover his composure and edge toward Pei Han. His own legs had become blocks of ice.

"Your future wife has gone on a trip," Tong said calmly. "You can see for yourself she isn't here, so why not sit down and join us? And after we finish here you can be our guest for lunch. We'll wait together."

Pei Han grimaced and lunged, his arm thrusting forward. Tong Xie crumpled to the floor. He moaned once and grew still, his face permanently surprised.

Within minutes the room was filled with school officials and government soldiers. They arrived so quickly that Sung Hongai wondered if they had been aware of Pei Han and had been waiting outside the room.

Lin Teu rushed to Tong's body. A long, rising wail came from somewhere deep within her.

Sung Hongai stared at the dead boy and cried inside, wishing he had been the target. He looked at the doorway and then at the soldiers and considered running away. His loss of face resulting from Lin Teu's attraction to Tong was understandable; after all, Tong was from Shensi; he had been on the Long March. But now, Tong had been killed because he, Hongai, had been paralyzed by fear.

10

The Rec Hall was decorated with makeshift wreaths and paper streamers. Someone had sent home for movie posters to hang alongside the pinup girls. On one, Deanna Durbin and Gene Kelly celebrated their *Christmas Holiday*. Facing them were William Bendix and Susan Hayward, advertising the stage version of Eugene O'Neill's *The Hairy Ape*.

GIs began arriving, stopping at the old upright piano to ladle punch into paper cups. Others rolled up their sleeves and plunged their arms into a garbage can of ice and beer bottles.

In their midst stood the "Old Man," General Claire Chennault. He was tall, with close, gray-brown hair that was swept back, as if by a strong wind. He appeared to be in his mid fifties, with the predatory face of an eagle: narrow eyes that took in small movements at great distances; a thin, unobtrusive nose above lips pressed as tight as his uniform. Smoke drifted from the cigarette in his left hand.

"Anyway, I don't see how a bigger gas capacity is going to change the war, sir," Paul Danko was saying.

"I appreciate the job you boys in the SCU are doing, but stick to your numbers." The General smiled patiently. "Some afternoon, when you've got three or four hours, we'll talk about gas capacity and how a drop tank will enable us to refuel in the air and maybe soon send bombers and fighters all the way to Tokyo."

Danko took a swallow of beer. "Just the sort of development that'll win us the war."

A thin lieutenant with deep set eyes and prominent cheekbones chuckled. "With all respect, sir, I hear the winter in Russia was what really turned the war."

The General raised an eyebrow and turned. "Maurice! Glad you could make it! What would Thanksgiving be without our resident Red? Come to thank America on Thanksgiving, did you?"

Maurice smiled. "Wouldn't miss it, sir."

*   *   *   *

Ken McPhee was standing with Mickey Warren off to one side. Warren tapped his feet to the music that crackled from the old phonograph.

"Looks like you've been getting into shape," McPhee said.

"Been working at it with some weights I made."

"Out of what?"

"Axles with brake shoes welded on the ends."

McPhee smiled. "Get a letter from your Dad today?"

Warren nodded. "Yup. Check out the nurses." They both watched the three young women who had come in. A crowd of men sprang up around them. "My dad's doing real well. All kinds of people're trying to get him to sell them rubber."

"Yeah, I guess it's in short supply."

"I'll say. They send him gifts, you know. Coupons mostly, for gas, cigarettes, all sorts of things. He's had quite a month for steak, he says."

McPhee folded his arms in front of him. "I'm going to wait for that crowd to die down, and I'm going over there and ask one of those ladies to dance. So, does he keep the coupons?"

"Sure, why not? Doesn't do the favors, though. Least I don't think he does." He looked at McPhee. "Yesterday, when the Colonel pulled you out of work, what'd he want?"

McPhee did not look at him when he answered. "Telegram."

Warren waited a long time before asking his question. "Was it..."

"Billy. No, he's not. Lost his," McPhee swallowed. "Lost his arm."

Warren shook his head. "Explains why you haven't said a word in two days. I'm sorry, pal. Glad to hear he's still alive."

"He's not glad. Wishes he were dead. Mom says he can't figure out why he's still alive. Just lays in bed drinking all day. Bunch of his buddies died and he wishes he was with 'em. Doesn't want any part of rehabilitation. I don't get it."

Warren took his friend by the elbow. "Let's go inside. I saw Major Drum..."

"To hell with Major Drum." McPhee's eyes stared ahead. "Now there's another guy I don't get."

"What? Because he's interested in what those Jewish guys..."

"That's right. Jews and Communist Chinese. Can you figure him out?"

Warren took a deep breath. "Listen, I think your first idea was best. Why don't you ask one of those young ladies to dance?"

*   *   *   *

It was cold for Kunming, and while he and Henry walked towards the Rec Hall, Jake looked up at the sky. He could just make out the silhouettes of high flying birds against the moon, and he wondered if they were circling to keep warm or if they were hovering, vulture-like, over the death of the war. Perhaps they weren't birds at all, but bats. He wished he were home with Blanche in cold, familiar New York. The way the Marines were mowing through the Pacific Islands, he hoped that would be by summer.

He remembered that when he had tutored Blanche in accounting at City College she had been intimidated at being in the very first class of women allowed into the school. He smiled inwardly. Imagine that, Blanche intimidated!

Think of Henry's problems, he told himself. At least I'm already married, and Blanche and I know where we stand. "Did I hear you tell our friends yesterday that you heard from Frances?" he asked.

Henry sighed. "I did. Yesterday. She talked about that fella who lives across the street from her parents' apartment. Gartman. A 4F. Some kind of eye problem kept him out of the service. Maybe they're at a movie right now."

Jake shrugged. "Just as possible she's looking out a window wondering what you're doing right now."

"Doubt it." Henry shook his head, slowing as they approached the Rec Hall and finally stopping altogether. "Maybe I should never have mentioned Mr. Ai and Neil Ku and our new friends when I wrote her. She wrote back that my letters sounded strange. I didn't sound like myself, she said."

"You just wanted her to know you were okay—that you'd made friends." Jake spoke slowly, not wanting to hurt his friend's feelings but wanting to be honest. "If you can't share your experiences with her, then maybe you really weren't meant for each other."

Henry blinked. "Maybe I oughtta forget about her."

Jake had started towards the door and turned to answer.

"Gentlemen!" A voice boomed and, startled, they saw that Major Drum had come up behind them, a Santa Claus grin on his ruddy face.

"I see you've started your holiday celebrating early," said Jake.

The major held the door for them. "Well, I've got a lot to be thankful for."

Henry leaned toward Jake. "First time I've ever agreed with him," he muttered.

They passed Mickey Warren and McPhee. "Hey, Mick," Henry called. "I walked by those lilacs you've got going out by the trenches. Smells just like my mother's house. No, I mean that in a good way. Half our backyard's one big lilac bush. Hello, Ken." He turned to Jake. "What's with McPhee? See the look on his face?"

Major Drum was nodding to everyone in sight and raised his eyebrows at Louis Stabler, who had a paper cup of punch in each hand.

"Thank you, Sergeant." He reached for one of Louis's cups. Stabler stepped back and drank it. "Sorry, Major. These are for me. The punch is over there."

The major frowned and wended his way through the cluster of pilots and Red Cross nurses surrounding the punch bowl. "Would any of you gentlemen by any chance be flying to Chengdu in the near future?"

A pilot spoke up. "How's that?"

"Ah!" Drum filled the ladle with punch and brought it delicately to his lips.

"In a cup please," instructed one of the nurses.

Drum smirked at the pilots. "It's what the nurses always tell you, isn't it? 'In a cup, please. In a cup.' Damn, lady, I was just smelling it."

"So, what's in Chengdu?" the pilot asked.

"Silver. Filigree silver. You know, weaved-like. Looks like lace. Can get it for a song there and I can get rid of it for—well, let's say for a medley at home. Want a part of that?" He put his arm around the pilot's shoulder. "Cassidy, isn't it? You're a wing man for the Shark?"

Cassidy shrugged and held an arm out for the nurse, who took it. "I'll drop ya a line, pal. Come on, darlin'," he said to the nurse. The couple strode to the dance floor, where the phonograph was blaring Glenn Miller.

Drum looked after them. "I could pull rank," he said weakly, edging toward Henry, Jake and Louis Stabler. "Those pilots," he forced a laugh. "Someone oughtta belt 'em now and then. Like the Brown Bomber did to Hitler's finest, Maxie Schmeling."

"Really?" Louis smiled bitterly as Jake watched him. "Did you ever think it's kind of strange, Major, that your hero, Joe Louis, is a Negro?"

"No," said Drum, his lower lip protruding. "I never did."

Louis had been staring into the cup in his right hand. Now he lifted it, drank, and peered into the cup in his left hand. "Ever wonder why, if the Army's so scientific, there aren't any Negroes in it? At least in our part of it, anyways."

Drum's moustache twitched. "Know what else happened in '38? Bob Feller struck out eighteen men in a game the Indians played against Detroit. He did! Ask Sergeant Freilich. He's an Indians' fan." He looked at Henry and Jake. "You guys ought to appreciate that feat. He struck out Hank Greenberg twice that day."

"Yeah," said Jake, still looking at Louis. "Like Goliath striking out David."

Louis did not blink. "Thirty eight. Yeah, Drum. Helluva year. Hitler invaded Czechoslovakia that year, didn't he?"

Drum turned slowly to look at Stabler. "That's *Major* Drum."

"Right." Louis's dark eyes seemed to recede into his skull. "You'd think some of them Negroes would be good pilots or soldiers or whatever. Seems pretty unscientific to me, though. Hurts the war effort, don't you think—keeping 'em out of combat?"

Drum shook his head. He looked at Stabler, curious now. "Well, I see your point, but if you look at it, you'll see the Army's right. Now, first of all, there are Negro divisions, but I guess you're talking about the real Army, so I see what you're saying. Now there's a reason for that. See, these Negroes have other problems that might get in the way of good soldiering. They're lazy for instance—like to drink too much, lack discipline. That's the real reason they aren't in the Army. Oh, it *is* scientific."

"Ohhh," said Louis. "I see. Now, these colored divisions— someone who worked for a friend of mine's in one, and they have a hell of a time getting supplies, I hear, much less any recognition for what they do. And they have to do all the cleaning and menial-like tasks for you white fellas."

Henry and Jake had been listening. Henry's mouth formed a silent 'o'. Jake stared at Louis, an idea dawning on his face. "...you white fellas?" he whispered.

Drum was too drunk to notice anything odd. "So? The brass have it figured, I'm sure. Teach them boys some discipline. Teach 'em to be civilized." He licked his lips. "Yup, civilized."

"Sergeant Stabler!" Jake interrupted. "Can I talk to you outside?"

The screen door slammed behind them. "You were lying back there about someone working for a friend of yours being in the Negro Army, weren't you?"

He looked at Jake for a long moment without saying anything. "What the hell," he said, finally. "It's my brother."

"Your brother?"

"Yeah, I changed my name—legally—before joining up." Louis looked relieved. "My real name's Luis, without the 'o'. And my last name's really Stablio, not Stabler. My brother, well he's a few shades darker than I am. So he's in, you know, the other army."

Jake's face had gone slack.

"You gonna turn me in, Sergeant Singer?"

"It's Jake, and don't look so miserable. Everyone around here's got some kind of secret—whether it's sending home supplies or making a black market fortune or bringing in twelve year old whores now and then."

Louis nodded. "I appreciate it. You ever been to L.A., Jake?"

"No, why?"

Louis lit a cigarette and walked slowly away from the Rec Hall. Jake followed.

"I used to live there," he began, his voice low. "We moved there from St. Louis two years ago, to be near my brother and his family. It was summer. We used to wear these suits—zoot suits."

Jake nodded. "With the collar like this and the shoulder here?"

"Right. There was lots of us with mostly Spanish backgrounds wearing these suits around L.A. that summer and I don't know, there was some kind of fight or something and I guess a serviceman got hurt, maybe even killed by a Spanish guy. Anyway, half the service must've come down to Los Angeles to gang up on anyone wearing a zoot suit. Pretty soon these guys really got going, thinking in the backs of their minds about the war maybe, and being soldiers and not being in a fight yet, and they started going after anyone Spanish. My brother, Antonio—I call him Tonio—and me, we got beat up pretty bad, and when we went home we found out these guys followed us so they could come over and kick some Spanish ass any time they felt like it." Louis half smiled. "I think these servicemen spilled more Spanish blood than Franco himself, you know?"

Jake took a deep breath. "Jesus."

"The upshot was we couldn't go home, so Tonio and I joined up and I stopped wearing zoots and started passing."

"That's why you looked like you wanted to strangle Drum."

Louis nodded.

Jake smiled. "Don't worry, it's an impulse we all get from time to time. He's not such a bad guy. Hank and I've been getting to know him better lately."

"He should watch his mouth about the Negro divisions. Tonio's gotta put up with stuff you wouldn't believe in France."

"I'm sure. Here's to you two seeing each other—soon. And here's to Louis Junior."

"Louis the Third, remember?"

"That's right. Sorry."

Louis dragged on the cigarette. "Well, at least my son got his all-St. Louis World Series. And thanks. I really wanted to tell someone, you know?" Louis put out his hand and Jake shook it.

"*De nada*. You want to come back inside?"

"I think I'll go for a walk. I'll see you later."

"Be careful Louis."

"Happy Thanksgiving, *amigo*."

*   *   *   *

Henry tried to join in the party but found the revelry false. This was, after all, a war—*the* War. He was frightened and a few drinks weren't going to take that away. He wasn't interested in kissing up to the General or making deals for silver with hot dog pilots. He went outside to wait for Jake and tried not to think of Frances.

He pictured his parents and sister sitting in low wooden recliners on their slate porch, relaxing in the shade of the wide yellow awning. His grandmother, Ette, lived upstairs but was usually at the dinner table, directing the conversation while his father bristled, grunted and found himself ultimately unable to keep from rising to her challenges. Boys played ball on the shaded street, and in the afternoons he played with them until he heard his father's shoes clicking toward him on the sidewalk, the Yiddish newspaper slapping his thigh.

"Whatcha sitting out here for?" Stan Freilich held the bottle out; Henry shook his head.

"Waiting for Jake."

"Don't wanna join in all that fun?" They both glanced through the screen and saw Marlowe and Mannion leading a line of GIs in a high kick in front of the phonograph.

Henry shrugged.

"I don't blame you. I'd as soon be out here thinking about the love of my life, too."

"What makes you think I'm doing anything more than waiting for Jake?"

"Look, the closest I've come to having someone who loved me was a drug store clerk named Irma who dumped me a year and a half ago, and a maybe from a Chinese farmer's daughter, who ran away as soon as this ugly mug tried to kiss her..."

"You don't know that's why she—"

"And now I'm stuck with her cold fish friend who manages, without the benefit of English, to convey her dislike for our whole country to me, the Army's representative to China, far as she's concerned."

Henry held out his hand. "Maybe I will have that drink."

*   *   *   *

At the talk the Chinese gave the following Sunday, the Rec Hall was nearly as crowded as it had been for Thanksgiving. Jimmy, the kid, was shipping out at New Year's. He'd be bombing Tokyo within a year, he promised. Marlowe came in with him. Weiss, Louis Stabler and Mannion had already arrived. Officers lined the back wall, the sun from the side windows glinting off the medals on their chests.

Henry and Jake Singer came in with four Chinese who were introduced as Neil, Jane, Sammy and Mr. Ai. A few officers in one corner scribbled their names and compared them with names on another slip of paper. As the athletic-looking one, Sammy Sung, was about to speak, McPhee, Danko and Mickey Warren came in, sat down in the back and lit cigarettes.

"He finally started rehab," McPhee whispered, as he leaned over to light his friends' cigarettes and then his own. "They work with him every day, and my sister-in-law says it hurts so much he cries half the rest of the time, except when he's unconscious from the pain or medication."

"He still drinking like he was?" asked Mickey Warren, snapping his gum.

McPhee shook his head. "Going to AA."

"All right! Shhh," Danko whispered. "Your brother will be okay, Kenny..." He saw everyone looking and fell silent, biting his lower lip.

Sung Hongai cleared his throat. "My name is Sammy. I was never quite as poor as some of the farmers and working people you see around Kunming. We had enough to eat and decent medical care." He paused the way Neil Ku had shown him. "I was one of a very small minority."

Jane Shiyan got up, whispered something to Mr. Ai, and went outside. Neil Ku followed, tapping Stanley's arm as he passed. He saw that the two were waiting for him.

"Mary Cha sent a letter to us," Neil Ku said, once they were outside, translating Shiyan's rapid-fire Chinese. "She is living on a farm. She made me promise to tell you that. Not my idea."

Ignoring Neil Ku, Stanley looked at Shiyan and she stared boldly back. He felt conflicting emotions: relief, self pity, loneliness and a self-serving depression that Jane Shiyan's news was not worse. He had the odd feeling that Jane understood these feelings and his embarrassment quickly turned to anger. He looked away. "So tell me something I don't know."

"She says now that Pei Han has been arrested she may be able to return soon, but the decision is not hers." She continued to look at him, said something to Neil Ku, and they both turned abruptly and walked toward the Rec Hall.

He felt a flash of anger. That this Chinese girl could bring such news and then walk away was just too much. He grabbed her shoulder and spun her around. Her shoulders were clenched, and the expression on her face was faintly resentful but not surprised.

Impulsively, he reached out with the other hand and pulled her to him, kissing her hard on the lips before she had time to react.

She did not kiss him back, but wiped her lips with the back of her hand and, without looking at him, returned to the Rec Hall.

Sammy was still talking. "We are not here to support any ideology; many millions are poor and sick and desperately need a program that can defeat the Japanese without being corrupt and exploitative."

"You think General Chiang is corrupt?" a voice called out.

Sammy started to laugh, but Mr. Ai whispered to him and he became very serious. Neither the American soldier nor his officer understood the simplest of things, or perhaps they saw but chose not to understand. A week earlier he might have been intimidated into silence. But he was not the same boy he had been a week earlier, before Tong Xie was killed.

"Chiang is preoccupied with being the only leader of China," he explained, "with the KMT being the only party. No sharing of authority, no matter how many might be against him, is permitted. What's best for China and the war effort takes a back seat. What people want takes a back seat." He waited but the voice in the back did not answer. "Some Americans have seen this, just as some have seen our successful war effort in the North. Now, I have a question."

Unused to being questioned by Chinese teenagers, the men shifted in their seats.

"If, somehow, American Lend Lease money intended for China's defense did not reach its intended destination because of corruption, if it went to fund something inappropriate, would that mean that the wealth and industry of the United States are working against the war effort?" Sammy Sung stopped when the commotion among the men grew louder than his voice.

"Sorry," an American voice called, "but we have to worry about American lives." It was McPhee. Paul Danko had him by the arm and was trying to pull him into his seat, but he shrugged away. "This is the only part of the war where American men are dying in vain."

"But it is not in vain—" Mr. Ai began.

"It damned well is!" McPhee continued, his voice rising. "If the Japanese aren't beaten back, it is! We're gaining ground in the islands but being stalemated at best—at best!—here on the mainland. It's because we haven't given enough money to Chiang Kaishek. We've wavered too much. He's our only hope. Don't tell me he's not!"

Overcome with grief and rage, Sung Hongai stepped in front of Mr. Ai.

"The answer is not aid to Chiang," his voice was choked. "Look at where there's been Chinese success against the Japanese.

Where was it? In the North! These are not small islands fortified by marines! This is China! No tea party here. And what part of China has been liberated and successfully defended? Where is there radio communication? In the North! The problem," Sung insisted, "is that the aid goes into the wrong hands, and those hands fill their own pockets!"

"But if we give every farmer a gun," one of the officers in the back began, "every storekeeper..."

Mr. Ai had succeeded in quieting Hongai. "No one suggests arming every farmer or tradesperson," Ai said, his voice calm and reasonable. "We only want to see all of the facts considered before a decision is made. My friend here, Sammy, does have some facts and is frustrated because not everyone has had a chance to hear them." His voice became quiet, humble. "We only wish to... inform."

Danko raised his hand. "What's your name? Sammy? Are you suggesting that the Army is keeping the truth from personnel who—"

"Not at all." Mr. Ai smiled; the only sign of tension was a tiny vibrating muscle in one cheek. "The findings of your Dixie Mission in the Liberated Areas are only now becoming known. We'd like to make sure that these findings are more widely distributed."

Jane Shiyan burst through the doorway holding three trays she had hidden in the truck. "For those of you who have never tried *jiaozi*, it is a stuffed pancake. And these are some of the best. Mr. Ai made them himself!"

Men clamored for the *jiaozi*, any questions they had forgotten, as the Chinese filed out.

The first out the door was Sung Hongai, who was looking straight ahead and trying to control the tears in his eyes.

I I

Henry was in New York, walking along frozen Fifth Avenue after a fresh snow. Frances was wearing a fuzzy white hat, and talking about seamstresses who worked at the rows of sewing machines at Henry's father's factory. No one looked out for their interests, she was explaining, with that intensity that came into her voice whenever she spoke about politics.

He loved the way New York lost its gray after a fresh snow, the way the streets and sidewalks turned to white, and the smoke and gas from autos and factories dissipated in the cold, as dissonant jazz riffed from the tattered doorway of a nearby club.

Henry blinked and opened his eyes as the door opened and Louis Stabler leaned against it, breathing heavily. "One of your Chinese pals just rode up on a bike...at the main gate...wants to see you...important."

Henry jumped off his still-made bunk, jostled Jake Singer awake, and dragged his friend out the barracks door.

Neil Ku Nuli was squatting low on his heels next to his black bicycle. He rose when Jake and Henry approached and vigorously shook their hands. "I'm glad you came. The Japanese have advanced to just northeast of Kunming. Mr. Ai says that if they advance any closer, we will have to take you with us."

Henry and Jake looked at each other. "We knew they were trying to push in this direction," Henry said, "but we've been bombing their supply lines and slowing them down. I wouldn't worry—"

Neil Ku shook his head. "No. The time to worry is now." He looked at Henry with steady eyes. "There are Japanese forces at Guiyang, in Guizhou Province. We met with Mr. Ai and other friends this morning, and we decided to take you to the Liberated Areas." Neil Ku smiled, unable to hide his pleasure at the thought. "You will be excellent English teachers."

Henry's face was hot; the roar of blood in his ears all but drowned out his own voice. "But you've known us for—? You'd risk—?"

"Out of the question!" Jake thundered.

Neil shook his head. "We're not strangers." He grinned, using a word he had learned from his friends. "We're *mishpocheh*."[8]

Henry and Jake looked at one another and laughed.

Neil continued. "In America, you would protect us. Like you say, this is our backyard. What choice do we have?"

Henry sat down in the tall grass; Jake and Neil Ku did the same. "We also don't have a choice. We can't leave," Henry explained gently. "In the American Army desertion is a very, very serious crime."

Neil Ku nodded. "When the Japanese Army arrives, well, that's pretty serious, too."

Henry took Neil Ku's hand. "Thank you."

"You didn't have to do this" echoed Jake, swallowing. "Besides, something like this could never be arranged...on your side of it, I mean."

Neil Ku laughed. "Anything can be arranged if the proper fees are paid to the right people." On the word "fees" he rubbed his thumb and forefinger together.

"Ah," said Jake. "The Chinese Squeeze. Thanks anyway, Neil. We joined the Army for hell or high water. You know the expression?"

"Kind of like a marriage," said Henry, smiling; he felt quick tears and swallowed against them. He was annoyed with his emotional reaction—*he was so like his mother!*

Neil Ku paused a long time, then rose and looked northward, as though assessing the danger for himself. "Mr. Ai predicted your answer. In that case, please accept his invitation. Chinese friends are taking a trip to visit minority area. Very interesting place. Mr. Ai suggest you both come along. Oh, and bring other skinny American friend."

"Stanley? I mean Sergeant Freilich?"

"Mm, yes, Stanley." He stood up and his American friends did likewise.

"We'll do that," said Jake, and he and Henry shook Neil Ku's hand.

The brown grass rustled in the warm wind; Henry looked around nervously. "Sounds good to me."

He and Jake watched Neil Ku pedal away. "You know he's not such a kid," Henry said.

"He's a piece of work," Jake said.

The grass had grown tall around the gated wall at the front of the compound, and neither Henry nor Jake noticed Kenny McPhee fifty yards down the wall, pretending to be reading a book. There was no printing on the book's pages—only a pencil scrawl. The message he had received had said the Chinese boy would be in a hurry and would probably not come into the compound.

He finished scribbling and tried to scrunch against the ground as the Chinese boy rode away.

*　　　*　　　*　　　*

Sung Hongai stood up. "I agree," he cleared his throat, which had grown thick from disuse. "Ahem. I agree with Ku Nuli about the need for more guards at meetings, particularly when we are putting together wall newspapers. There are sure to be more like the one who killed Tong Xie. I would like to volunteer."

Everyone in the room applauded and Sung felt a surge of pride. Even without Lin Teu's presence—she had not appeared at class or political meetings since Tong's murder—he felt changed, curiously lifted, like a newly colorful butterfly from its long, cocooned sleep.

Neil Ku rose to his feet. "Think of the necessity of armed guards as a sign of success. Who would want to break up a *failed* political movement to kill one of its members?" There was a general murmuring of agreement. "Besides," he gave a wave of his hand, and a fly that had been buzzing around his head flew away, "they've failed in one respect. Tong Xie is now a martyr. He has more influence dead than he ever had while alive." There was nodding all around. As usual, the budding journalist had summed up the group's feelings.

A student who rarely spoke at the meetings, Chin Chuzi, who was heavyset and wide at the shoulder, stood up and adjusted his thick framed glasses. "This man, this killer or fish seller, Pei Han, was probably not a spy. Tong Xie probably was killed because he exercised bad judgement and in this crazy man's opinion, tried to interfere with an arranged marriage. But Neil Ku's right about one thing. Is it possible that the wrong people figured out what Tong Xie's name really was? That he was on the Long March? Perhaps we do need to be more watchful."

He smoothed the front of his shirt. "So Hongai and I will stand as additional guards at our meetings, and I will personally discuss the possibility of firearms with the proper authorities. I realize no one is ever allowed to have guns, but when a student is murdered, well, this is a special case."

Chuzi paused, looked down at the ground, and continued. "Ai Wenti has contacted the Chief of the Minority people and arranged for a meeting next Sunday. The Chief and Mr. Ai will discuss where the minority tribe will stand should civil war break out. Neil Ku Nuli has asked our American friends to join us on this trip, so they can learn still more about us, and about China. Always a good thing..."

In the back of the room, Shiyan was barely listening. She badly wanted to dislike American Stan for his brazenness, as she had the other Americans who had made similar advances at her father's store—often in full view of her father and brother.

He had demonstrated the intention, the li, of being for Wulin already. But Wulin was in hiding, on a farm far away from Kunming, so perhaps this American did not belong to little-sister-turned-big-sister. Perhaps now that Pei Han was in custody, Wulin might feel safe enough to come back, and the American might turn to her again. It was all so confusing!

She wondered whether her attraction to American Stan was a result of her feelings of competitiveness with younger sister, Cha Wulin.

In spite of all of these thoughts, she hoped Stan would accept Neil Ku's invitation to visit the minority people.

*　　　*　　　*　　　*

"Say, Jake! Speed up. Didn't Willie say we had to have the truck back at the PX by dinner?"

"He wanted the truck an hour ago, Henry." Jake turned his head, grinning his crooked grin. "We're already late."

The Chinese, who had stopped talking at the question, all began talking at once, all except the two young women, Lin Teu and Ju Shiyan, who sat together and bounced in unison every time they went over a bump.

"We could learn a thing or two from these minority folks," Sung Hongai was saying, in Chinese.

"Speak English," said Mrs. Ai. "Not polite otherwise."

Sung looked at Henry and concentrated, as he did every time he had the opportunity to practice his English. "I was pointing out how interesting I thought it was that the minority tribe has given up, ah, the practice of passing one's possessions down to eldest son."

"There is a reason for this," said Neil Ku. "With these people, no one can be certain that the eldest son is legitimate."

There was an embarrassed silence. Stanley, who was sitting stiffly next to Jane Shiyan, coughed sharply.

"They *were* a..." Henry searched for the right word, "an *uninhibited* people."

"Promiscuous," said Mr. Ai. "What else did our American friends think of these Chinese people?"

"Very different from everyone we've met so far," Jake called from the cab. "No offense."

"None taken," Mr. Ai said. "Yes, these minority tribes are particularly uninhibited. Not like most Chinese people. Very healthy, I think. Bah-haa!" He gave a bellowing laugh.

Henry saw Mrs. Ai's eyebrow go up and couldn't keep from chuckling.

In the back of the truck, Stanley inched closer to Shiyan. The green wool blanket that was folded beneath them itched through his uniform.

Lin Teu spoke up. "I don't like the way their Chief takes the young girls to bed whenever he wants, nor the way he orders the other young men around. There is no consensus, not even a committee." She gave her head a defiant little toss to one side, her short hair bouncing.

Sung Hongai stared at her, wanting to speak but unable to break the wall that had been erected between them. It was as though Tong Xie were still alive. When he had seen the minority couples not bothering to hide their intimacy, he had hoped that the sight would break Tong's hold on his own beloved Teu. He sighed and looked up at the ceiling of the truck. A spider dropped from a thread and hung for a moment over his head, then inched upwards again. He could learn from the spider, he realized. *Yes, he could do that as well. Inch back into Teu's life, despite his long drop from her favor.*

Neil Ku was taking notes, practicing his journalistic techniques, trying to use his senses as he had been taught. He recognized the odor of the truck's gasoline as it mingled with the sweet spring smells of pollen and trees. He noted the relief on the GIs' faces, possibly to be away from the unpredictable minority people, more likely due to the end of the Japanese threat now that their forces had exhausted themselves just short of Kunming.

At the minority village, the air had been thick with mosquitoes; only the Chief in his brown brimless hat and animal wrappings had seemed unaffected, never once slapping at his arms or scratching. The people of the village had danced most of the day, and he remembered that Henry and Stan had compared this to a kind of dancing they had witnessed in America, a dancing without form, to a music also without form.

Neil closed his eyes, wondering whether he would marry Bing Po and what their home would be like. Would New China require the traditional sort of home he was accustomed to or would daily life be formless, like Henry's music? And if the latter were the case, what would his father, who had been so taken with Sun

Yatsen in the early years, think of that? He opened his eyes, and saw that Henry was looking at him. He smiled, and his friend smiled back.

*   *   *   *

Henry watched Neil Ku, wondering what he was thinking. The wild abandon of the minority people was like nothing he had seen thus far in China. It reminded him of America in his very early childhood—in the 20s. The Chinese he had met until now had all been either cowed or rebelliously organized.

He turned to watch the red and yellow flowers by the roadside blur to orange and recede until they became a distant pool of color. They reminded him of Inwood Park. He reached into his pocket, took out the barrette and held it in his lap for a moment, then cupped it to his face. The faint Rose of Sharon scent brought tears to his eyes.

"What is that?" Neil Ku asked.

"B-barrette," Henry managed to whisper. He calmed himself. "It holds a woman's hair in place."

"Ahh," said Neil Ku, looking at Henry's face, then quickly out the window.

The truck arrived at Mr. Ai's shop, chasing bicycles and chickens before it, and once everyone was assembled at the roadside, Mr. Ai asked that the whole group come inside to share the dinner Mrs. Ai had prepared.

Mrs. Ai replied sharply in Chinese to this, and everyone laughed and even Henry could see she had not prepared anything. It was then that Jake, climbing down from the cab had said, "Say, anyone seen Stanley?"

And Neil Ku noted that Jane Shiyan had also disappeared.

*   *   *   *

"I'm afraid, I guess," Henry said, surprised to hear himself say so. Mr. and Mrs. Ai nodded slowly. Their apartment in the back of the dumpling shop was crowded; everyone had stayed for dinner.

"Well, we've spoken before about how natural that is in a war," said Neil Ku, who was sitting on the floor along with everyone but Mr. and Mrs. Ai. "Remember Jacob's dream?"

"Let's not start that again," Jake said, and Neil Ku hid a smile.

Mr. Ai had tipped his bowl of white rice and was scraping the remainder down its sides with his chopsticks. "I don't think that's the fear he's referring to. Henry?"

"No, it's not." He put down his bowl and sat back, sipping from the small cup of warm tea and wishing it were cold water. He was suddenly sweating. His pants were stuck to his thighs. "The trip to the minority people made me miss my girl—my ex-girlfriend." He felt himself blush. "I can't believe I'm talking about this. Frances wrote to me saying that I've changed since I've been here." He folded his hands in his lap and stared down at them. "I guess I realized how much I love her."

There was a long silence, punctuated by some Chinese words from Lin Teu, who was playing jacks with little Ai Wei.

Jake clapped his friend on the shoulder. "It'll be alright, buddy."

"I know." Henry sighed. "I've always worn my heart on my sleeve—I'm like my mom, I guess." He laughed weakly. "War is hell."

Jake, Mr. Ai, Sammy Sung and Neil Ku began a debate—in English—about the nature of fear, and Henry's mind wandered, as it often did after big Thanksgiving and Passover meals. He considered courage and bravado, which so often seemed the same on the outside but which were actually more like opposites. He thought of the Central Government soldiers and their swagger and the way they brandished guns and how the men in his unit drank; these were responses to fear. They were bravado, attempts to cover up externally. Courage was entirely different—the acceptance of fear. He remembered the way his father's friends would cross the street on their way to synagogue when he was a boy, striding in their black suits and yarmulkas, ignoring the oncoming traffic, as though unafraid—never deigning to notice whether cars were coming or not. He realized that this also was bravado, while Frances tearfully watching him go to war despite her fear, was truly courageous.

Their jacks game finished, Lin Teu was clapping hands with Ai Wei, who squealed and giggled each time they touched.

Mrs. Ai's voice woke Henry from his thoughts. "So you will write to ex-girlfriend and ask her to marry you?"

Henry froze, then laughed at himself. "I'm such a hypocrite," he exclaimed aloud.

Jake looked at him. "Why's that?"

"Because I'm afraid, but—never mind. What the hell. Yeah, I'll do it."

Everyone stopped what they were doing to applaud.

*   *   *   *

American Stan had whispered to her to follow him—he wanted to show her a place he knew and, without knowing why, Shiyan had followed. She liked him no more now than she had when she had first seen him, less perhaps. And when he kissed her, she had been furious. But she had also been surprised and thrown off her footing. No American soldier had ever had such an effect on her before, though many had tried to kiss her. And worse.

The brown wooden hut he had found in the field between the city and his base was open on one side so they could see the grass ripple in the wind and the birds hopping near to inspect them. He took a book from his back pocket and began to read out loud, and though her English was improving with Neil Ku's help, Shiyan could only understand part of what American Stan read, but what touched her was the quiet intimacy in his voice, as though his words were a hand lightly caressing her. His eyes brightened and reached out to her when he looked up between words.

He put the book down and spoke softly and what she understood was "Mary Cha," and from what she had learned of the tones of American speech Shiyan knew he meant to reassure her, like a younger sister, and she was at once comforted and annoyed. Once again, because of Cha Wulin she was demoted to younger sister, and now this sweet foreigner was her own sister's accomplice.

The affront was too much for her, so she found a compromise between her confusing feelings for this American and her upbringing, which told her to run away.

She reached out, her hand open, fingers spread, to a spot in the air next to his arm. The gesture told him to be still and listen. She recited a poem she had learned as a child, and her gestures told the surprised American that she was talking about the trees, the sky, and the earth.

Afterwards, as the wind blew through her hair, she listened, only half understanding, while he explained that he was different from his friends. His family had no leader with a kind heart, like Henry's mother or Jake's grandmother. He had learned to be a good person as a little boy, in synagogue. And when after making *bar mitzvah* he had stopped attending synagogue, such values had disappeared from his life. Until now.

"Coming to Kunming has changed me," he said, looking her in the eyes. He reached out to touch her face, and Shiyan leaned back, just out of his reach, but she allowed his hand to linger in the air, inches from her.

"I don't know why, or how, but I feel I belong here. I don't understand it, but I feel the way I felt in synagogue as a boy. Something that was missing is back. Don't ask me to make sense of it." He shook his head. "Maybe it's just that you don't run away, or laugh."

Shiyan smiled, understanding little, but enjoying the sound of this gentle American's voice.

*   *   *   *

Henry was trying to coax Ai Wei out from behind a counter. He held out three sticks of gum, carefully opened one and put it in his mouth.

"Gum, see? Want one?" He handed a stick to Lin Teu, who turned it over in her hand before shaking her head and handing it back. Ai Wei appeared at Henry's boot and was holding a small hand out.

"Okay," Henry handed him the gum, which was unwrapped and in the boy's mouth in one motion. "Have a seat, young man. I'm going to tell you a story about a girl, named Red Riding Hood, who lived next to a dark forest. You know what a forest is, Ai Wei?"

At the table, Mr. Ai was waving an animated finger. "But the Depression is over. Didn't President Roosevelt's programs...?"

Jake interrupted. "His programs were part of it, but the bigger part was the war itself. The country went to work to produce arms and supplies for us. That's what really ended the Depression."

"I see," said Neil Ku.

"My fear," Jake said, "is what's going to happen after the war. There's this streamlined sort of prosperity now, but it's all for the war—War Bonds and rationing and double shifts and so forth. Everyone's willing to do without. But what about when there's no war to keep it all going?"

Mr. Ai shrugged. "The end of the war can bring many kinds of changes. Why worry now?"

Henry looked up from his story. "Yeah, Mr. Worrier. Listen to the man."

Jake pointed an arching finger over Neil Ku's head, at Henry. "You stick to your stories and don't start calling the kettle black."

"Kettle?" asked Mr. Ai.

"It means that he's the one who's usually afraid. It's a joke between us." Jake folded his arms on the table, and took a sip of tea. "I just wonder what kind of country we'll come home to. Will there be jobs, or will it go back to the way it's been for the last fifteen years or so, which was pretty bad?"

"The war has had a unifying effect on your people?" Mr. Ai wanted to know.

Jake nodded. "For the most part. Although there's been a big to-do with some of the unions, who aren't happy that folks have to work double shifts, for low pay, and so forth."

Mr. Ai looked concerned. "I see."

"What do you think about this?" Neil Ku asked.

Jake shrugged. "Well, I see both sides. Look, there's a war on. Everyone has to pitch in to win it. But they should be compensated. I've always been very much in favor of unions. It's the only way I can see to insure fairness to the average guy."

A tinkling melody came from the other side of the room, followed by excited shrieks. Ai Wei and Lin Teu were dancing in a circle around Henry, who had a lap full of paper scraps.

"I see you gave Wei his present," Jake said, beckoning everyone to get up from the table. "It's a music box. A dancing bear to go with his friend, furry bear."

A formation of bombers flew overhead, briefly drowning out the music, but the Ai family closed their eyes against it, and focused on the musical dancing bear.

*   *   *   *

The sign on Xiang's door said "Bargains" and young Tao thought he heard a woman's voice from within, singing a song he had heard as a child. The finch chirped in its cage over the bed and on the walls hung movie memorabilia and a large portrait of Madam Chiang. A thick, curling smoke enveloped the room, so young Tao did not see Xiang at first.

Tao tried to follow the smoke back to its source with his eyes. "I want to buy some cigarettes."

"Cigarettes?" Xiang leaned forward, his eyes gleaming. "I have the finest opium. They say the Japanese are approaching Kunming. Already they are halfway through Guizhou Province. Think about that and tell me you have no use for a small amount of opium to clear your mind of fear should they finally overrun us." He did not say that the Japanese had already pulled back, having exhausted their supplies.

"We are men; our enemies are also men," said young Tao.

"Oh, yes, I've heard that saying." Xiang sat back and lit another cigarette. "All well and good for Mao Siansheng, but do you really believe our enemies are men? Our enemies are monsters. Ask anyone from Nanking or Shanghai. You will meet my friend Liduo. Ask him about our enemies, but be ready to run when you do."

"A friend told me they are men." Tao pictured Tong Xie in the days before his death, stern faced, his long, fine hair in his eyes.

Xiang leaned forward suddenly and spat. Then, his eyes widened and he jumped out of the heavily cushioned chair and fell to his knees, peering at the thick, brightly colored carpet that was now dotted dark and wet. He looked up at young Tao. "What do you want?" he asked, his eyes narrowing.

"Cigarettes. A carton of American cigarettes."

"Is that so?" said a voice from the doorway.

Tao peered through the smoke.

"Liduo!" Xiang waved to him, straining his eyes. "We were just talking about you! Come in." Indeed, it was Chen Liduo. Yet it was not. "You've been through some, ah, training I understand." He laughed nervously.

"So you're here for cigarettes, young Tao." Liduo stepped into the room and the cat-quickness in his step, all balls of the feet, heels never touching the floor, inspired fear in both Tao and Xiang.

"I remember you, Tao. Friendly with Chong Lingxiu and Tong Xie, weren't you?" His voice was relaxed and something about this ease of manner terrified Xiang. Only one kind of training brought the physical agility and cold confidence that radiated from his old friend.

"Tell me, Tao. Have you seen Chong Lingxiu around school lately? Where do you suppose I might find him?"

*   *   *   *

Henry and Jake came in, nodded to the group of pilots crowded around the Rec Hall's radio, then saw Stanley.

"Say, Stan," called Jake. "Where'd you disappear to yesterday?"

Stan smiled back. "Hey, we get time off. It's not like I was AWOL."

Henry and Jake looked at each other. "Sergeant Freilich, you go on a nature walk or something?" Henry grinned good naturedly. "What's with the Houdini act?" But Stan turned back to Mannion and Marlowe and resumed his discussion.

Henry nodded in their direction. "Nice to see the boys're back okay."

"You bet," Jake agreed.

A waltz, complete with string section and lead clarinet, crackled over the airwaves and Stan picked up a chair and hugged its metal frame close, doing a few quick steps.

"Not much to look at, but she sure can follow, eh, boys?"

Marlowe laughed; Mannion shook his head.

Jake said, "Did I just imagine we were good buddies with that guy? Weren't we just talking about how to help him find his girlfriend?"

Henry raised an eyebrow. "Must be I forgot to shower this morning."

"Look," said Jake. "Stan's going into the PX. You thinking what I'm thinking?"

"How would I know what you're thinking?" Henry chuckled at his buddy, who rolled his eyes. "Let's head him off."

The 14th Army Air Corps PX was separated from the Rec Hall by a small doorway. Henry and Jake arrived at that entranceway just before Stanley. Jake leaned against the doorstop, one of his legs blocking the doorway at thigh level.

"Why hello, Stanley. Long time no see."

"What do you think you're doing?"

"Just saying hello to an old pal—a pal I share my scotch with, a—"

"What, you want money for that?" He reached for his back pocket.

"No, I don't want anything," said Jake. "I was just surprised at the difference in you today as compared with yesterday."

"Oh, really? Well maybe there is a difference."

"Well," said Henry, "wouldn't you want to tell your buddies about it?"

Stan's eyes shrank until they were green pinholes. He smiled suddenly "Maybe. But not right now, okay?"

Jake stood uncomfortably close to Stan. "You know you made such a good impression with our pals—really you were representing America. Our new Chinese friends liked you a whole lot."

Stan nodded. "And I liked them a whole lot."

"Some more than others, it seems," Henry teased.

Stan changed the subject. "So, Henry. Have you heard from your girlfriend yet?"

Henry nodded. "Yeah, she's written a few times."

"And what about that Gartman fella? She happen to mention him?"

The confidence drained from Henry's face. He chewed his thumbnail. "No. I ah, haven't heard his name much."

Jake cleared his throat. "Don't get off the topic, Stan. Now, there's something I don't understand." Jake hitched up his belt and rose to full height, which was to about the base of Stanley's neck. "I'm wondering, Stan. You're an inconsistent fella. Friendly sometimes, not so friendly other times. Buddies with us. Buddies with them. I wonder if it doesn't somehow have something to do with our last names."

"Your...you're kidding, right? I'm as Jewish as you guys. You didn't know that?"

Jake's eyes glittered. "Oh, we knew. It's not your blood—it's your attitude."

Henry nodded. "When it's to your advantage, you're Jewish. When you're around certain people and they have certain attitudes," he nodded towards Marlowe, "who you are kind of changes."

"It's not true."

"Really? You and McPhee, for instance."

"So, we've had a drink, went downtown a few times."

Henry looked at him. "You make friends with who you want. We're all in this together. I know. But let me ask you this: did I ever tell you about my first conversation with that guy?"

"With McPhee? I don't think so."

"He walked all around me. Said to me: 'Just tell me something, Neiberg. Where are they?' I asked him what he's talking about, and he says, 'the horns.' He thought all Jews had horns and he just couldn't figure out where mine were."

Stan folded his arms. "So maybe he was pulling your leg, or maybe being my friend showed him Jews don't have horns. Ever think of that?"

"You're a real educator," Henry laughed uneasily. "You've just seemed, I don't know, inconsistent, and I'm concerned about you."

Stan turned away, fingers snapping to the Benny Goodman beat. "Don't patronize me."

*   *   *   *

"Jacob, go easy on the guy." Henry said when they'd sat down. He leaned across the table, speaking in low tones. "He didn't come from any kind of family. How can you expect anything from him?"

"I can expect him to be proud—at least not ashamed—of what he is. I can expect him to be consistent with his friends, us, and with our new friends. If he doesn't like Mr. and Mrs. Ai and Neil Ku and the rest, fine! If he doesn't like us, fine. But be consistent, please. And don't try to pick up the Chinese girls." His voice went up a notch. "For the most part, the Jewish GIs stick together. Something about us is the same, and its more than spelling. He should be what he is."

"Maybe that's what he is. Maybe taking that young girl behind the barn or wherever they went is what he does when he has a new group of friends with a pretty girl among them." Henry began biting his thumbnail.

Jake frowned. "What's gotten into you? Grab yourself a napkin. Your thumb's bleeding."

12

Cha Wulin had been in this same field since dawn, listening to Gong Fu Ma's twin daughters laugh as they filled their baskets with freshly picked rice. Mary Cha could squat on her heels for many minutes at a time—but her ankles ached and her thighs were damp with sweat, and each time she rose to her feet a slow wedge of pain began in her toes and edged up toward her hip, while Guelo and Ting Siao leaped up, laughing their coarse country girl laughs, easily transporting their overflowing rice containers.

Mary Cha had thought she would be happy to escape Pei Han and his mother's wedding plans, and so she was until she found herself collecting ox dung in a dark field after five hours of sleep on a dirt floor. And once the sun came up, she had thought she would find solace, or at least a comfortable repetition she might lose herself in, in the wet green rice paddy, but the red-faced twins with their bad teeth and loud, laughing games had driven away any such idea.

They were very like her old image of herself—a coarse country girl with big, ugly teeth and fat ankles. How ironic to have found her way home to twin images of herself!

What she wouldn't give to be in Kunming—never mind New China and her new friends and her upwardly spiraling political education. Never mind the warlords and the Kuomintang and the Long March. What she wouldn't give to be younger sister again, sitting at Shiyan's foot, listening to her false city wisdom!

But that was all before the New Year. Now, after a few months, she did not mind the Gong family's illiteracy and bad teeth quite so much. She did not mind eating the same meal most evenings, and she had even found a new sleeping place: high up in a storage bin for chicken feed. She had made a crackling bamboo shoot bed with a headboard of farm implements bundled in burlap and old grass.

Her body had found an advantage in farm life. While she had been a strong child and adolescent, Wulin thought of herself as uncoordinated, unable to effectively compete at the children's games requiring speed, agility and accuracy. Farm chores helped. Feeding chickens, chasing ducks, planting and reaping all developed her hand-eye coordination. She had once seen a book with pictures of men throwing spears in competition with one another, and in the afternoons she practiced throwing Mr. Gong's pitchfork from her sleeping area up in the feed bin. But while she improved, she never developed quite the throwing skill she desired.

But being a stubborn young woman, she continued to practice.

She had grown accustomed to the twins' silly jokes and too-loud laughing. They were a hard working family who knew nothing of Sun Yatsen or the bridge at Tatu Ho or even of Chiang Kaishek. Her stories of Kunming politics and even the war itself were met at first with stares of disbelief and incomprehension, but later, as she softened toward their countryside ways, the Gong family adopted some of Mary Cha's Kunming sensibility. They were, she admitted, entirely incapable of disliking an individual who had not personally done them harm. Such people would be the mainstays of New China, she decided, devoting their time and energies to their families and work and communities rather than to landlords and local thugs.

She squinted in the afternoon sun, trying to make out the shimmering silhouettes coming toward her. One was Chong Tanshi, the boy who had been staying with the Gong family, but the other man was much taller than the farmer, Fu Ma, and she could now see that he wore round framed spectacles. Tanshi bounded toward her, leaping over plants and branches.

"Wulin, look! Look who it is!" he screeched. "Come meet my father, Chong Lingxiu!"

*   *   *   *

Sung Hongai watched fearfully from his hiding place as Xiang stood high enough on his coughing friend's shoulders to rip down the posters Neil Ku had put up. He was filled with rage and an urge to jump out from behind the fence, but he was too afraid of the beating he would surely receive.

The boy holding Xiang up began to retch and his shoulders heaved until Xiang spat on the top of his head and barked down at him to be silent. If he wished to die of consumption later, that was fine, but for now, hold still! Xiang began to mutter disgustedly about the poor rabble in this awful town—how low it had sunk this past year! After the war, he said, fine houses would be built; compounds would spring up sporting dozens of servants made up of the very rabble who put up such vile ideas as these. He would start his own business and it would grow and his family would become a landed member of the aristocracy!

He spat on Neil Ku's poster, and the boy holding Xiang up began to giggle, and the dark boy holding the two bicycles they had arrived on demanded to know what was so funny. Seeing his chance and having entirely lost control of himself, Sung Hongai leaped out from behind the fence and gave the boy holding Xiang up a mighty shove, knocking them both over. The short, dark boy dropped the bicycles and ran toward him, scooping up a large rock as he ran. Sung Hongai heard Xiang moan just as the rock crashed into his ear.

The next voice he heard was that of his beloved Lin Teu.

"You shouldn't have done such a ridiculously dangerous thing," she said, bending over him, washing the side of his head with a wet rag. "But it was," she whispered, "incredibly brave."

Sung Hongai smiled for the first time in weeks, and again lost consciousness.

*   *   *   *

Shiyan had never known how much she loved to sing! Of course, part of the enjoyment was being surrounded by new friends, she thought. Professor Shin caught her eye and smiled. Singing about New China's future was invigorating too, but the singing itself was good for her spirit the way running was for her legs or wrestling with little Weima was for her arms and back.

And when the song ended she wanted to begin again, no matter that she enjoyed studying and in ten minutes would certainly be immersed in that. No doubt about it, singing joined her with her friends, and the fact that she was a newcomer became irrelevant as dozens of young voices joined, rising and falling and growing together.

Shiyan saw him standing in the doorway—the classroom had no door, only a loosely attached splintered molding. She was used to seeing American Stan in her mind's eye, and so the sight of him in the doorway of her classroom did not at first startle her.

But his doleful eyes did.

One by one, heads turned.

"Neil Ku found me and told me. I don't know how, but he did."
He looked at Professor Shin. "I'm sorry, sir. I—" The professor
bowed his head; Stan went on. "Neil thought I should be the one.
Here, come outside." He took her hand and led her out, and she
heard the murmurs sweep the room behind her. She strained to
understand his words; her English was improving but she wished
he would speak more slowly!

"Some soldiers were taking target practice behind the fruit market." His voice was low, lacking its usual bravado.

"Chinese soldiers?" she asked, not knowing why.

"Yes. They were surrounded by trees."

"Bees?"

"Trees. You know how it is on that road behind the market, all
overgrown. Anyway," his hand reached tentatively for hers, "your
brother was playing there—"

"Alone? Weima?" She fought to keep the hysteria out of her
voice.

He shook his head. "I, I don't know how—"

"He was probably coming from Mr. Ai's store. He and Ai Wei
play in back room…"

"Jane, they swore it was an accident." Stan's eyes overflowed
and he began to sob on every other word, clutching her to him.
"They said they didn't know he was there. The commander apol-
ogized." He looked away, letting go of her hand, which fell to her
side. "I'm so, so sorry. I arranged for transportation of, of his
body to your father…"

American Stan seemed to vanish and it was a moment before
Shiyan realized that it was she who had disappeared, running as

fast as she could to her father's store—but of course, no one was there.

*   *   *   *

When Neil Ku had found him and told him about the shooting, Stanley had listened more intently than he remembered ever listening to anything that was not jazz or his own thoughts. He listened to the details of the shooting as though they were chord changes; he listened to Neil's suggestions that Stan be a source of quiet strength as though Neil's voice were a melody and his own ideas a counter melody.

Stanley listened also to Neil Ku's description of Shiyan's home-life, the father-daughter relationship, respectful but strained by the long-ago loss of her mother, which had left the two children, so far apart in age, with little to cling to but one another and traditions eroded by time and war. Stanley saw how he could help. No one, not even Irma, had ever needed him before.

*   *   *   *

He waited for her to return; and after several hours she did trudge back to Lianda. Mr. and Mrs. Ai invited them to supper—no doubt that was Neil Ku's idea. Their own little son was out of the house, as were all signs of him—toys, clothes, even his furry bear and music box bear. Stan wondered where he might have been sent.

They talked about school and Stan recounted his own school life and was surprised by how much he remembered: the horse-face of his science teacher and how he'd hated gym class and even the playground with its drab green see-saws and dull, squeaky slide.

At one point he realized he had been talking for hours and he put down his teacup and laughed and then smiled sheepishly at Shiyan. "Sorry, but I'm not used to talking about myself for so long."

And when he walked Jane Shiyan back to her dormitory, neither of them spoke, but the silence was not at all uncomfortable.

*   *   *   *

Stan thanked whatever God there was that Major Drum was in charge of the SCU. Unless the major had an interest in what one of his men was doing he was not apt to notice that particular man. He had tunnel vision; he played checkers with McPhee, read in the library, smoked his pipe and wrote letters to his family. And so when Sergeant Jacob Singer gruffly responded when Stan's name was called, the major never looked up from his ledger. Stan did not think of himself as AWOL. He thought of himself as providing a needed service that happened also to be a labor of love.

Stan stayed with Neil Ku in the Chinese students' dormitory and did his best to occupy Shiyan's attention when she had free time. He cultivated his own instinctual curiosity about the world around him and used it with the persistence of a child to question Shiyan, keeping her diverted and busy. Rocks, trees, even politics and language became so fascinating that Stan was compelled to share his observations and elicit ever more particular details from her. This benefited them both; he kept her mind from her brother, and he had not had a drink in a week.

The language barrier proved an ally to Stan's cause. The crude common ground of verbs and nouns and simple adjectives they shared became a topic for discussion. Stan noticed subtleties of meaning and intricacies of insinuation that opened whole new areas for his diversions. And when Shiyan became exasperated and sighed or, as she did on occasion, said sharply "Shut up, Stan Siansheng!" Stanley would smile to himself, having won not one but two victories: he had distracted her, and he had coaxed her into exhibiting emotion, and one does not show emotion when immersed in self pity.

Jane Shiyan built a small shrine to her brother in one corner of her father's room in the back of the market, and Stanley helped her, remaining AWOL, while Jake ever more reluctantly covered for him. She collected scraps of her brother's clothing and a piece of rice bread he had been eating the afternoon he was killed, and to these Stanley added a phonograph record. She had once told Stanley that Weima had loved to sing and dance, and Stan could not help but notice the flicker of gratitude in her eyes as she took the disk between her fingers and placed it with the other items.

A week before her brother died, Shiyan had given him her old shirt puppet. She had made the puppet when she was about his age, and it had become a friend as well as a way of sharing with both Cha Wulin and little brother. With Stan Siansheng beside her, she now knelt beside the simple commemoration and laid the piece of cloth, string and beads across its top.

*   *   *   *

On a Wednesday that same week, Henry visited Mr. and Mrs. Ai for dinner while Jake worked late.

He told Ai Wei the story of the Three Bears while Mr. and Mrs. Ai had a conversation in low tones in the cooking area. When the story was finished, Ai Wei beckoned Henry to a corner of the room and with great delicacy took down his new music box, wound it up and began to dance around it. He marched, thin thighs pumping to the equally thin melody, tiny head tipping to either side, while Henry clapped time.

Henry kissed the boy on the cheek when the music wound down and finally stopped. "You're an excellent dancer with a fine sense of timing." He tousled Ai Wei's hair.

Ai Wei hugged Henry's knee.

"Very good," said Mr. Ai, laughing. He pointed for his son to bring the box back to his corner of the room. Mrs. Ai went into the cooking area.

"It's good you keep him busy and happy." Mr. Ai was suddenly serious. "My son's best friend was killed in a shooting accident, and we're trying to keep him from finding out." He gave a helpless shrug. "He'll have to find out some time."

Mrs. Ai had returned with a bowl of sugar dumplings in water. She pointed to it and said something in Chinese that sounded to Henry like a partially held back sneeze.

"When you eat them," she explained, "you must eat the entire dumpling at once—to taste it properly."

Henry tried one. "They're kind of big to eat whole." He popped one into his mouth. "But delicious. Very sweet and... mmm." He swallowed and took another.

"Have some of the water," Mr. Ai suggested. "Sweet."

Henry ate another three dumplings; Mr. and Mrs. Ai shared the rest. When they were finished, Mrs. Ai looked directly at Henry. "So, what did Frances say to your proposition?"

Mr. Ai said something in Chinese.

"Excuse me," Mrs. Ai corrected herself. "Your proposal."

Henry shook his head miserably, not saying that he never asked. "I feel like a fool. Before the war, she cared for me, at least she seemed to, but she wouldn't marry me because I didn't care enough about people less fortunate than myself. Now, she says she hardly knows me. Before was bad enough. Now..." He shrugged. "I've changed somehow, she says—I don't sound like myself! Who do I sound like? Not Gartman, the fella who lives across the street. Her letters are short, like she's annoyed, and those words run through all of them. I'm different." He snorted. "If I wasn't good enough before..."

Mr. Ai pointed to Henry to finish the last dumpling; it made a wet, sympathetic sound as it went down.

"Maybe things will change."

"But if I'm not there to change them..." Henry shook his head, unable to find the source of his friend's optimism. He sighed. "My sister writes about trying to avoid talking about the war around the dinner table. Early in the war, she used to ask me about places like Bataan and Chongqing like they were names on a test at school. But to my parents they were more than just school work; they were where the neighbor's boy's ship was heading, or where their best friend's son was killed.

"Now my parents talk about business, the weather, food—they avoid mentioning the war, but it's still there, like the smell of a fire on East Fifteenth street—that's the way Enid puts it." Henry shook his head. "In the backs of their minds, they're scared because the war's winding down in Europe, but here?" He sighed, wondering if they knew that he was more afraid than his sister was.

Bell-like music from the windup bear drifted in from the back of the room. The tiny tune played prettily, over and over.

"I asked one of the officers about the Japanese getting close to Kunming," Henry said. "Boy did he give me a funny look." He hesitated. "I'm beginning to think this war'll never be over." He changed the subject. "You know, my family is slightly more well off than that of my friends."

"Many of our best students are from—"

"They're political, my friends and their families are, and to them, I think, struggle is more a way of life." He looked pained. "What I mean is they don't like political struggle but they're more used to it."

Mr. Ai was nodding. His wife came into the room and said something in Chinese. "Ah, Wei is going to sleep soon. Why don't you stay here tonight?"

Henry nodded. "Maybe I will, thank you. Long as I'm working at the SCU, that's Stat Control, in the morning, no one'll miss me."

"Huida will get you a blanket," Mr. Ai said. "Please, continue."

"A lot of Americans think that minding one's business is the most American way. And I was like that too, but now," he shook his head, "I don't know. I think I'm more like Jake than I used to be. I never really cared about the Spanish Civil War—it was so far away. But I'll tell you, I'll never get used to seeing bodies by the side of the road, whether they're Chinese or American or whatever. When you see them up close, they always look like someone you once knew."

Mr. and Mrs. Ai were silent.

"The pilots bring in bodies sometimes and what gets me is it rolls off their backs or it looks like it does, though I guess that's the reason so many of them get so drunk. I don't see how they can fly—back and forth and back and forth—knowing what they're doing and that it's going on and on and they're just getting drunk and doing it again."

"They're doing their job," Mr. Ai said, with the air of someone who's own job might occasionally require that reminder. "And they're doing it for a common cause."

"And just when that stops, they bomb our airstrip. Not a heavy bombing by some people's standards but I'm telling you, between you and me, it's enough to scare the pants off me and make me want to do something about it."

Mr. Ai changed the subject. "One of the articles you gave us," he said, "was about your Presidential election..."

Henry brightened. "Roosevelt was elected to a fourth term, unprecedented—no one's ever done it. And let's see, his running mate is a man named Truman. I don't know much about him."

"What happened to Mr. Wallace?" Mr. Ai asked. "Wasn't he your vice president?"

"The answer depends on how cynical you are."

"My American friends tell me it is important to be cynical when talking about American politics." Ai Wenti leaned back on the couch. "What do you think about Stilwell returning to the United States?"

Henry raised an eyebrow. He had been sitting next to Mr. Ai, but now got up and went to the wooden bench on the other side of the room, perhaps twelve feet away. "General Stilwell, from what I understand, was—is—a man who has a great deal of knowledge about China and about how to win wars..."

"There are some who disagree," said Mrs. Ai.

"Chennault," said Mr. Ai.

Henry agreed, "Chennault is a very knowledgeable military man, particularly concerning air power. Controversial to some— but smart."

Mr. and Mrs. Ai nodded.

"But in my opinion, Stilwell probably understands China as well as any American, with the possible exception of Edgar Snow. He understands Chiang Kaishek, he understands the need for social reform."

"And the need to include all of China in the struggle," said Mr. Ai.

"I think he does, at least to the extent any American does." Henry's voice was rising. "What I don't think Stilwell understands—no, no more tea, thank you—is politics." Henry bounced on the bench, which rattled on the bare wood floor, nearly tipping over. "He did not understand what Roosevelt wanted to hear about China and America's future. Patrick Hurley, he's one of the political bigshots, he does—he's better, it seems, with American politicians, whether or not he cares about them. Stilwell, on the other hand, just told Marshall and the bigshots how he saw it here, about the real conditions, and the only real prospects for a decent future as far as China's, not America's, priorities. And he got dumped for saying it." Henry sat back, smiling sadly.

An hour later, he was nestled under the dinner table, wrapped in a green wool Army Issue blanket he would never have been able to find at the base. And it was some minutes before he realized that the light, beautiful tones lulling him to sleep were not the music box he had brought, but little Wei, singing its melody.

*   *   *   *

The library was quiet, as most of the men were at dinner. The sky was quiet and empty; no planes had gone out since morning.

"You're red; you go first," said Drum.

McPhee edged a checker at a diagonal. "You know, I didn't really want to play."

Drum moved a checker with a chubby finger. "I appreciate the favor. How's Billy?"

"Mom says what's left of his arm's pretty well healed. Getting fitted for a hook. He says we won't need a gaff for fishing next summer." McPhee smiled faintly. "Guess if he's joking about it, he can't be doing too badly."

Drum grimaced. "Didn't see that jump coming."

McPhee went on. "His best therapy has been Lady. Not so much what she's done, but the way she keeps him company, keeps his spirits up." He rubbed the sides of his face between thumb and forefinger, his blond stubble making a scratching sound. "Don't think I ever asked. You have a dog?"

Drum shook his head. "They make Marie sneeze. Besides, she's always at that damn plant. Double shifts, you know? If we had a dog, it'd probably starve."

McPhee shook his head. "Nothing like a dog. No offense, but I find them more faithful than girls."

"Doesn't seem to keep you from trying. Anyway, some day that'll change."

McPhee shook his head, starting to get angry. "Lady'd never..."

"Not Lady. You. You'll change."

"We'll see. Now, don't tell me you didn't see *that* jump coming! Don't snow me here, Major!"

Drum cleared his throat. "So what's Bill going to do?"

"Mom says he's talking about becoming a teacher."

"That's ironic. Marie's being taken away from being a teacher in favor of building planes and all."

McPhee's eyes went dull. "Billy'd love to be building planes, believe me." He exhaled, long and slow. "I dream about Lady, you know. We're running together. No place in particular. Just running. King me."

Drum nodded. "Been doing any reading?"

McPhee shook his head. "Just magazines mom sends. You?"

"History, as usual. Chinese history, lately."

McPhee eyed him. "Those Chinese fellas Neiberg and Singer brought around got you interested."

"Yup. Interesting fellas, I thought. Didn't you?"

"What do I care about a bunch of local Chinks?"

"Well, even if you don't, what they said was relevant to the war. I had coffee with Neiberg yesterday, and he was telling me more about his friends. You know, I like knowing about it if there're some adept Chinese units someplace, especially if they're establishing communication links, freeing up areas. And if Chiang is threatening to switch sides, I'd like to..."

McPhee pushed the table away. Red and black disks slid across the table, clattering to the floor, some rolling across the room.

"What's the matter with you?"

McPhee shrugged as he walked towards the library door. "I didn't feel like playing in the first place."

* * * *

"I'll watch for Xiang," Bing Po said, holding the bicycle as Neil Ku Nuli stood unsteadily on its seat and tacked up the wall newspaper. He wondered how woman-who-talks-too-much managed to concentrate so well on so many things.

"Xiang has a new ally," Bing Po said. "He's been away for spy training—Professor Shin told me so."

Neil Ku knew Chen Liduo had been trained by a special Army division. He knew also that these wall newspapers and the recruitment and sympathy they might bring would fight the tactics of people like Chen Liduo and Xiang and the powerful Dr. Wu. He knew also that civil war was inevitable and that it would be no "tea party," and he longed to discuss these things with Bing Po, who, he imagined, would be a typical woman of New China—speaking her mind on all, even taboo, subjects.

But instead, what he said was, "hold the posters; I'm coming down. We'll put the next one on that dormitory at the bottom of the hill."

What had changed? He leaned forward on the bicycle, his chest against her back, and tried to remember when this roadblock in their conversation had arrived. His lips accidentally brushed the soft skin at the nape of her neck, and he remembered.

"You were writing in your journal this morning?" she asked. He did not answer. "And you will again, tomorrow." She turned around until he could see the right side of her face. She was smiling subtly and, as they dismounted, he wondered about his feelings. He was glad of her interest in his future, annoyed by what he perceived as meddling and yet, physically aware of her as he had never been of anyone before. He traced this awareness to the visit to the Minority People. His even disposition, the calm that had pervaded his life since leaving Chengdu for school life in Kunming, had been shattered, not by war, not by social upheaval, disease, poverty or corruption—but by a woman.

13

Lin Teu ignored the green-eyed American GI standing outside the dormitory, wondering only briefly why he might be shivering. For a Chinese to be improperly dressed on a chilly Kunming evening was commonplace, but an American GI ought to be well supplied. Oh, well. There had certainly been many a lovesick American GI hovering around Chinese student girls, even after the liquor wore off!

She found Shiyan in a chair, reading a child's storybook in English, which she knew her friend had been practicing. She quickly sized up the situation. The American GI was feeding Jane's grief, reminding her of her poor brother so that she might be more dependent on him.

She sat down on the nearest mat. "I'd have thought you'd have outgrown such children's stories." She saw Shiyan's eyes move in her direction; the rest of her face remained motionless. "Wouldn't a school text or a political newspaper or even a wall newspaper be more..."

"Why are you so interested in what I read?"

"Little sister, I—"

"Don't call me that!"

"I only meant..."

"I don't care. Don't *ever* call me that!"

Lin Teu stood up and took Shiyan's hand. "I understand more than you might think. Tong Xie was like my brother. I had hopes that someday..." She shrugged. "I know now that I can never marry..."

"Why have you come here?" Shiyan interrupted.

"I have a fantasy." She let go of Shiyan's hand and sat down, facing her. "I imagine I am well. That is the fantasy. Simple, isn't it? I pretend that Tong Xie's spirit is with me, and I can go about my life. I can work, study—I can live. I can function."

Shiyan looked up, her eyes full of doubt, her expression pained.

"I know," Lin said quickly. "It would not be like before. There's still no feeling; I am like a nutshell with no meat inside, but I can serve a purpose. I leave my room in the morning, do what's expected of me, using my fantasy to hold me up, like an old man's walking stick."

Shiyan's eyes filled with tears. "I was not reading this book for my brother..." She began to cry, and then to sob, her shoulders shaking. Lin Teu's arms went around her neck, and as Shiyan cried, a memory came to her of two little girls playing with shirt puppets and their imaginations.

＊   ＊   ＊   ＊

It was dawn in Kunming, and the sun came up red over the green rice paddies and light brown fields. The ground was wet, glistening until the dew dried in the morning sun, leaving only the hot, pungent aroma of fertile plants. Normally, Cha Siansheng would make his way among the stores in the marketplace or, if he were too ill, the merchants might send their sons by bicycle or oxcart to his farm. Either way, storekeepers such as Ju Shaotse would find a way to receive their supplies.

Today, Cha Siansheng found Ju Shaotse's store empty, his ovens cold, and utensils and platters scattered. Old dough had hardened on the countertops. Since the death of his wife, Shaotse had relied in his thoughts on his only son, Weima, for his future. Everything he had done was with an eye and a hope toward Weima's future. Now there was none, and Shaotse's future was dead, and the suddenly old storekeeper stayed in his room, flat on his back, waiting for his own life to end.

*   *   *   *

In the evening, Shiyan danced with Stan Siansheng. Before the shooting he had been American Stan. Now he had earned the title of respect: Siansheng. Slowly, her face pressed against the smooth green of Stan Siansheng's uniform collar, and they swayed to the absurdly rapid beat and watched the moon rise and the sky brighten through the wide Rec Hall window. The radio was too loud and Stan moved to turn it down, but Shiyan held his wrist and his normally excuse-filled mind was blank and for once turned outwards, towards Shiyan.

"Before I came to school, Mary Cha told me in a letter about the three scramblings," Shiyan said.

"What are they?" Stan murmured, the Rec Hall's walls seemed to be turning, carousel-like around him.

"For rice in our bowls, for a seat in the library, and for a classroom in which to learn." She breathed a sigh against his cheek. "I like this music, even though it's too fast."

He knew there would be a lot of trouble when they were caught, and a small part of his mind searched and sniffed for escape. But the greater, newly born part of his mind made a decision from which there was no turning back. It was a choice born of the few sentences Shiyan had spoken about Mary Cha, and of his own experiences with her; it was born of the expression—not of fear, but of need—in Shiyan's beautiful, upturned eyes.

The decision made, he closed his eyes, patted Shiyan's hair with the tips of his fingers so that she leaned against his shoulder, and together they felt the music and the cool evening air on their hot skin.

*   *   *   *

Xiang lit a cigarette and tilted his chair back. The others were leaning eagerly forward while Dr. Wu discussed the difficulty of infiltrating and gleaning information from the newly organized students and citizens. There were difficulties, too, the professor remarked, with the local politicians and school administrators.

"The army," Wu said, with a sly glance at Colonel Yin, "can do things in a more straightforward way. But here in civilian life, we must organize carefully, more subtly. We must watch our adversaries like the cat watches the bird—while pretending to do something else. We wear no uniforms here."

Xiang spat on the floor, and ground his cigarette in the wetness. He ran his fingers back through his stubbly hair, comforted somehow by this contact with himself. He noticed that the Colonel alone among the others in the room seemed to share his boredom with Dr. Wu's speech. The Colonel's eyes were heavy-lidded beneath the brim of his cap, so Xiang was as startled as anyone by the whip-snap of his words.

"Ridiculous!" the Colonel declared. Dr. Wu stepped back, and Colonel Yin rose slowly as though those in the room ought to have known what he was about to say, and his effort in standing and speaking was unnecessary.

"All this talk of subtlety and the nature of military versus civilian operations—nonsense!" The Colonel barked a laugh and Xiang laughed too, in spite of himself.

"None of this matters, you see, once we employ a plan." The Colonel cleared his throat. "Yes, a plan and the services of a professional."

Xiang's laugh turned to a gasp when into the open doorway stepped his old friend, Chen Liduo.

*   *   *   *

The SCU was dismissed and, free for the day, Henry went to Grandview Park to watch the ducks. Grandview reminded him of New York City's Inwood Park, where he had walked so often with Frances, except that Grandview was more open, less shaded, and it lacked the huge tulip tree that was Inwood's centerpiece. With fear and loneliness as a motivation, convincing himself that the grass and sky were Brooklynese, rather than Chinese, required little effort. His eyes strayed upward less than at the base, and loud noises and sudden movements were few. Sounds, smells, and the slow pace of ducks and families comforted Henry, reminding him of home. He watched a young couple strolling and holding hands, and a family laughing and pointing to the ducks that paddled under the bridge.

He wondered what Frances was doing at that moment. Was she sleeping; was she dreaming of him? Did she think of him as much as he thought of her? Was she starting to forget him, and was forgetting him easy? Perhaps she was strolling the Coney Island boardwalk with Gartman right now, he thought, then remembered that New York was probably cold.

Back in the barracks, Henry had a few minutes before dinner, so he climbed onto his bunk, took out his writing paper and pen, and tried to write the letter Mr. and Mrs. Ai had suggested. Why not just go ahead and propose? That way, she could write back, telling him he must be crazy, and that she was already engaged to Gartman, who was sympathetic to every poor person walking the earth. Then he could set about forgetting her.

But the pen refused to cooperate, and Henry flipped onto his back, staring at a bit of darkened wood over his bunk. The twin knots-for-eyes looked down at him. The wood's grain reminded him of the barrette. He reached into his pocket, took the barrette out, and looked at it for a long time.

*   *   *   *

Neil Ku Nuli had been sleeping only three hours when Chin Chuzi came to wake him; the dormitory was still dark and for a moment he thought Chuzi was his grandfather, up early to treat a patient on the other side of Chengdu.

"I know you want to sleep, but it will be light soon and they will see us putting up our newspapers."

"Right, as usual." Neil Ku pulled himself up and took two of the four bundles of papers Chuzi had brought. Sung Hongai would go with Chuzi to the far end of Lianda, and he and Bing Po would begin at this end.

Outside, he blinked in the darkness, waiting for his eyes to focus. Under the tree at the other side of the road, he could make out the youthful shape of Bing Po, who, it seemed, never tired and never became hungry. The thought of food often sustained him through the walking and climbing and confrontations with other newspaper associations. Bing Po seemed to need no such crutch. She was able to carry bundles of newspapers as long as necessary; her ability seemed to grow with the size of the task.

"Come on," Bing Po laughed, "the sky is becoming light. Chong Lingxiu was right. You prefer sleep to putting up newspapers."

He stared at her a moment before he realized she was teasing him. As he woke up, he tried talking more, but she seemed to become engrossed in their work and increasingly reticent—or perhaps this was another kind of teasing.

"So you like getting up in the middle of the night and putting up newspapers?" He had to reach up high to cover the top of a poster bearing Chiang Kaishek's likeness.

"I like to do what's necessary."

"And not sleeping or eating doesn't bother you?"

"You ask silly questions, Neil Ku Nuli."

As he stepped down from the seat of the bicycle, Neil Ku saw her smile to herself.

"So you think I'm funny." He began walking towards the next wall, but Bing Po stopped and put her hand to her mouth. "Look what they've written!" Neil Ku's lips moved as he read to himself: "Chong Lingxiu Disrupts Learning and Was Forced to Run Away" and "Neil Ku Nuli is Insincere and Should Step Down" and, in the largest letters, above the others "Neil Ku was Seen Taking Money from Landlord's Sons."

With a cry, Bing Po slammed the bicycle against the wall, leaped atop its seat and tore the posters from the wall, pinning Chin Chuzi's words over them. Neil Ku stood in the road, open-mouthed.

"'The Government Hoards American Supplies for Civil War,'" he read, with satisfaction. Bing Po climbed down and stood next to him. "Who would write lies about you?"

"You'd be surprised at what some people know about Neil Ku Nuli." Three tall students stood on the other side of the road, their arms folded. The one who had spoken carried a thick tree branch and a bundle of wall newspapers. Bing Po hopped onto the bicycle, ready to pedal away. Neil Ku got between the three young men and the wall.

"People know the truth when they read it, whether about me or where the Lend Lease money goes—where we all see it going." Neil's voice was soft, but steady. "I understand the Chen family's doing very well, not to mention the Soongs, Chiangs and Kungs."

At the mention of the famous Four Families, Chiang Kaishek's relatives, the student with the branch ran forward and whacked Neil Ku across the legs. His two friends ran to the wall, one climbing on the other's back to tear down the newly placed paper. The branch-wielder had gone to give his friends one of their own papers to tack up.

Neil Ku started after them, but his leg collapsed beneath him. "Think about why you're doing this! Think about who the enemy really is! What would your brothers and fathers and grandfathers say? We're trying to help everyone!"

The student with the stick whirled around. "What would they say? They'd be proud we're taking revenge for their deaths. We want revenge for Nanking, and without a unified China, that will never happen." He took a step toward Neil Ku.

"Nuli!" Bing Po cried, sliding forward on the seat. Something in her voice was not to be disputed, and Neil Ku limped quickly to her, swung his damaged leg over the seat and held on while Bing Po pedaled away.

*   *   *   *

The knock was Chen Liduo's special code and Xiang hastily lifted the needle from the crackling record and the operatic aria was replaced by the creaking hinge on his door.

Liduo came into the room and stood before him, his hands crossed in front of his belt. Except for a stiffer way of standing he looked no different than usual.

"You seem afraid of me," said Liduo. His tone of voice was such that Xiang was compelled to light a cigarette, clear his throat twice, and spit onto the floor next to the rug before answering.

Xiang laughed and sat back in his cushioned chair, unable to meet Liduo's eyes. "I've always been impressed by athletic training. It's not for me, though."

"But you played soccer."

"Only now and then. Soccer's a game. Your athletics—no game."

"That's right. We're not in one war; we're in two. And we've got to be willing to do anything to win."

"Remember, Liduo," Xiang used a patronizing tone, "you are my 'little brother'."

"I used to believe that. Now, I think the tables are turned. Experience and courage more than age are what make an older brother."

Xiang scrambled to retain the upper hand. "There's a place for both of us. It is a virtue for me to know my limitations, don't you think?" He laughed nervously and ground his half smoked cigarette into the rug.

"You're a disgusting hypocrite, who lectures and poses very well but does nothing." Liduo squatted on his heels so that he and Xiang were eye to eye. "I've learned a few things, Xiang. Not only about extracting information and inflicting pain, though there was that, too. I've learned that when the Japanese finally surrender, we will be brought to receive the surrender."

"How?" Xiang was astounded. This was no longer little Liduo—the instructors had changed him, added years to his life experience.

"How?" Chen laughed. "We'll be there. With help, if necessary. And I've learned that we don't need the weapons and money we've received from our allies, at least not to fight the invaders; it will all be put to better use."

"I knew that," was all Xiang managed to say.

"Did you?" Chen Liduo stood up and lifted a corner of the cloth covering the bird cage. He smiled and the smile terrified Xiang.

"But most important, I've learned that my former teacher, who I thought was a warrior, is only a field mouse."

As Chen Liduo closed the door behind him, there came a sharp cackle from the covered birdcage, and Xiang took the record from the victrola and flung it against the wall, but the disk struck the cloth tapestry broadside and fell to the floor, unbroken.

*   *   *   *

On spring mornings there was normally a bustling, perpetual motion in the air at the 14th Army Air Corps. Planes roared from runways, men shouted and cursed in English and Chinese, children warred over bits of food in garbage bins and exclaimed at a glimpse of some never-before-seen trinket shown to them by a GI opening his mail out-of-doors. Noisy birds cawed above growling jeeps and trucks; dogs and officers barked at the enlisted men.

But on this particular morning, when Henry and Jake opened the door and stepped outside, there was such silence that the slam of the barracks door behind them was as startling as a gunshot.

One would have thought that the base had picked up and moved, were it not for the men standing or sitting along the road.

They looked at one another, each thinking the same thought. Blanche wasn't the only one who had sent pictures of the German camps. Henry and Jake had sat, stunned, when they read the accounts she had sent. Death camps, gas. Thousands, perhaps millions of civilians, Jews mostly, murdered in Europe.

Dozens of men from their unit were milling about, some shaking their heads, others crying, all looking lost.

Colonel Root walked by, one eyebrow up, the other curled low over a cold eye. "Yeah, I know. But, you'll get over it." He waggled a thumb. "Just remember, you've all got jobs to do, whether the President's alive or no. So don't sit around crying too long."

And he was gone.

Henry ran up to the nearest soldier. "Roosevelt's dead?"

The soldier was swaying slowly forward and back. He looked right through Henry, not answering.

Henry and Jake sat down where they were on the ground. Silently, Jake's face twisted and he began to cry; Henry was too stunned to speak. In his head he heard The Voice of the *Fireside Chats*, which seemed to speak to him personally. With no disrespect to his own father, who, he knew, felt exactly the same way, Roosevelt had been a father—he had been all their fathers.

And he felt his chest constrict and the air rush from his lungs.

*   *   *   *

Lin Teu washed each piece of clothing and handed it to Shiyan, who wrung it dry and laid it over the fence. Lin nudged the wash basin over.

"He surprised me," said Shiyan, hesitating. Speaking of such things was nearly impossible, but not speaking of them had become out of the question. "He was kind, understanding. I never expected that. Wulin would be furious." That last thought was not as amusing as it once might have been.

"Huh," said Lin Teu. She rubbed the shirt with extra energy.

Shiyan thought for a moment. "I think he wants to stay with me."

Lin Teu didn't answer her right away. They finished, and Lin rinsed the basin and put it away in the dormitory, after which they washed themselves and lay down on their mats.

"You don't have to decide anything now," said Teu. "Wait. See what happens." She did not admit that she was jealous.

"I miss my brother so much," said Shiyan, and her tone of voice made Lin Teu roll onto her side and stroke the side of Shiyan's face.

"American Stan isn't so bad," she whispered. "Some of the other Americans aren't so bad, either."

Shiyan lay on her mat, listening to her own breath. It was only when she cried quietly for a few minutes, the way she did each night, that her body felt comfortable enough, her muscles loose enough to relax and sleep.

14

The woman with the new clothes was buying the entire con-
tents of her father's cart, and there wasn't a thing Cha Wulin
could do about it. She knew that when they arrived at elder sister's
father's store, there would be nothing left to sell. Why was her
father allowing such a ridiculous thing?

Soon they were on the dust covered road to Kunming, Cha
Siansheng coughing and urging the old water buffalo on. Wulin
was in the cart, cross-legged in the coarse straw, thinking how
strange the empty cart seemed and how scratchy the straw was
against her legs.

She awoke with a start, the well-dressed woman a vanishing
image while the straw in the loft around her rubbed white marks
on her legs. Her arms ached from trying to throw the pitchfork the
previous afternoon the way the men in her picturebook threw the
javelin. She was improving. What she wouldn't give to be graceful
and elegant! Chickens pecked and clucked below her, and as her
eyelids drooped again and fell, she thought of her green eyed
American soldier friend and his western smell.

Several miles away a man was standing so close to a thick tree
that his grey, loose clothing blended with its bark and his face
resembled a round spot of mold between its boughs. He stood so

still that the birds forgot about him and resumed their noise and the field animals downwind grew accustomed to what little scent he had.

Without shifting his weight, he looked up at the sky and imagined the planes, the red dots on their wings like droplets of his family's blood. He remembered his mother and sisters, and his grandfather's futile efforts to protect them, while he, the supposed protector, the strong grandson, could only watch from afar.

He remembered his orders, however distorted by rage and loss they might have become. He had become useful, and that was enough.

The spot of mold shifted ever so slightly and, after being still a moment, disengaged from the tree, along with the rest of Chen Liduo, and headed for the Gong Family farm.

*   *   *   *

The twins danced around the yard, singing and playing the chicken feed game, leading the chickens in concentric circles by leaving winding trails of feed. Once the chickens were well along this route, Guelo would follow them, strutting and gaggling, like an oversized hen. So persuasive was her imitation that more than a few hens would join her conversation and waddle after her, never missing a beat. Ting Siao would sprinkle feed from the other direction, and in this way the twins passed an hour each afternoon, teasing and feeding their father's chickens.

Occasionally, young Chong Tanshi would join them and watch or try to imitate Guelo's chicken calls—which was impossible since hers had been perfected over an entire lifetime. More often though, Tanshi would do as his father had taught him and ignore the twins in favor of his textbooks. Chong Lingxiu's academic standards had been high, and even the twins were occasionally influenced into giving up their chicken game in favor of the appearance of study.

Today, Chong Lingxiu was in the village, and Tanshi's head was so overwhelmed with his studies that he joined the twins, as a long, winding line of feed, chickens and children snaked around the yard, clucking, bricking and bracking.

"Wait, do you hear them?" Guelo asked, stopping so suddenly that her sister ran into her back, and they tumbled to the ground.

Ting Siao brushed bits of feed from her elbows. "Two or three are still in there." She pulled open the door to the shed.

"Let me get them," Tanshi said. "Those hens will listen to reason from me." Laughing, he went into the shed. There was a quick bumping sound followed by silence.

The twins looked at one another. Ting Siao stepped into the shed and found herself instantly on her back, a hand over her mouth, a knife at her throat. Instinctively, she began to struggle, but a voice interrupted.

"Call your sister into the shed. Do as I say, or I'll kill you both." The voice was quiet, flat, like that of the neighbor's boy, who was unnaturally slow-witted.

In a shaky voice, she agreed, and did as she was told, and in a moment, she and Guelo were sitting next to Tanshi, who was face down in the straw. Blood seeped from the side of his head, staining the straw brown.

Facing them, the man with the knife watched her with an animal's eyes.

Chong Siansheng and Daddy will be back soon enough. They'll have something to say about this!

Guelo had begun to whimper, and the man with the knife hissed at her to shut up. He was tanned dark from the sun and his accent was from the North.

Taking her sister's hand, Ting Siao was comforted by her own ability to wait for that inevitable change in their circumstance. She had been able to out-wait Cha Wulin and even Chong Tanshi at all their games. Only Tanshi's father, Chong Lingxiu—or Chong Siansheng, as she called him out of respect—had bested her at waiting games. And now she waited for Chong Siansheng himself, comforted by the knowledge of inevitable change. Chong Siansheng had explained to her that he had perfected his own waiting technique in prison. He had, for a long time, avoided thoughts of his son, Tanshi, who, he told people, must certainly be dead. But he had never truly believed his son dead. Convincing others that this was his belief was a great convenience, but he had refused to believe it himself. He neither believed nor disbelieved, but avoided the thought entirely.

By waiting very well.

He focused on each day as it came, the experiences, the thoughts, the physical feelings. And he was able to learn to wait quietly and so, to finally see Tanshi again.

Ting Siao sighed and settled down in the straw, her body relaxing around the thoughts of inevitable change, but as her eyes focused on the man from the North, she grew cold because she saw in his flat, animal eyes that he, too, was waiting.

*   *   *   *

The low wooden Statistical Control Unit was lit by two bare bulbs that hung from the rafters. In the afternoons, the shadows given off by the bulbs lengthened, and a faint smell of human sweat overcame that of the bare wood.

Major Drum leaned back behind his desk, rubbing one edge of his blond moustache between a thumb and forefinger. His eyelids drooped. The rustlings of pencils on paper lulled him along with the echoing chirps of hundreds of early crickets.

"So, what's the big news today?" Warren asked.

Danko answered, laying his pencil down. "My sister says the law firm around the block has got a Negro lawyer."

"That so?" Warren said.

Jake looked up. "People who weren't getting jobs before are sure getting 'em now. Women, too."

"Yah. My sister'll be graduating in a few weeks," Danko continued. "Goin' to the prom with that fella she's been dating. The girl needs a chaperone. She was at this fella's apartment the other day, listening to records."

Drum blinked awake. "In, you mean in the apartment?"

"That's what I said. She's got no sense."

"Maybe they were just listening to records."

"They'd better've been. It's her reputation...And another thing, she reads the papers too much. She's sure that, what with all these suicide attacks, they're going to bomb over there. Lot of folks're pretty scared about that now."

Drum shook his head. "Wisconsin? They'll have to make it over a whole lot of America to bomb Wisconsin."

"Well, it's an attractive target, what with them building those planes..."

"Excuse me," said Henry, "but those kamikazes want to do more than damage. They want to scare the heck out of people. Wouldn't bombing one of the east coast cities be the way to really cause a panic? And they could fly right in, unlike Wisconsin."

"Is this the stuff you think about?" McPhee asked, shaking his head.

"How're they going to fly right in from the Atlantic?" Warren wanted to know.

"Heck of a lot easier than bombing Racine, Wisconsin," Henry answered.

"I'd think that Detroit'd be a much more attractive target for them," Warren said, with more than a hint of pride.

Everyone had stopped work now, and had put down their pencils. Only the occasional clatter of adding machine keys punctuated the conversation.

"Well, but again," Henry said, "they'd have to fly over—"

"We're talking about the most important targets," Warren said. "This is, what d'ya call that word, imaginary."

"Hypothetical," Jake corrected.

"Tell you this," said Henry. "They're safe in Cleveland. Jeez, what'd you do that for?" He rubbed his shin where Jake had just kicked it. "Oh." He looked around, but it was too late.

"Where the hell is Freilich?" Drum asked suddenly.

"Infirmary," Henry said, hoping that saying it quickly would make the lie somehow less offensive.

"Dysentery again?" Drum asked.

Not wanting to compound the lie, Henry didn't answer.

"Don't say that word," Stabler moaned. "I crapped blood the first week we were here. Besides, everyone knows if they bomb us, they'll bomb California, for sure. My mother's got it all figured out."

"Then they'll be bombing a lot of their own people," said Jake. "Those camps we've got 'em in are an awful lot like the ones in Germany, and guess where they are?"

"They're not at all like the ones in Germany," McPhee said. "Don't put it that way."

Drum tried to clear the air. "So, Kenny. Pratt and Whitney'd be an attractive target. And Connecticut's on the coast…"

"Wrong coast," Stabler pointed out.

Drum frowned and made an "easy, guy," gesture, pressing his palm down. "Say, how's Bill doing?"

McPhee shrugged. "Well enough, I guess."

"Lady taking good care of him?"

McPhee didn't answer.

"What's the matter, Ken?" Drum sat forward, his uniformed stomach pressed against the desk. "Want to play a few games of checkers when we get off?"

"I don't think so." He swallowed. "Got a letter from Ma. About Charlie."

Drum continued to look at McPhee. "Something happen to Charlie, Ken?"

McPhee nodded. "Guess maybe Lady needed some help with Bill. That's the way Ma's looking at it, anyway."

"What happened, Ken? How're you looking at it?"

The adding machines stopped, as did the rustling of clothing and pencils.

"He was in a place called Los Banos, near Manila."

Stabler muttered, "the bathrooms," then shrugged to himself and looked at the ledger in front of him.

McPhee didn't seem to hear. "In late February. There was a camp there. A couple of thousand people, not just men, but women and kids. The 11th Airborne Division was supposed to try to get them out. That's what MacArthur's plan was, anyway. Problem was, the camp was behind enemy lines. I don't know exactly what the plan was, or what Charlie was supposed to be doing, but he turned up missing. The raid itself was a success, but I don't even know if my brother got there, or maybe it happened afterwards because he was missing at sea and the raid ended with the prisoners in amphibious vehicles."

The only sound in the room was McPhee's hard breathing. "The men came to my mom's house with the telegram. My dad had some kind of attack or something. Collapsed right there on the porch and it was a good thing Bill was there because Dad had to be helped inside."

"This was in February?" Drum asked.

McPhee nodded. "His obit was in the paper back home. They didn't want to tell me, so no one sent it. Well, then, they found him. They didn't tell my family, but they found him a few days later, alive, floating with some debris. The reason they didn't say anything for nearly a month was they were grilling him."

Drum nodded. "That's what they do with men found at sea. They could be saboteurs put there by you-know-who to be picked up. So they ask a lot of questions."

"I suppose so." Elbows on his desk, McPhee squeezed his eyes shut, then yelled at the top of his lungs. "I've gotta get outta here!"

"Way it's going in the Pacific," said Warren, "you will be soon."

"So, ah, Warren." McPhee turned slowly, his voice dead calm. "How's your brother?"

Startled, Warren pulled back, as though from a slap. "I don't have a—"

"Sure, you do. Curley told me you won't accept his letters. Why is that, by the way?"

Warren stood up, fists clenched, the veins in his forearms standing out. "He's a CO, that's why."

McPhee spoke as though talking to a child. "Doesn't approve of the war, does he?"

"McPhee, that's enough," Drum ordered.

"Come on, Major," McPhee continued. "This guy spends half his time in his little garden. If I had to pick which guy's brother was chickenshit..."

"Sit down, Warren!" For a heavy man, Drum could move quickly. He was on his feet and between the men before either could move. "I said, sit down. And Kenny, better watch what you say. Warren spends the other half of his time lifting those home-made weights of his. Getta load of the build he made for him-self…"

"We've got some real winners in this outfit," McPhee was grumbling.

"Ken," Henry said, gently. "We know how you feel."

McPhee whirled, glaring. "And you're at the top of the list. Don't pity me. I don't need that, especially from you. I know they've been censoring your mail for months now, and I'm pretty sure the brass wouldn't be too happy about you two sheenies making such good friends with our ally's enemy…"

Jake looked at McPhee. "You know, if I had a brother and—"

McPhee turned on him. "Well, you don't have a brother. In fact, from what I remember, you don't even have parents. Why don't the two of you kikes leave me alone. I've had enough of you, and your Chink buddies, too. Who told you to make friends with those guys, anyway? Since they're our ally's enemy, wouldn't that make them our enemy too?"

"They're good people, Ken." Jake spoke calmly, reasonably.

"Well, maybe that's what they want you to think." McPhee's face was red. Danko had gotten up out of his seat and was stand-ing over McPhee. "And you, sit down!" He turned back to Jake. "And just maybe you did exactly what they wanted you to do, bringing 'em here to the base, so they could look around, size things up. You know, Neiberg." McPhee pointed at him. "I've got a mind to—"

Jake interrupted. "You have a mind to what?"

"Warren," said Drum. "Why don't you punch out early, and take McPhee here for a spin around those dumbells you made."

"Not me, sir."

"I don't think you get it, Warren. I wasn't asking."

Jake saw an opportunity to diffuse the situation. "How're those carrots doing, Warren?"

Mickey Warren smiled. "They're doing their job. I haven't had a cold in months. Now I'm trying to grow roses and impatiens."

McPhee was looking at Henry. "You guys'll get yours."

"Our what?" Henry said. "We're not doing a thing wrong, Kenny. You're forgetting that there were plenty of brass at our forums. If anything was out of line, they'd'd've—"

"Neiberg, let it be," Drum said, pressing both palms slowly down in front of him.

*   *   *   *

Chong Lingxiu thought of his son, as he and Fu Ma sat at the front of the wagon. They had grown comfortable together and he was glad of that. It was something that had worried him. How would he get along with his son's surrogate father? For that was what Gong Fu Ma was. Would he disapprove of anything and if so, how would he manage to refrain from showing disrespect? And how would his son receive him after five years? Here he was, suddenly intruding on his son's new life, and not even on a visit— he was hiding! A revolutionary on the run! Not the best of circumstances. Certainly no tea party, as the saying went.

But Tanshi understood that was how his father must arrive because, the boy explained, that was who his father was. And Lingxiu had laughed at that, because it was so simple and so perfect, and because he was proud that such a thought had come from his own son.

Lingxiu had been waiting to deliver a letter from Jane Shiyan to Mary Cha Wulin. He had wanted to wait for the proper time to bring such difficult news. Cha Wulin undoubtedly had known Shiyan's brother and would be grief stricken at the news of his death, particularly coming as it did at the hands of government soldiers, accident or no.

Lingxiu sighed as they entered the farm grounds. Perhaps Mary Cha would be heartened that Shiyan had been comforted by Lin Teu and that the two girls were now the closest of friends. Or perhaps Cha would be jealous that her place had been taken, with both her best friend and with the American GI. This was his dilemma, yet it was not. He had no control over these circumstances, just as he had none over Mary Cha's reaction to them. He sighed again as they stopped the cart. Sometimes he wished he had had at least one daughter!

He helped Fu Ma place large stones against the rear wagon wheels and removed the reins from the waterbuffalo. Fu Ma held the shed door open for him.

There was a wet sound of flesh giving way, and a hot light passed through his leg, tearing muscle and tendon, and damaging bone as it plunged in and then downward. A dull thud and Fu Ma was beside him in the dirt. In a corner of his vision, he saw his son's closed eyes and the blood on the shed floor.

An ant crawled near his face. He could see its antenna feeling curiously toward him; an instant later it was swept away on a brown tide of blood. The scream he heard told him two things: at least one of the twins was alive, and Chen Liduo had captured them all. The reports he had received told him it could be no one else.

He heard one more faint noise, and this sound he could not place—a tiny scrape from high above him.

*   *   *   *

Henry Neiberg sat on top of his neatly made bunk, oblivious to the noise of the GIs around him. Letters from Frances were scattered on his bunk. He read each one through, and then began again, closing his eyes and imagining her voice reading them to him.

He piled the letters on top of one another, reached into his pocket, took out her barrette, and lay it gently on top of the pile. Then, with the barrette in their center, he folded them into as small a square as he could, swung down from the bunk, and hurried out the door.

"Where ya going?" Jake called after him, but Henry was gone, towards the outskirts of the base.

When he reached the trenches, he found the spot he was looking for and began to dig. He had forgotten to bring anything to dig with, so he scooped up the loose dirt with his fingernails, lay the letters and barrette at the bottom of the hole, and replaced the dirt.

"So I've changed," he muttered, as he patted down the pile and clapped the dirt from his hands. "Well, maybe I have."

He walked around the trenches, within sight of the base's outer wall. He knelt beside Warren's gardens, inhaling the familiar fragrances, and trying to dispel the fear brought on by McPhee's tirade.

Jake talked about what life would be like when they got home. And this became a new fear to obsess over. Would all that American ingenuity and hard work that was winning the war continue afterwards? Would the Depression return? Would anyone ever have faith in the stock market? Would he get back to college?

He hadn't thought about college during his entire hitch. It was where he'd met Frances, yet the thought of college had flown out of his mind once the war began in earnest, after Pearl Harbor.

What kind of living could he earn without depending on his father's position?

Would he ever see Mr. and Mrs. Ai and Neil Ku and the others again?

Suddenly he was running back towards the base, towards the motor pool, hunting desperately for someone, anyone, who might be heading into town.

"There you are. I've been looking all over for you!" Danko ran up, breathless. "McPhee's on the warpath."

"I know. I saw. What's it got to do with me?"

"He's going to Root to talk to him about your Chinese buddies. He's got it in for you guys."

Henry shook his head. "The guy needs a doctor. His brothers' had some bad luck, so he's coming after me?"

"Just watch your back, okay?"

*   *   *   *

A few hours later and several miles away, Stan Freilich leaned back against a tree and strained his eyes against the darkness. The sky was moonless and cloud-covered; he could barely see Shiyan. Beside him was a box containing what he knew was the last package he would ever receive from home. It had been sent at his request by an old Cleveland buddy he had not seen since their *bar mitzvahs,* which had been one week apart.

He had never been a brave man, nor was he anything but patriotic, yet here he was seriously considering desertion. He wondered if he ought to tell Jane; he suspected she knew.

He was in love, and love had made him whole. He had courage, a sense of himself, a sense of a family. And he did not need a drink to celebrate it.

He tried to kiss her, and when she held him away, he could feel in her touch that this was not a rejection, but a way of saying "wait."

He breathed in the scent of her, relieved that she had agreed not to wear white just this once. Her mourning could go on when she returned to school.

"It was nice of Lin Teu to spend so much time with you," he said.

"She understands," Jane Shiyan whispered. "She can teach me to cope."

Stan nodded, and they sat down together on the cool earth. She leaned back, her shoulder all but touching his.

"Tong Xie was a revolutionary. Lin Teu will teach me his ways so I can kill the men who killed my brother."

He had begun opening the package and examining the books inside, running his fingers over the embossed gold on their covers. Now he drew back. "For God's sake, Jane, you're not going to kill anybody."

"I am going to be a soldier. You expect we will be a married couple? You are an American GI. You will be going home. If we had a family, who would feed...?"

"I'll help."

She laughed and he covered her mouth with his hand. "Stan Siansheng," she whispered. "American Stan."

"No. I'll stay with you, Shiyan. No more GI."

And Shiyan looked at him for a frozen moment, and she was drawn in two directions, straining against her own fear.

She threw her arms around his neck, kissing his face and pulling him fiercely to her. "We must find younger sister and tell her."

*　　　　*　　　　*　　　　*

At dawn the next morning, Stanley led Shiyan to a spot an eighth of a mile down the road from the front gate of the base.

"Wait here," he told her. "I'm going to my barracks to pick up a few necessities. I'll be back in five minutes."

He jogged to the barracks, slowing as he approached the enlisted mens' living area, and walked quietly into the barracks. He wrapped some clothes, shaving supplies and his clarinet in a blanket and slung it over his shoulder.

"What do you think you're doing?" Jake Singer stood, arms folded, at the foot of Stan's bunk.

Stan faced him. "I'm going to stay with Shiyan."

"You're deserting, Stan. You know what that means?"

"It means I've found the life I was meant to live. Think this'll hold together?"

"Stanley. They're going to come looking for you. You're not just romancing a local girl anymore. You're deserting. Let that sink in a minute. You'll never see anyone back in Cleveland. You'll never see another baseball game. And that's not to mention what they're going to do to you when they catch you. And they will catch you. The Army's really good at certain things, and that's a big one."

"Jake, I appreciate your concern, but I know what I'm doing." Stan smiled grimly.

Jake raised his eyebrows. "Well, you sure look more confident than I've ever seen you look. I'm sure they'll question Henry and me pretty thoroughly, so don't tell me where you're going. I only know you're involved with a local girl."

Stan nodded. "I understand you have to say at least that to protect yourselves. And I suppose it won't reflect very well on your other friends, Stabler and the rest."

"Never mind that. What you're doing reflects on you, no one else." He started to clap Stan on the shoulder, but pulled back. "I just hope you've thought this out and it's not, you know, infatuation."

"I've thought this out more than I've ever thought anything out. It's what I'm supposed to do."

Jake looked down, grounding his boot tips against the floor. "I don't know about that. Listen, everyone'll be up in a few minutes…"

They looked at one another for a moment, then Stan strode out the door, which bounced once off the sack on his shoulder, and banged shut. Jake stared at the door for several moments before gathering his razor, brush, and soap and heading for the latrine.

*   *   *   *

Chong Lingxiu sighed with what little breath he had. So it would end so simply for him. He would bleed to death in a hay shed on a farm, killed by one of his own son's schoolmates gone mad for revenge, his son dead beside him. A flood of rage rose in him, but he breathed again, ignoring the pain, until it receded and he heard the drone of Chen Liduo's voice—something about his family and the Japanese and this being his retribution. Something shifted again above them, and Chen Liduo stopped talking, stood up and pointed his knife up at the dark loft. He picked up a rock, threw it in that direction, and two startled doves flapped into the light, whipping around and around the shed, panicked, until Liduo opened the window, freeing them.

"Why don't you let the girls go?" Chong whispered.

"Shut up! You're here to pay for war crimes! For atrocities!"

"But I committed no atrocities. It was the Japanese, who are both of our enemies…"

"Shut up, I said! You are the enemy of my superiors. That is enough! You are trying to trick me! They told me you were expert at word fighting."

Lingxiu saw that Liduo was deranged with grief, and that those who had trained him had fed his sickness while strengthening his muscles and honing his reflexes.

"Yes, I confess," Chong said softly, and a slow smile spread across Chen Liduo's face. He grunted approvingly, as Chong continued. "I have committed crimes and I will pay..." He forced a look of confusion to come over his face. "But these children are innocent. Why not show me how a true war hero administers justice? Send them out the door, then kill me, and be on your way to punish some other war criminal. Why not—?"

The knife tore through his leg again. Lingxiu gasped.

"Shut up! I said, shut up!"

The pain shot up into his back, and Lingxiu moaned and watched Chen Liduo turn toward the first of the twins, raise his knife, and as he was about to bring it down, lean forward, as though his body were wracked by a cough. He continued to lean forward and Guelo managed to throw herself back so that Chen Liduo fell forward on his belly, just short of her lap, the iron pitchfork protruding from his back.

Mary Cha Wulin leaped down from the loft and began shouting orders. First Guelo was to help her sister, then the girls were to press clean rags torn from their shirt sleeves against all their wounds. She would take the oxcart in search of a doctor.

*   *   *   *

Mail call was the most exciting time of the Army day. Pictures of loved ones arrived along with news of the old neighborhood and detailed accounts of sporting events. Sights and smells of home towns, the fresh faces of girlfriends and kid sisters sprang from those paper God-sends delivered by Larry Curley and filtered through the censors. Mama's cooking and grandpa's catch-of-the-day traveled overseas along with little brother's report cards and Dad's business news.

But for weeks the mail had been the same. Eulogies and shared shock over the President's death and news of the German camps. While the war news seemed good, the future was confused without most everyone's surrogate father or uncle filling them in regularly over the radio. Whatever the new days would bring would certainly be different from anything anyone had imagined. And different could be frightening.

So the SCU was quiet; men soberly tore the ends off envelopes, read their contents, and looked away.

No one met anyone else's eyes. Henry was nowhere to be found. Jake was napping, snoring softly. He had fallen asleep on his back, a letter from Blanche resting on his chest. Louis Stabler fitted a picture of his new son between the springs of the bunk above his, so he could see it at all times. He cooed at it and tickled it as though it were his real son.

Four GIs ran into the barracks, the door slamming behind them. One did a flip in the air and landed in front of Jake, who snorted and woke up, blinking.

"Whoo-hoo! Boys. Whatdya gonna do when you get home?"

"Are you guys nuts?" Jake demanded.

"Ah, I don't know," said Danko, who had also been asleep. "What's it to ya?"

"What's it to me? What's with you, boys? In love with this place? Wanna settle down here, or you got plans?"

The one who seemed to be the leader threw back his head, laughing wildly. "Or didn't you know? Hey boys! I think these guys might be the only ones on the base who haven't heard!"

From the direction of the Rec Hall came the blare of a brass band accompanied by war whoops and gun fire.

Danko jumped up and grabbed the railing of his bunk. A grin broke across his face.

"Doncha get it?" One of the four GIs cried, laughing drunkenly. "The war's over! The Japanese surrendered!" He slapped his leg and fell to the ground, laughing. "These boys didn't know. They didn't know! Where yas been? In China? Ha, ha!"

"...over?" Jake said, turning the words over in his mind. His fingers folded and unfolded Blanche's letter. "Over?"

"We were firebombing them," Louis said, bewildered. He spoke slowly, as though dazed. "Trying to get 'em to give up, but they wouldn't give in, no matter what LeMay and his superfortresses dropped on 'em."

"...over?" Danko began to giggle.

"That's right, Stabler," said the fourth GI. "That's what we were doing, only it wasn't working. So we dropped something else on 'em. Something no one's ever heard of before. Some kinda superbomb. Gotta give it to that President Truman. He killed a whole city with the damn thing. Two cities. Two whole damn cities!"

Louis Stabler jumped down, went to the door, and stepped out into the light. *"Dios mio...hijo mio!"* He smiled and the smile came not only from his mouth but from his whole face.

Everyone except Jake ran outside to watch the celebration and after a few minutes, Jake rubbed his eyes and stumbled after them, watching the GIs laugh and yell and run in circles.

15

"I was a typesetter before the war," Stan said, his right hand around Shiyan's waist, helping her along the narrow path that zigzagged up the side of the hill. Once Stan Siansheng had made his intentions clear, she had begun to allow small physical displays of affection.

To either side of them were tall, delicate trees with thin, light brown trunks and tight clusters of tiny leaves high above the ground.

"Type...setter," Shiyan said, looking at him for an explanation.

"Before printing—books, newspapers—we made the letters. But not with brush—with lead. Hot metal letters."

This seemed to satisfy Shiyan, who nodded. "Now you are teaching. Stay here with me and..." She stopped walking and turned to him, her palm to his chest. "American Army angry with Stan Siansheng." It was not a question; it was a statement, an understanding.

"Oh boy, are they!" He did not look at her. "Yes. Very angry." Then, he looked her in the eyes. "But I don't care. Well," he looked at the ground. "I do care, but we belong together and I, I don't know any other way to go about it. I've never had such an opportunity before." He paused, touching her face with the tips of his fingers. "Don't worry. We'll find a way to give our family a good life now that the war's over. I'll work hard. Besides," he smiled, "in for a penny, in for a pound."

"Penny? Pound?"

"Whatever happens now, I'm in plenty of trouble already. I heard a rumor that the base is moving to the capital this week, and you can bet that Colonel Root knows I'm not there now. They'll be looking for me. Whatever happens from here on is just icing on the cake."

"Cake?"

"Bing,"[9] he said. "Something sweet." He kissed the tip of her nose. "Like you."

*   *   *   *

Mrs. Ai served the soup while Mr. Ai took Henry's jacket. It was as chilly a summer evening as anyone in Kunming could remember. Just after five the rain had begun and within minutes it had become a steady downpour. The main road was a winding brown puddle.

"Take off shoes, please," said Mrs. Ai.

"Shoo Spees!" cried Ai Wei, rushing over and hugging Henry's knee.

Mr. Ai bounded into the room. "Congratulations! The war is finally over!" He shook Henry's hand vigorously. "Now you can go home, get married."

Henry smiled for the first time in what seemed like days. "Yes, thank you. I, that would be very nice. I guess you'll be staying put, though, and fighting another war."

Mr. Ai looked at Henry. "What's wrong? Something happened." He shrugged and looked thoughtful, his forehead wrinkled. After a moment, his features relaxed. "Come, sit down. Dry yourself. Mrs. Ai will serve soup. Ah, here is Neil Ku. Come in! Come in!"

Neil Ku smiled shyly and sat down at the table with Henry and Mr. Ai. Behind them, the music box played over and over, and Wei hummed along with it.

Mr. Ai noisily pulled in his chair. "Perhaps it's for the best. Now, perhaps we can have first stage of a better life."

Mrs. Ai spooned a vegetable broth into wooden bowls. "Now will be the real beginning of New China." She glanced at her husband and then quickly away as she put down the bowl.

Mr. Ai straightened up and looked over at Ai Wei. "I saw an American movie today with Chuzi and Sung Hongai."

"How Hongai feeling?" Mrs. Ai asked.

Henry grinned, his spoon poised. "You really like to help the lovesick, Mrs. Ai, don't you?"

"Sometimes that kind of happiness is only one available. Did you make proposal to girlfriend yet? She said yes, already?"

Henry looked from his spoon to Mrs. Ai and back again. "You're a true optimist, Mrs. Ai."

"Hongai is fine," said Mr. Ai. "He's been very busy. He's found new energy. He writes, he puts up wall posters. He's even volunteered for guard duty at meetings and study groups." He nodded to his wife. "He loses himself in his studies and...extracurricular work." His expression showed that he approved. "As I lost myself in this movie. It starred famous American—" He tapped his bowl with his spoon, trying to remember the name.

"—Shirley Temple."

Henry's eyebrows went up. "Shirley Temple?"

Mr. Ai nodded solemnly. "Movie about sad little girl who loses her father. She loves her father and wants only to find him again. Though that seems impossible, she believes she will find him." He dipped his spoon into his soup, and as he ate, no one spoke. "She endured terrible things—" He hardened the r's, emphasizing the adjective.

Henry smiled. "Terrible in the context of a Shirley Temple movie, perhaps!"

Mr. Ai's seriousness never wavered; he shook his fist. "She had unshakable belief. This was important aspect. Never give up. She said...she would dream such a beautiful dream that it would come true." He put down his spoon as though this were a momentous revelation.

Henry was about to explain to Mr. Ai the difference between a Shirley Temple reality and that of wartime China, but the look on Mr. Ai's face stopped him.

"You must understand," Mr. Ai said, "that we are in a struggle for all China."

"I know," Henry began.

"It is a historical struggle but it is a personal one, equally so for all of us. You've heard me speak of the atrocities at Shanghai?"

Henry looked at his plate. "Yes."

"That loss is no less than that of a child losing her father. It is the same. My future, my life, my support, my home. We saw terrible things there. But we know our home will be restored. This is my beautiful dream. And I know—" he took his wife's hand, "we know it will come true."

Mrs. Ai nodded, her jaw set.

Mr. Ai continued. "Only the movie, perhaps, does not show the terrible violence behind the feelings, the actions that bring the emotion." A round tear gathered and rolled down one of Mr. Ai's cheeks. "Now, we have the opportunity for something new. With the Japanese defeated, there is a void...and an opportunity. If the wrong avenue is taken, if the chance is passed up, the result will be worse than a child losing her father. It will essentially be the reverse. The opportunity—the child—will be lost. And what can be worse than that?"

No one spoke for some minutes. Henry slurped hot broth from his spoon. The line from the movie ran through his head. *To dream such a beautiful dream that it came true.* Easier said than done.

He slapped the table, his voice bigger and deeper than necessary. "Well, Neil, you've been awfully quiet."

Neil Ku looked into his soup, seeing his home in Chengdu and his childhood friends. He thought of his father and mother, and how he loved them so singularly when they were the only authority he understood, when they filled his sky. The second authority he learned of had angered him deeply. He remembered the raw rage he felt upon learning the truth about the taxes his father and grandfather had to pay. Years of wages gone, food taken from their table. And for nothing in return! Strangers restricting what school he might attend, keeping him from having a brother or sister.

And look now, fifteen years later, at the change! The government was preparing for civil war, calling for the arrest of dissident students! Yet here was the governor of the province refusing to arrest them. Wait long enough and you might see anything!

As the rain drummed against the bamboo roof, Neil Ku remembered a similar rain in Chengdu half a lifetime ago. Thoughts ran through his head like bicycles and rickshaws rushing down the city's main road.

The Americans seemed more bothered by the rain than he was. Even the soldiers, the men under Stilwell's command, particularly the English who were supposed to be 'worldly' colonialists, had not found the jungle fighting in Burma to their liking.

He wondered how he would feel if Mao Zedong died suddenly. President Roosevelt had been a father to these friends, and Neil Ku suddenly understood the depth of his new friends' grief. He saw political wisdom and the old, Confucian wisdom of respect in Mr. Ai's idea to send condolence cards to Mrs. Roosevelt in Washington. He got up and went to the door, opening it enough so that a muddy trickle ran over his bare feet, cooling his toes. He felt something around his leg and looked down. Ai Wei was clutching his calf. He patted the boy's head.

He pictured Chongqing, so different from the green and comparatively quiet streets of Kunming—more like rainy, poverty stricken Chengdu, but bigger. And hotter. He imagined Mao in that hot basin, ready to meet with Chiang Kaishek, the city inundated with summer bugs.

He wanted more than ever to become a journalist and to record those events for history, for his father and grandfather.

He dreamed such a beautiful dream…

He remembered Chong Lingxiu's reaction to his ambition:

"You know, you won't always be so happy about such a position. To be a witness can be dangerous. And a journalist is not quite an innocent bystander."

And Jake Singer had reminded him of a western expression: "to kill the messenger."

And Mr. Ai had reminded him, "like a worm on the ground after a long rain, you would be exposed for all to see."

Henry looked at Mr. Ai. "Have you seen our friend Stan?"

"He is missing?"

"AWOL, the fool! There are men all over the countryside looking for him. He's going to be in a helluva lot of trouble when they find him." He shook his head. "Going to hell in a handbasket."

Mr. Ai frowned. "Hand basket?"

"It's an expression."

Mr. Ai looked uncomfortable and seemed to struggle with his thoughts. "Jane Shiyan is also missing." He stroked his chin. "We will see what we can learn."

Mrs. Ai came out of the kitchen with a tall, rolled up piece of material. Mr. Ai cleared the remaining plates from the table and helped his wife lay it down and unroll it. The eggshell-colored scroll hung over the table's edges.

"Neil Ku, Shiyan and Lin Teu did most of the lettering; Chong Lingxiu helped with the writing before he left, then Chuzi and Neil helped."

"We wanted to have it finished before American Army moved to Chongqing," said Mrs. Ai.

Mr. Ai had to stand on a chair to see the scroll with enough perspective to be able to read it. "Our friends from other side of the world are trustworthy, long life friends. Wartime struggle together has made our friendship close and strong. We will always remember and be grateful."

Everyone raised their glasses.

"Gambei!"

*   *   *   *

"Well, I haven't got all day." Colonel Root looked up from behind his desk. He looked small, but perhaps that was because his desk was so large. McPhee waited in the doorway.

"Look around, son. You can see I'm busy. We'll be in Chongqing in three days, unless you keep me here wondering what in the hell you want."

"It's about some of the men, sir. The Jewish ones. Corporal Neiberg and Sergeant Singer."

"What about 'em?" Root straightened in his chair. What little neck he had disappeared below his shirt collar.

"Well, you know they've been friendly with this bunch of Chinese, sir. Even brought 'em here, pretending they were talking about Fascism, but it was more some brand of Communism, if you ask me."

Root made a sucking sound out of the side of his mouth. "I see. And you're telling me this because..."

"Because it's my duty, sir."

"So...you think these men are some kind of threat? Let me ask you, son, they doing their jobs?"

McPhee looked past the Colonel at a knot in the wood on the wall. "All except Freilich, who doesn't seem to be around."

"That's another matter, a matter for the MPs. But we were talking about these two other men, Neiberg and Singer. Isn't that right?"

"Neiberg and Singer, sir. Yes. I believe they are doing their jobs. But these friends of theirs are the enemies of our allies."

"Well, in a sense you're right, but have you ever heard of the Dixie Mission, son? Well, they're a group of Foreign Service fellas, commissioned by our late President, to look into what the Chinese Communists are doing. Now, let me tell you, son, I'm a career man. I was in the Great War when I first came up. You didn't know that, did you? No, I can see you didn't."

"No, sir. That's great, I mean..."

"I know what you mean, and it was anything but. Now, between you and me, I wasn't much for the way FDR did things. Found ways to get what he wanted. And I don't think much of his wife, neither. But he's the Commander in Chief, dammit, and I have to do what he says, like it or not. You see?"

McPhee shuffled, looking at his shoes. He exhaled, his face pale and mottled. He looked at the ceiling.

"You okay, son?" Root got up, opened the outside door and sat down again. "A little air'll help. That's better. Now, these Chinese, all of 'em, are our allies. The Dixie Mission said they're okay. And these men here, all of 'em, are our fellow soldiers. We're in this together, son. There's a war on, or there was, and the only way you win a war is by sticking together."

Root came out from behind the desk. He was a head shorter than McPhee, and stockier, thicker in the chest and legs. He stood in front of McPhee, grasping him suddenly by the upper arms. "I want you to listen to what I have to say, son. You've had a rough couple of months."

"But, sir. I—"

"I ordered you to listen. The war's over now. Ken, look at me. The war's over. For you, too."

McPhee looked as though he were about to cry; his mouth drooped and his eyes tightened to slits.

"You don't have to be buddies with these fellas. And put their religion out of your mind. You've just got to function in this man's Army alongside them for whatever's left of your hitch. Okay, son? Now you go back to your men and carry on. And remember, we'll be going home soon. The war's over."

*   *   *   *

As the sun disappeared behind the hills, Henry and Mr. Ai stood outside. Inside, Wei was singing and his mother was clapping her hands to his beat.

"I heard a rumor," Henry said. "The base is full of rumors, all the time. That the officers are eating prime rib, we're going to be bombed on Tuesday at oh eight hundred hours, the base is moving to the capital, Chongqing. Those are just examples. This one's about one of the men at the base who has it in for me. Actually, he has it in for everyone. He's upset and isn't handling it very well. Anyway, he's a bit of a bigot and he doesn't approve of my friendship with you guys, and he's aiming to do something about it."

Mr. Ai pointed as a huge bird flapped over their heads, tilting and gliding with the light breeze until it disappeared into the last gleam of the sunset.

"This man is an officer?"

Henry shook his head.

"He has special friendship with General Chennault?"

"No, I don't think so."

"So why not worry later, when something happens, not just sport worry?"

Henry considered this. Then he laughed. "I guess, to answer your question...because I'm very good at sport worrying. Perhaps I might make a living at it when we ship out."

Mr. Ai smiled and turned to Henry, who marveled at his friend's wide smile and perfect teeth. "You have helped my family, Henry. You are in the war; my family is in this war. Jacob, Stanley. We are all part of history. Go inside and ask Nuli. He'll tell you about historical events. We have no choice but to help each other."

"That's not the way everyone sees it."

"It's right thing to do. You learned that from your honored mother. Jake learned from his grandmother. I learn from my father. And from study of the man you call Confucius. It's the right thing. You brought us news, information, food, ah, all kinds of things. Shaving supplies, treasured presents for my son. It means so much. Shanghai was terrible, a nightmare. So we have beautiful dream, a Shirley Temple dream, today. You help bring this dream to us."

It was a moment before Henry could speak. He felt in his pocket for the barrette, and realized it was no longer there. "That's how we feel. I was scared to death. I missed my family and Frances terribly. And when they bombed the base, my God, I thought the world was coming to an end. You brought us into your home. You fed us." He smiled shyly. "You were even a matchmaker."

Mr. Ai waved him away. "This was all the natural thing to do."

Henry looked at Mr. Ai's face, so serious behind its smiling mask; and his black laughing eyes, which hid such a deep reservoir of pain. "Why don't you listen to Wei play his music? There's something I have to do. Do you have a shovel I can borrow?"

*　　*　　*　　*

As if preparing for the sweltering new base, Henry, Jake and Louis Stabler sustained the momentum of glorious relief in their sweat-stained uniforms. Chongqing would be a stop on the long road home. But while the base at the capital was readied, the SCU had its hands full.

"If we have to inventory the whole move," said Ken McPhee, "we'll be here 'til 1950."

"Well," said Danko, "if we get it wrong, you know who's gotta pay for it, doncha?"

"Who?" said Stabler.

"Our moms and dads," Henry said, from the Rec Hall's piano, "that's who."

"Oh, please," Jake waved him away, "get it wrong? Do you know how wrong we've already gotten it? We might as well be working as arms suppliers for the Central Government."

"Hey, Singer." Marlowe danced past, thrust a wooden chair out in front of his chest. "Wanna cut in?"

Danko was looking at Jake, shaking his head.

"No thanks, maybe later. What's the matter with you?" Jake looked right back at Danko. "You don't agree that most of the equipment we loaned the Chinese government isn't coming back and wasn't ever used? It wasn't destroyed. So where is it?"

"Who cares?" said McPhee.

"Maybe they sold it," said Danko.

"To who?" Jake said. "Maybe they're hanging onto it for their own purposes."

"So what if they are?" said McPhee.

Jake shrugged. "So nothing. Except it costs the U.S. Government, meaning our families, money. And it gives whoever has it now a big say in who's going to be in charge here."

"We all know who's going to be in charge here," said McPhee. "Besides, who cares? When I leave this place, I never want to hear about it again. I don't care if they bring Mussolini over to run the show, to tell you the truth. Our job was to win the war in the Pacific. That's it. And it's done. The rest is crap."

"I don't think the citizens over here see it that way."

"I don't give a—"

"Yeah, well that's just it." Jake raised his voice over McPhee's. "Is that all the Army cares about? Is that the impression we want to give? That we're here to win the war and not give a rat's ass about the people whose country we're guests in? Shouldn't they have a say in who's going to run this place?"

McPhee shrugged.

Paul Danko shook his head. "He's right. We've got our own problems, Singer." He looked at Marlowe, who was dancing by, not with a chair, but with Mannion as a partner. "Some people are so greedy," he said, jerking a thumb in Singer's direction. "You save the free world for 'em and they just want more."

*   *   *   *

When they were within sight of the two bare wood structures that made up the small farm, Shiyan began to run. Stan chased her, breathlessly trying to convince her that running in this heat might dehydrate her and make her sick. But Shiyan wanted to see younger sister, and burst triumphantly into the farmhouse.

Wulin was tying a blue rag over an ugly wound on a little girl's leg. The girl was whimpering but was otherwise very brave. A similar-looking girl was bent over a boy who was screaming in pain. The girl's hands were spread open just above his head, as though she were afraid to touch him. The floor and mats were stained brown. Wulin looked at Shiyan, open-mouthed.

"Shiyan, how did you get here? Is this a dream? What a gift that would be, if all this..." The boy cried out and slapped at the little girl, who tumbled backwards, crying.

Stan had come in behind Shiyan, and she felt a sharp pain in her back. "Who are you and why are you here?"

Out of the corner of her eye, she saw a middle aged farmer thrusting a pitchfork, first at her and then Stan. Beside him was Chong Lingxiu, his leg swathed in bandages.

"It's all right, Fu Ma," said Cha Wulin, her voice more authoritative than Shiyan had ever heard it. "This is the friend I told you about, Shiyan."

Part of Shiyan relaxed, but another, older part of her heart performed acrobatics, confused at who this woman, this leader was. She looked almost exactly like her former younger sister.

*   *   *   *

At dinner, Shiyan translated the Mandarin into what English she knew, and Stan found that he understood many of the words and tones of what she was unable to translate.

Mary Cha watched everyone talk and eat. She motioned for Guelo to help her clean up, then brought a pile of dirty plates and chopsticks into the kitchen.

Young Tanshi was excited. "Mr. Gong said that now that I am here and have no city to divert me, no classmates or soccer-buddies, I will be forced to study." He looked at his father. "I am turning a negative into a positive."

Chong Lingxiu grinned. "Exactly the way I taught you." He took a piece of paper from his pocket. "I have a note for my American GI friends." He looked at Stan.

Stan nodded. "Right. Henry and Jake. I don't know how much help I can be."

"Stan Siansheng is a fugitive," said Shiyan, in Chinese.

"What's it say?" Stan asked.

Chong unfolded the paper. "It's directions to a building in Chongqing, near the place the base moved to. It says to go to Number 17 of the Marble Rabbit. That's an address. They're to look for a beautiful young woman dressed in western clothes."

"Why?" said Stan. "What's it about?"

Chong shrugged. "They must find the right people in Chongqing."

Shiyan took the note from him and examined it. "Chinese friends from Kunming know friendship with American GIs is very important. Very special. Chinese friends know that only few Americans understand details of Chinese war. Henry, Jake, and," she took Stan's arm in her hands, "Stan Siansheng part of select group that understands."

"You're right." Stan took a deep breath. "I'll do whatever I can—if you want me to."

"No," said Shiyan, alarmed. "That's not what I meant."

"But it's what *I* meant."

Mary Cha had returned and sat down. Gong Fu Ma shooed the twins into the kitchen to play with their dolls. "Maybe Wulin go?" asked Fu Ma.

"To Army base to deliver message to GIs?" Mary Cha nodded. "No problem," she said, in English.

Shiyan squinted at her. "You have responsibility here, now. The farm needs you."

Fu Ma started to protest.

"No," said Shiyan. "I see it now. Cha Wulin likes to be running whole show all the time." She turned to her friend. "One show at a time, little sister. You are needed here, and your big sister will stay and help."

Mary Cha took her hand. "You are not really my big sister. Never were."

"If Stan deserted American Army," Chong said, "he cannot deliver note."

"Well, hold on," said Stan. "Cha Wulin's not going. You, Chong, can't be seen. I'm not going to allow Shiyan to go. So guess what? I'm the one."

"Bad idea," said Chong. "If caught, you executed."

*　　　*　　　*　　　*

As he rode the rickety bicycle, Stan decided that the safest way to deliver his message would be to seek out someone unconnected with the 14th Army, someone who might be able to slip onto the base unnoticed. He thought of Chung, the General's houseboy, but decided on Neil Ku Nuli because his trustworthiness and judgement were unquestioned.

Stan wore his uniform and stayed in the most crowded teashops, keeping his cap low over his brow and trying to walk quickly. The black market was in full swing, everyone making every deal he could before leaving for Chongqing. As convoys of equipment wended out of town, Chinese agents bought weapons and field accessories, GIs bought precious metals, fabrics and other local goods. Stan listened with half an ear while keeping his eyes open for the thin, bright-eyed aspiring journalist or any of his acquaintances. After an hour, he walked to Mr. and Mrs. Ai's store front and left Chong Lingxiu's note there with instructions for Neil Ku to wait two days before attempting to deliver it to Henry and Jake.

*   *   *   *

CHONGQING

Although well north of Kunming, in Szechwan province, Chongqing is by far the hotter of the two cities. The air is oppressive, weighed down by the waters of the Yangtze. Clouds of mosquitoes cluster around any living thing, and without netting around one's bed, one might wake up at night swollen and scratching as the temperature plummets to the mid 90s. Chongqing clouds are either wispy and distant, as though even they are afraid of the wet heat, or they are dark and jagged and peaked, like dirty wet snow, filled with rain ready to burst from their pregnant bottoms.

If Kunming was the City of Eternal Spring, Chongqing at the end of the war was not far removed from Eternal Hell. Statistics swam together in the shimmering swelter of the SCU, while outside the hazy sun and airplane exhaust made each breath an effort and walking an Olympic event.

The lush greens of Kunming shrivelled and dried here to browns and straws. The only bright colors in the new capital were the brilliant yellow of the sun and its magnificent orange and red, as it lingered full in the evening sky as long as it dared, sometimes remaining into the evening as a gray ghost of its daytime self, breathing heat into the reluctant night.

The note tucked away in his pocket, Neil Ku Nuli scribbled as fast as he could; he wrote until his fingers cramped, then wrote some more. He wrote details of everything he saw: ships, generals, the brightly colored flags, the black suits and top hats worn by the Japanese leaders. It was September, 1945, and the sun glinted off polished gunships and the chests of generals at the American ship, *The Missouri,* the site of the Japanese formal surrender. As expected, the Chinese Nationalists had been flown in to accept the handing over of authority from the Japanese. Neil Ku continued to write carefully, watching, taking notes and putting pen to paper, his emotions detached and compartmentalized.

He had been unable to locate Henry and Jacob to deliver the message Mr. Ai had received from Stan. He did find Louis, whom he recognized as their friend from the forums at the base. He had waited nearly four hours just beyond the edge of the new base, squatting on burning heels. The temperature was one hundred fifteen degrees, and his legs screamed with cramping pain, but at last he saw Louis, who was with two other men, and he walked quickly past them, glancing back and catching Louis's eye. Then he circled back, as Louis bent to tie his shoe, while his friends continued walking. To them, all Chinese looked alike. As he passed, Neil Ku dropped the piece of paper next to Louis and continued walking, never varying his pace.

16

Young Hui Mingtian did not answer, and Stan had to concentrate and remember all the Chinese Shiyan had taught him to remember how to ask the boy what had become of his homework.

Mingtian was fearful of the only foreigner he had ever seen. Blond hair and green eyes were novelties that, once seen, did not soon wear off, so he did not want to answer at first. The boy was ready to accept whatever punishment came his way rather than explain why he was not able to complete his assignment.

It had been a good day. The children were less intimidated than they had been yesterday by this tall foreigner with the short hair who spoke in such a funny way.

Shiyan was happier than Stan had ever seen her. They would be married within the month.

Mary Cha and Jane Shiyan ran the farm together, caring for and entertaining the children and coordinating much of the farm work, despite the fact that Mr. Gong was technically the leader of the household. Stanley brought the twins and Chong Tanshi to and from school and, according to Mr. Gong, the farm had never been run so well nor been so well organized. The animals and land produced as never before, and the children seemed to forget the violence that had been thrust upon them.

Chong Lingxiu had become known as a literate, inspiring organizer around the town. After an appropriate waiting period, he brought Stan to meet some of the village's respected elders, who gave him the opportunity to explain who he was and why he was staying at the farm. The elders decided the matter was none of their business.

The blue of the afternoon sky was turning to orange, and the sweet smell of green leaves and flowers under the sweating sun had just begun to rise up from the ground when Stan dismissed the children. He asked Hui Mingtian to stay a moment. He attempted, in his broken Chinese, to convince the boy to talk about his missing homework.

Mingtian looked at Stan, as though trying to see deserved trust or the lack of it on his alien face. He looked away, and a stream of Mandarin poured from his mouth. Stanley was able to glean a meaning from every few words. Only this morning his father had been conscripted, and his mother had run off, grief stricken, to try to find him. His only brother, six years his elder, had joined the Communists, while his aunt, a widow who lived in the same compound with another aunt and a step-uncle, dragged him away from this scene and brought him to school. He had done his homework—he really had, only he had not had time to retrieve it, and the aunt would not allow him to return to do so. He would be living with his aunt now and had been forbidden to return to his family's house, though it was only across the courtyard.

The boy hung his head. He would have to buy a new notebook. His old one was in his mother's kitchen.

Stanley nodded and patted the boy's head. "I understand, Mingtian," he said. "You cannot go back. The way it was—" he flicked his hand in the air, "gone now." He looked at the sun, which cast purple mountain shadows into the valley that was now his home, and he marveled that such sunsets he had once considered

American could now appear so Chinese. His eyes filled with tears. "No, Mingtian, you can never go back."

This was the first Friday with his new family. That evening, Stanley took out the books that had arrived in his last package from home, and arranged them next to the best rice bread he could find, an adorned cup, and two candles. For the first time in more than eleven years, Stanley recited Shabbat prayers.

*   *   *   *

Henry and Jake tried to ignore the sweat running down their backs as they squinted at the piece of paper Neil Ku had been instructed to give them, and then back up at the brick buildings lining the steaming street. Chongqing was even hotter than they had been told.

"It should be right here," Henry said, pointing to a low, dust-covered structure. Jake didn't answer. He had stopped and was looking down at a Chinese man perhaps twenty-five years old. The man's clouded eyes looked up as though he were begging; the man was dead.

"Found it," said Henry, pulling on Jake's sleeve with one hand. In the other he carried a paper bag containing several cartons of American cigarettes. "It's over this way."

They knocked on the heavy wooden door. A slot Henry had not noticed opened and an eye peered at them and, for a moment there was silence. The eye said nothing and Henry backed away. Jake held the note up and pushed it through the slot. After a moment, the door swung open.

"Friends of Mr. Chong!" A short man shook their hands vigorously. "I am Ne Ting. Welcome! Come in. Have some tea!"

Henry and Jake looked at one another and stepped inside. They followed Mr. Ne down a carpeted hallway to a sitting room and sat down on a yellow sofa that was plush by wartime Chinese standards. A black porcelain teapot and matching cups were already set out.

"Were you expecting us?" Jake asked, joking.

"Yes!" Ne Ting nodded. His expression reminded Henry of Mr. Ai's perpetual look of happiness.

"This is some place," Henry said, looking at the dark wood shelves adorned with green figures. He wondered if they were jade. "What is this building?"

"It is generally referred to as the residence of Zhou Enlai," said Ne Ting.

"Zhou Enlai!" Henry breathed.

"Excuse me?" said Jake.

An attractive woman appeared in the doorway and, upon seeing her, Ne Ting's face lit up even more brightly than before.

"I am Tia Ganjing," she said, in English as clipped and perfect as Mr. Ai's.

Miss Tia led the GIs from the tea room to a smaller room that smelled of fresh paint. Along one wall were wide windows that overlooked the valley and the rushing brown river. She was a dark, pretty woman whose lively eyes and engaging smile put the soldiers instantly at ease. She explained that she was a press attaché, as well as Zhou Enlai's secretary and interpreter.

They sat at a corner table and talked and sipped strong tea for over an hour. The GIs explained about Mr. Ai, Neil Ku Nuli, Chong Lingxiu and all they had learned at Kunming. They spoke of their interest in the Liberated Areas and speculated about life after the war in both their countries.

Jake withdrew the two red cartons of American cigarettes from the paper bag. "We understand that Mr. Zhou and Mr. Mao enjoy American cigarettes."

Henry nodded. "We just want to say thanks for—" The thought of explaining about all their experiences in Kunming was too much and he shrugged and closed his eyes for a moment. "Please express our appreciation." He handed her a folded sheet of paper.

Tia Ganjing nodded and dipped her head graciously. "Thank you. We are lucky," she said quietly, "to have such educated friends." She read the note, glancing from it to Henry and Jake, and back again. She then placed the folded note under the carton of cigarettes.

"That's the whole story," Henry said, pointing to the note. "We feel we're in our home away from home, as absurd as that might sound."

Ganjing smiled, her eyes twinkling. Henry could not help thinking that though they did not look one bit alike, something about Ganjing reminded him of his mother.

"It is not at all absurd," she said. "It is the truth." She stepped back. "Well, Zhou Enlai has appointments and it's getting late."

"It's been a privilege meeting you, Miss Tia."

*   *   *   *

A tall, thin student was standing by the side of the road, outside of one of the Lianda dormitories. He had come out after smashing a victrola and two framed paintings. The Three Uglies, he called these items, since he had begun vainly looking for the slip of paper that had caused his frustration. He had written a name on the slip of paper because he knew he would forget. He dug his hands into his pockets, though he had done this five or six times already. They were empty. A barely audible cry escaped his lips, and he lit a cigarette to calm himself. He looked around, saw the groups of students, some walking, the wealthier ones pedaling their black bicycles. He scratched one of the sores on the back of his neck. His time was nearly finished, and he hadn't the stomach to whole-heartedly join the other side. He hadn't the stomach for violence. The name on the paper was his only hope for survival, short of leaving the country.

So he looked again for the slip of paper. The name on it was that of an old man who had once been the servant of someone he knew well, a trusted friend of his father's. The man was of the old ways. He would have the political connections to help him, and a willingness to use them. He would find Xiang a place to stay and a way to survive. The old man owed a debt to his father and would be uninterested in the new ways, since all he understood was caring for the rich—washing clothes, preparing meals, help-ing with baths. Xiang, whose clothes were soiled and who had not bathed in a week, dribbled spittle down his chin and puffed his cigarette as he tried vainly to remember the man's name.

17

Henry had hoped his fear would dissipate at war's end, that the end to the possibility of the base being bombed would instill a confidence born of having been through an ordeal and survived. The fear for his own physical safety did diminish, as did the sleepless nights of listening, wide-eyed in the dark, snapping alert at sudden sounds, his nostrils keen to the stench of gunpowder and grease. But a new fear arose: the fear of going home to an uncertain future. He had left Brooklyn a boy, focused on the war with no thought to what might come after. But now, what would come after had become the unknown. Frances claimed he was no longer the Henry she had known; he had changed. Exactly how far had he fallen in her estimation? Her letters were short and curt, like her sentences when she was annoyed. Perhaps she was right, he had changed.

Henry's mother—loving, warm and fearful—had taught him to wear his heart on his sleeve, and so he continued to write Frances about his day-to-day life, and the sights and sounds of postwar China. Not for Frances' benefit, but for his own, he included in the letters feelings that rose up from his stomach and had no place else to go but his pen.

*   *   *   *

In early September, the frantic pace of the basin city of Chongqing slowed to a more natural one. No sudden movements, plenty of loose clothing and wide brimmed hats were required to survive the sweaty celebration in the wet heat.

Jake and Henry stopped on a street corner, and Henry closed his eyes and let his head loll back, feeling the hot sun on his face. City noises washed over him. Chongqing after VJ day was not unlike the mid-town New York of his childhood on the Fourth of July. Even a week after the surrender, the streets teemed with happy Americans and Chinese, finally released from years of tension. Mothers cooed to long-lashed daughters, trucks honked and threw off clouds of black smoke. Whole families waved tiny American flags, and little boys darted, chattering, between GIs' feet.

Henry opened his eyes and sighed, the illusion gone. So many of the people around him were so desperately poor. Though they had survived the war, many were sick, teeth rotting, skin mottled. Children battled over scraps of food in garbage heaps.

He and Jake watched two fast talking black marketeers in Army Air Corps uniforms.

One hawker spotted them. "Gentlemen, you look like you could use a bargain. Now that the war's over, I can get you all sorts of supplies, even a gun or two if you want 'em. We've got genuine Moose Dung[10] suits. He's coming to town, you know, to negotiate with Hurley and Chancre Jack.[11] Want a gen-u-ine Moosey Dung suit for the occasion? Show it to the missus and the kids! And hey, I can get it—well, let's just say it's for a song."

Jake sidled up and fingered one of the Army issue blankets on the folding table. "Isn't this stuff supposed to be shipped stateside?"

The second marketeer swung around and squinted at Jake. "Listen sarge, we're doing you a favor, selling this to our guys. We can get a fortune from the slopes for it. I know a coupla Kuomintang officers who'd pay big..."

Jake hesitated, hating the derogatory term. "Yeah, but it's our money they'd be paying with," said Jake.

The second marketeer leaned over, his voice low. "Sarge, ya gotta understand. I got a little daughter back home I ain't never seen, and I'm trying to save for a nice little house to put her and the missus in, see? You wouldn't want to take that away from my little Sweetie, wouldya?" He pulled out a worn picture of a wide-eyed little girl. "She's nearly four now, ain't she cute?"

"Mmhm," said Jake.

"Let's go," said Henry. "We've got to get back to you-know-who."

*   *   *   *

When they arrived at "Zhou Enlai's Residence," Tia Ganjing was polite but seemed distracted, less attentive than she had been at their first meeting. She asked them to sit in the freshly painted side room, and through the veil hanging in the doorway they heard a clamoring—urgent voices accompanied by drumbeat foot-falls. The GIs looked at one another; Henry had an impulse to jump through the window and roll down the river bank into the muddy water below. It was what Fairbanks or Barrymore would have done. Tia Ganjing poked her head into the room.

"There is someone here who would like to meet you."

She held aside the curtain, and a group of soldiers filed into the room. In their midst was a tall man with bushy, dark eyebrows, thick black hair and enormous eyes.

The man smiled and held a hand out to Jake Singer, who was nearest the door. "I am Zhou Enlai. Pleased to meet you."

"Jake. I mean Staff Sergeant Jacob Singer, sir." Later he would admit to being tempted to say, "Yeah, and I'm Jack Benny."

It was all Henry could do to stay upright. "Corporal Henry Neiberg," he muttered.

Tia Ganjing acted as interpreter. She then bid them all sit while tea was served.

"If we were to go along with the proposals put before us," Zhou was saying, in response to the questions he had invited the GIs to ask, "we would have to recognize Chiang Kaishek as the leader of all China." Zhou spoke freely and without hesitation, smiling and delicately sipping his tea while Ganjing interpreted.

"But the governments in the Liberated Areas must be incorporated into, not just absorbed by, the National Government here," he explained. "It is the least Chiang Kaishek can do for those who best resisted the invaders." He made a circular gesture with one hand. "We insist on so little. The KMT would be recognized as the number one political party in China while the Communist Party would be number two. Very reasonable." He smiled, and Henry felt that his charm and warmth were genuine. Zhou pronounced the last words in English and the GIs smiled.

"We understand that some of what we ask might take time." Zhou seemed amused while he spoke, as though by a private joke. His eyes crinkled in the corners, reminding Henry of someone— who, he could not recall. The entire circumstance, in fact, bordered on the absurd. He had the feeling of being in a dream, or fairy tale.

"Very important," Zhou said with sudden seriousness, "is that our troops be able to accept Japanese surrenders. But as you know, this has not been the case."

"I see," said Jake.

Zhou nodded and shrugged as if to say: "*You* see but it is not so obvious to others." He laughed suddenly and said, "Miss Tia tells me that one of you is a musician."

Jake pointed to his friend. "Henry is always fiddling on the piano, playing along with the radio. He's not bad, really." He giggled. "Can't be too bad if he can get half a unit of grown men to dance with a bunch of chairs!"

Mr. Zhou laughed for nearly a minute when he heard the translation. He got up and opened a door behind them, revealing a closet-sized room into which a dusty upright piano barely fit. "Play, please?"

Henry looked around, unable to move. Mr. Zhou rattled off a few singsong syllables and Miss Tia giggled as she translated.

"If you do not play, I will have to sing."

The piano was badly in need of tuning but no one seemed to mind, and Mr. Zhou sang anyway, despite knowing neither the melody nor the words of *"Summertime."* He gamely invented his own composition that more or less fit the chord changes. When he was finished, Henry wiped the sweat from his eyes, Jake applauded and Mr. Zhou laughed and laughed.

"Have you been to Guilin?" Mr. Zhou asked, when he'd gotten his breath. Henry shook his head.

"You must go. It is a popular spot for honeymoon."

"A honeymoon?" Henry eyed the Chinese leader, wondering whether he had been speaking with a certain dumpling maker.

One of his entourage interrupted, and Zhou nodded and spoke to Tia Ganjing.

Miss Tia stood up; everyone else followed suit. "Mr. Zhou says he has enjoyed meeting each of you and that you represent your country well. He has another appointment now but asks that you return next week, the sixteenth, to enjoy a full meal with him."

"That's *Yom Kippur*," Henry whispered.

Jake nodded. "We'll figure something out."

Zhou Enlai nodded vigorously before Tia Ganjing could translate. "You are welcome," he said, in English.

"Maybe we can say we're going to some kind of storefront synagogue or something," Henry said out of the side of his mouth as they walked toward the front door. "There's no way we can pass this up."

"Just remember to bring a camera," Jake said. "Besides, maybe there *is* a storefront synagogue."

As they closed the heavy door to the "Marble Rabbit," Henry pointed to three uniformed figures across the street.

"Look who's keeping an eye on us," he said.

"Yeah, they were here the first time, too," said Jake.

One of the soldiers spat in slow motion, the spittle dribbling off his lips.

Jake called to them, waving, "How you fellas been?"

*   *   *   *

"You've got to introduce me to some of these friends, Jake." Louis was lying back on his bunk, one leg crossed over the other.

Jake was laughing, giddy from the day's meeting. "Sure, Louie. Anytime."

"I like that you're friends with all these different people, you know? I like having some perspective on the situation here. McPhee was trying to tell me it's dangerous because we don't see the whole picture. But I think it's healthy. We can judge for ourselves, you know?"

Jake got up. "Let's go down to the Rec and hear some music."

"*Vamanos*, my friend." They walked a ways in silence. "So, when you going to bring me downtown with you?"

"Well, we're going next Sunday." Jake was lost in thought. The end of the war had amplified the emptiness he felt without his wife. Since the surrender, his thoughts and feelings had returned home, and he had been seeing her face in his mind. She wore her sky blue nightgown and her smell was sweet and her touch light.

"The sixteenth?" Louis asked.

"Right. Sure." Jake smiled.

"I'll be there, my friend. Thank you."

18

Enid Neiberg was engrossed in her novel, her mind thousands of miles and dozens of years away. Her parents were in the kitchen while she sat near the window, in the waving shadows of late summer leaves that were just starting to dream about turning. Like the previous two, the summer had been odd without Henry, but the war was over and he would be coming home within the next few months. All she and her parents waited for was news of the date and place.

The book was a romance set in turn-of-the-century England, and so successful was it in drawing her into its milieu, that Enid never saw the shadow cross the window, nor heard the knock at the front door.

"Could you get that, Eenie?" her father's gravelly voice called from the kitchen. When she opened the door, the fifteen-year-old stepped back, surprised.

"Fran! Mama didn't tell me you were coming."

"That's because I didn't tell her." Frances stepped into the living room, past the paintings and charcoal sketches of rabbis and representations of Torah scrolls. "Would you ask your parents if I might speak with them a moment?"

Nettie hurried into the living room, fingers over her lips. "What is it? What's happened to Henry? Why didn't the telegram come here?"

"It's okay, Mrs. Neiberg. He's fine, as far as I know. I didn't mean to upset you."

"As far as you know? You don't write each other?"

Fran looked down at the pleated blue skirt she wore below her plain white blouse. "Maybe not as much as he'd like."

"Come, sit with us in the kitchen." Nettie beckoned. "Eenie, you go back to your book. This is no place for—"

"If you don't mind, I'd like Enid with us. What I have to say concerns her, too."

"Let me get you a piece of *babkah*." Nettie guided Fran to a seat as Morris folded his newspaper, took off his black-rimmed glasses and lay them on the lace doily in front of him.

"Henry has written me letters," Fran began slowly, "and it seems he's changed. It's, it's unsettling."

Morris nodded. "He believes the Chinese version these new friends feed him. But don't worry, when he gets back I'll..."

Fran shook her head, her fingers played with a loose strand of tablecloth. "He's more openminded, more interested in the, the, what would you call them, difficulties of these Chinese friends of his." She took a deep breath, looking from Mr. to Mrs. Neiberg. "We haven't always seen eye to eye, but I need to know. You see, I haven't written him much about...because I can't really be sure he really..." She stopped and looked out the windows, her eyes red-rimmed, watering.

Nettie Neiberg put an arm around Fran's shoulder. "You're a smart young lady. You have a science degree, no? They teach you to observe. Mm, I see you're good at observing. Oh, Henry's changed, all right. Not so focused on himself anymore. He grew up over there."

Morris cleared the phlegm from his throat and waggled a finger. "Don't be so sure it's for the better."

"Morris!"

Fran hesitated. "You see, Henry wanted me to wait for him, for us to have an understanding. I refused because I felt he wasn't compassionate towards people with different backgrounds—people less fortunate..."

"Well," Morris began.

"Don't start," Nettie wagged a finger back, with a friendly glance towards Frances, who saw in her eyes the same kindness that transcended Henry's letters. She took Nettie's hand. "Thank you." She kissed her on the cheek. "I'd like to ask a favor, if it's okay."

"Ach, now a favor she wants!"

The finger shook. "Morris, I won't tell you again!"

Morris shook his head.

"Well, its a small favor. Would you let me know when his ship is coming in?"

Enid giggled. "I think it just did."

*   *   *   *

There was a strange restlessness to Chongqing by the middle of September, 1945. With the war over, the GIs were impatient to return home. Thoughts were with girlfriends, wives, families. Boys who had interrupted schooling to go to war were suddenly men ready to return to incomplete lives. But could they simply resume those lives? Could they finish school or would they go right to work, and what sort of work would there be in the strange, changing world they were returning to?

*   *   *   *

Corporal Firaldi looked over his shoulder, keeping one hand on the wheel. "You're damned right it was a good thing. Later on we'll all look back and say 'if it weren't for President Truman and that bomb, a lot of our friends might've died invading Tokyo or Yokohama.'"

Louis nodded, keeping his reservations about the bomb to himself.

"You know where nearly everyone I know is today?"

"Where, Jake?" asked the Corporal.

Henry answered for him. "*Kol Nidre* service."

Jake nodded, leaning to one side as the truck made a turn. "That's right. In Philly, you can hear most of the *Yom Kippur* service from half a block away." He grinned. "And Louis, I think it's terrific that you've taken such an interest in the Jewish religion."

Henry's eyes lit playfully. "Guess you must be Sephardic."

"I believe learning about other cultures is important," Louis said, seriously. "Besides, you said there's a lot of singing at the service. I like singing."

"I always had a heck of a time sitting through that night," said Henry. "I'd go to the service before, but *Kol Nidre*—sheesh, a long evening. Three, four hours. My butt hurts just thinking about that."

Jake waved a finger, his face serious. "Show some respect."

"My butt hurts in this truck!" Louis called toward the front.

"I know how both you guys feel," said Firaldi. "I've been to masses that felt like they were going on into the early Fifties. And Louis, I practically live in this truck. My butt's a rock. Say, that's how you guys got to go downtown, isn't it? Said you're celebrating your holiday?"

"Well, in a way," said Henry. "*Yom Kippur* isn't exactly a day you celebrate. Sort of like Ash Wednesday, if you see what I'm saying."

Jake shrugged. "So, we told a little fib. Is that such a big deal? Besides, I seem to remember something in the *Torah*." He tapped the side of his head. "If a person has the opportunity to serve or help many people, but it's a holiday or *Shabbat*, it's okay. Maybe this falls into that category."

"I can almost smell Brooklyn," said Henry. "Imagine, we'll be home soon. Home! Oh, hey, turn here, Corporal. You know, there's a smell there on those streets..."

"Garbage?" Firaldi asked, as the truck made a right turn.

"You just watch the road, Corporal." Henry shook his head. "No, it's the butcher, the dress shops, the bakery, mothballs in people's clothes as they come home from work or go to shul. It's leaves burning in garbage cans, and it's all rolled together into one big home smell. But you don't realize that's what it is until you're gone."

"I'm going to tell everyone," Jake said, "strangers even, that I met Zhou Enlai."

"Better be careful about that," said Henry, turning to Jake. "Bring your camera this time?"

Jake patted his knapsack. "Be nice if Zhou Enlai were to show up again."

"Whaddya mean, show up?" said Henry. "He said he'd be there. He invited us. Besides, it's supposedly his residence."

The truck lurched to a stop and the three GIs were thrown against the back of the Corporal's seat.

"Some guy's wagon broke down," Firaldi called back to them. "Look's like half the town's watching him try to fix it." He leaned out the window. "Hey, move aside there. Army business!" He took a deep breath. "Movee waggee so I can drivee through, okay? Yes, yes. Chop, chop." A few minutes later, they were moving again. "You'd think out of that whole crowd someone'd be a mechanic."

By the time they arrived at Zhou Enlai's "residence," it was midday and well over a hundred degrees. The GIs were shuttled into a side room by another young woman, not Ganjing. At one point, Tia Ganjing did peek in, waved, and was gone.

Outside, a black limousine waited, its windows curtain-covered. After each of the GIs had several cups of tea, Tia Ganjing reappeared and led them outside to the limousine, held the door and got in after them.

"Where are we going?" Henry asked.

"Red Crag Village," Ganjing answered. "Safer for you there." She smiled easily.

After a half hour ride into the countryside, they arrived at a small white cottage. From inside came the wail of a crying baby.

"My son," said Tia Ganjing, as they entered. She ushered the soldiers into a bare living room whose dirty wood floor was covered with a fine layer of sawdust. Three men came in; one was smoking a cigarette and Henry stepped back involuntarily.

The smoking man was Mao Zedong.

Mao uttered a few syllables in a rising and falling tone and smiled at each of them. "We thank each of you for your generous gifts and for your appreciation of our efforts," said Tia Ganjing.

"You're welcome," said Henry, looking at Mao and then down at his own shoes. "...sir," he added, as an afterthought.

"We would like to know," Ganjing began, but Mao interrupted her with a few words punctuated with the name "Hurley"[12] and a friendly shrug.

"He says that your gift was far more generous than that of Mr. Patrick Hurley, American negotiator." She laughed and Henry wondered whether this was her own laugh or a translation. "He asks that you join us for dinner."

"Tell Mr. Mao that we would be honored," Jake said softly.

As they walked into the dining room, Louis whispered to Jake, "Pinch me, ok? And when I wake up, give me a lecture never to eat whatever it is I ate last night!"

They sat at a simple wooden table, and Henry wondered if it had been built especially for the occasion, hence the sawdust. Each place setting consisted of one bowl and a plain pair of chopsticks. Besides Mao, his aides, and the three GIs, there were only Tia Ganjing and her baby, Huan Gaoxing. In the kitchen were two waiters and two cooks, who might have been Mao's cousins, so at ease were they with him and vice versa. Gaoxing's crying and needing diaper changes were human elements that put the GIs at ease, reminding them of Ai Wenti and his family. Louis, particularly, hovered over the baby, cooing and grinning and when he finally looked away there were tears in his eyes.

"In a few months," he whispered to Henry, "I'm going to see my son."

"To our friendship," Mao said, and as Tia Ganjing translated, the Chinese leader lifted his glass and drank the clear liquid, and everyone but Ganjing and her son followed suit. *"Gambei!"* he said.

Henry coughed as the fiery fluid caught in his throat. "What is this stuff?" he said, holding his glass to the light.

Mao waited patiently and signaled to the waiter to refill their glasses. *"Mao Tai,"* he said.

"To the memory of President Roosevelt," Ganjing translated, and Mao downed the drink and held his glass upside down.

"Mr., ah, Mao," Jake Singer cleared his throat. "Everyone's working so hard to bring about peace, tell us what we can do."

Mao's high forehead wrinkled. The answer came quickly. "You can go home to your families and friends and tell them what you saw in China. Tell them the truth." He looked closely at each of the GIs. "Tell me," he said, looking not at Tia Ganjing but at each of them, "what is your opinion of your President Truman's under-standing of China?"

Louis cleared his throat. Until this moment, he had been too shocked to open his mouth, but alcohol had given him the courage to speak. "I don't think we know that yet, sir. We haven't been home since the campaign and election, and besides, when you're elected Vice President, your job is to agree with the President. We don't yet know Truman's views, but they're probably affected by...you see, Mr. Truman's from a different sort of background. From the countryside. President Roosevelt had been governor of New York; he was concerned about social issues, his wife..."

"Louis," Henry hissed, "you're making no sense."

"Ah!" Mao interrupted Ganjing's translation, shifting gears, "tell me about the American labor movement."

"There's a lot of debate about that," said Henry. "Many fami-lies argue, even among themselves. My own father owns a factory, and I think he finds the labor movement..." His voice trailed off as the absurdity of the situation dawned on him. Here he was explaining the American labor movement to Mao Zedong! "Excuse me," he said to a waiter. "Is there any more of this?" He pointed to his shotglass.

"Our people," Mao said, "even our most devoted followers come from all sorts of backgrounds. One must know what one struggles against." He leaned toward Jake. "Tell me, why did Henry Wallace lose his vice presidency?"

"The vice presidency," Jake explained, "is offered to a person, not because he is a good politician or good worker, but because he is from the background that'll best help the president get reelected. A presidential candidate from the North, for instance, might choose a vice president from the South to achieve a bal-anced ticket. Mr. Wallace, I'm afraid, had only leftist support and mainly in northern cities."

Mao nodded. "Please understand, just as the contents of our talks with the Central Government are secret, so are the contents of our talks here." He made a circle with his finger including them all and looked each GI in the eye. Henry felt that the look was giving—and asking for—trust.

"After the observers came to the Liberated Areas," Mao explained, as he lit another cigarette—Henry noticed they were the same brand as the gift they had given, "we became hopeful. What you called the Dixie Mission promised that the truth about China would be told to the people of the United States. But," Mao paused, "during these past months, your government seems to have forgotten, and shifted its point of view even further away from ours. Perhaps it is the newspapers giving an inaccurate representation, or that those who observed us, the foreign service officers, have lost influence. As you say, Mr. Truman's background is different," he waved the cigarette in a what-can-we do gesture. "Leaders are subject to pressures just as a bird must contend with all winds."

Mao sat up straight and slapped his palms on the table. "The Chinese people have been through difficult times—and there will be more difficult times. I'm very pleased to know that some American people understand." He looked at the three GIs and a smile broke across his face. "All of our circumstances," again he included them all, "are so difficult, and your friendship means much. My friends in Kunming have told the same story of meaningful friendship." He raised his glass.

Henry wondered about Mr. and Mrs. Ai. Could it be that they were the friends Mao spoke of?

"Your friendship to so many has given me hope for a long and strong friendship between the people of our countries. We must be patient. It is a beautiful dream, and we can make it true." He quickly drank the *Mao Tai* and exchanged a glance with Tia Ganjing.

Jake and Henry looked at one another, startled by the reference. Henry smiled inwardly. Mr. Ai was a clever man who remembered everything!

Mao stood up, pointing to the camera on the back of Jake's chair. "If you would like to take pictures, please—before the sun goes down. American people believe you more with pictures."

Jake jumped up. "You know, I've been sitting here trying to figure out how I'll ever get Blanche to believe this. I forgot all about my camera!"

"I don't know if I can stand up," Louis said, pointing to his glass. "This stuff takes away my legs!"

Mao laughed and waited in the doorway, the setting sun in front of him to make for a better photograph.

Two rolls of film later, Mao had gone, asking that the GIs remain and enjoy "a few simple dishes" prepared by his cooks.

The food came in waves. Leafy vegetables in sauces, bean curd soup, chicken in a spicy brown gravy, mung beans, dumplings with more vegetables, and on and on...

Jake took a piece of chicken from between his shaking chopsticks. "I'll never learn to use these." He turned to Tia Ganjing. "Today before sundown was *Yom Kippur,* the annual day of atonement in the Jewish religion. We make our peace with God and with ourselves on this day."

Tia Ganjing nodded respectfully.

"I was surprised to see that no rice is being served with our meal," Henry said. "Is that because no rice is grown near here?"

Tia Ganjing laughed. "No, there's plenty of rice. Not serving rice is an honor. Only an important meal for an important guest would be served without rice!"

"Of course," Jake said. "Mao is in town to talk to Chiang Kaishek and Hurley! How much more important do you get than that?"

"Oh, no," said Tia Ganjing, looking at the cradle on the bench behind her to make sure her son was asleep. "Mao would never allow such an effort on his own behalf. This meal without rice was in *your* honor."

19

Before enlisting, Henry Neiberg had secretly suspected he would die in the war, perhaps not in combat, perhaps in some freakish accident. And so when he arrived home, in New York Harbor, though he had no idea what kind of life he was returning to, Henry really did kiss the ground, and when he stood up, Jake was next to him, pointing in the other direction.

"Aren't you going to introduce us?" he said, with a toothy grin.

"Aren't I—?" Henry turned, and there she was. "Fran? I never expected, you didn't tell me—"

Her dark eyes barely restrained an excitement he had never seen. "Why spoil the surprise?"

They stood and stared at one another for a long moment. Then Henry reached into his pocket and took out the worn, wooden barrette. He held it out.

"I think you dropped this."

She fell into his arms, clutching the new hat she'd bought only that morning as it tried to fly into the wind that blew off the water.

Henry held her at arm's length. He had never dared imagine this moment; he had forced it from his mind on the transport ship, thinking instead about getting an apartment, a job and other frightening, but not impossible events. But this, this was something out of a Shirley Temple movie!

"But you said I'd changed. That I wasn't the same Henry who'd left for—"

"Stop shaking me. I'm not a bottle of soda pop! Oh this silly hat." She took it off and handed it to Jake. "Here, hold this. I was never much for hats anyway. I only bought it because all the women were buying them before meeting their—" She bit her lip and looked away.

Jake stepped forward and put out a hand. "I'm Henry's buddy, Jake Singer."

Fran took his hand. "You must think I'm awfully impolite."

"No, I think you haven't seen one another for—here," he gently took her by the shoulders and turned her towards Henry. "I'm going to try to find Blanche."

Around them, a kind of euphoric pandemonium was occurring. People were shouting, crying, hugging, screaming. Couples twirled, parents pointed at ships' railings, from which hundreds of GIs waved their hats.

Henry laughed and looked straight up in the air. "You bought a hat because all the other girls were buying them? I should be the one telling you that you've changed."

Frances looked at the ground, then at Henry. She took his face in her hands. "I wasn't very clear in my letters. I'm afraid I don't write my feelings very well and, and I guess I was afraid I was wrong, so I didn't want to say too much. When you wrote about China and your friends—who were so poor but so rich with friendship, and how they made you feel so at home and took away some of the homesickness—that seemed unlike you. It's—Henry, those're the sort of things I'd always wished you'd say. That was what I meant when I said you'd changed. From your letters you sounded grown up, compassionate, understanding. And that—"

"Fran, don't say anything else." Henry glanced around; the words came out in a rush. "Marry me?"

For a long moment no one said anything. They looked at one another, the wind rippling their clothes. GIs and families rushed around them on the dock.

Slowly Fran began to nod.

And as he kissed her, Henry made a silent promise. Someday, somehow, he would find Mr. and Mrs. Ai, and thank them.

Footnotes

1 "When luck comes in, give him a chair."

2 "A miracle! A fool makes children!"

3 "When hitting your head against a wall, at least you should have a wall!"

4 "A dead person is mourned seven days, a fool is mourned his whole life."

5 Chiang Kaishek

6 "A little."

7 "A drunk. Whatever's on his mind comes out of his mouth."

8 "Family"

9 One meaning of her family name, "Bing," is "cake."

10 Mao Zedong

11 Chiang Kaishek

12 Patrick Hurley was mediating the negotiations between the two Chinese factions in September, 1945.

References

Sources include:
Approximately 10–12 hours of taped interviews with individuals upon whom the characters of Henry Neiberg, Jake Singer, Neil Ku Nuli and Mr. Ai Wenti are based, as well as two other China Veterans who were with the 14th Army Air Corps.

Print Sources:

Chen, Janey. *A Practical English-Chinese Pronouncing Dictionary.* Tokyo: Charles E. Tuttle Company, Inc., 1970.

Hoopes, Roy. *Americans Remember the Home Front: An Oral Narrative.* New York: Hawthorn Books, 1997.

Kedward, H.R. (Harry Roderick). *Fascism in Western Europe 1900–45.* New York: New York University Press, 1971.

Kristof, Nicholas and Sheryl Wudunn. *China Wakes.* New York: Random House, 1994.

Chang, Iris. *The Rape of Nanking: The Forgotten Holocaust of WWII*. New York: Basic Books, 1997.

Schaller, Michael. *The U.S. Crusade in China, 1938–45*. New York: Columbia University Press, 1979.

Snow Edgar. *Red Star Out of China*. New York: Grove Press, 1938.

Stilwell, Joseph and (arranged by) Theodore White. *The Stilwell Papers*. New York: William Sloane Associates, Inc., 1948.

Suyin, Han. *Wind in the Tower—Mao Tsetung & The Chinese Revolution, 1949–1975*. Boston: Little, Brown & Company Ltd., 1976.

The Swing Era, 1944–1945—The Golden Age of Network Radio. New York: Time Life Books, 1970.

Tuchman, Barbara. *Stilwell and the American Experience in China, 1911–1945,* New York: Macmillan, 1972.

White, Theodore and Annalee Jacoby. *Thunder Out of China*. New York: William Sloane Associates, Inc., 1946.

About the Author

David E. Feldman lives in Long Beach, New York, with his wife, Ellen, and sons. *Born Of War* is his first book. He has recently completed his second, *Bad Blood,* and is working on a third, *The Universe Principle*.